DEVIL IN THE DEADLINE

A NICHELLE CLARKE CRIME THRILLER

LYNDEE WALKER

SEVERN RIVER
PUBLISHING

Severn River Publishing
www.SevernRiverBooks.com

ISBN: 978-1-64875-514-9 (Paperback)

ALSO BY LYNDEE WALKER

The Nichelle Clarke Series

Front Page Fatality

Buried Leads

Small Town Spin

Devil in the Deadline

Cover Shot

Lethal Lifestyles

Deadly Politics

Hidden Victims

Dangerous Intent

The Faith McClellan Series

Fear No Truth

Leave No Stone

No Sin Unpunished

Nowhere to Hide

No Love Lost

Tell No Lies

To find out more about LynDee Walker and her books, visit

severnriverbooks.com/authors/lyndee-walker

For Avery. You are truly my sunshine, and you make me proud every minute. I love you all the way to the moon. And back. Always dream big.

1

Near-bottom on my list of ways to spend a Saturday night: going to work dressed like an extra from *Flashdance*. Criminals have such little respect for reporters' social lives.

I ducked under crime scene tape and glanced around a decaying concrete building, the holes left by missing sections of wall offering moonlit views of the colossal boulders of Belle Isle. Boulders I was out of breath from scaling in heels and a miniskirt.

And it looked like I wasn't through climbing yet.

"Did I miss a memo about Halloween moving to June?" Aaron White, the Richmond police spokesman, called from ten feet above my head.

"Aw, c'mon, Aaron—all the cool kids are wearing lycra and leg warmers." I put one Manolo on the bottom rung of a circus-length extension ladder. "One step at a time, don't look down," I muttered. Ladders and stilettos aren't really meant to mix.

"I'm firmly out of the loop on two counts, then—no one's called me a kid in at least a decade." Aaron chuckled.

"One count. You're the coolest not-kid I know." Stepping into the loft, I shot a bracing hand out for the graffitied wall when my foot slid under me. "Do I want to know what I'm walking in, here?"

"Not blood. I make no guarantees beyond that," Aaron said, a snicker slipping through his teeth as RPD floodlights illuminated my racing-stripe plum blush and the cloud of White Rain and frizz surrounding my head. "What are you supposed to be? You look like a h—"

"Shut up," I said, shooting him a warning glare that'd probably be more foreboding minus the four layers of neon eyeshadow. "No, don't. But lay off the costume—haven't you ever seen *Flashdance*? I bailed on my best friend's eighties night in the middle of her margarita-fueled performance of 'Material Girl' to come out here and climb rocks in four-inch heels."

"You match the scene, anyhow." He walked down a narrow hallway lined with tiny stalls, waving for me to follow. "This looks like something out of an eighties movie. Just not one with dancers."

The tangy, metallic smell of blood—a lot of it—slowed my breathing as I followed Aaron around a corner. My stomach tightened around bites of hors d'oeuvre, making me wish I was back at Jenna's house. Two sips into my Midori sour, my scanner had started squawking. Combine the body-discovery chatter with Aaron's text (*come across the rocks—have exclusive for you*), and the party didn't stand a chance.

I paused when Aaron turned back, his wide shoulders blocking a brightly-lit corner of spray-paint-tagged loft. I'd worked with him long enough to know that look. Probably a good thing I didn't have much in my stomach.

"Stay back here," he cautioned. "Forensics is still working. I've got a uniform out by the bridge keeping the cameras at bay, but I wanted you to get a look at what we're dealing with here."

"At the risk of getting myself thrown out after I played Frogger across the rocks in this getup, why?"

His lips disappeared into a thin white line. "People who won't talk to us will talk to you. We need your help, Nichelle."

He stepped to one side and ice washed over me in the balmy summer air, a scream sticking in my throat.

"Evil. Evil is the only word I've got." Aaron's low voice barely crossed the blood pounding in my ears. "I've been a cop for twenty years, and I've never seen anything like this."

My eyes fell shut—not that I'd ever get the blood-splashed walls and makeshift sacrificial altar out of my head. The young woman's matted, soaked hair and glassy eyes were the stuff of nightmares. I turned away.

Aaron laid one hand on my shoulder and stepped around me, bending his head to catch my gaze. "Sorry. I should've warned you."

"I never thought I'd see the day I minded an exclusive." I gripped a pen like a tether to my sanity. "Jesus, Aaron. When? How?" I leveled a what-the-everloving-hell gaze at him. "Tell me the story."

"I don't have to be a doctor to tell you she hasn't been here long. Couple of vagrants who sleep here sometimes called it in from a pay phone at the 7-Eleven on the corner," he said. "If they hadn't, we might not have found her until the trail runners started complaining about the smell."

Ah-ha. That's why he'd called me. Street people wouldn't tell the cops the grass was green, much less anything about a murder.

"Where'd they go?" I asked, my feet itching to put as much distance as possible between me and the Wes Craven gore-fest the forensics crew milled around. "Can I talk to them tonight?"

He nodded. "Hopefully. I had a squad car take them to St. Vincent's for a psych eval," Aaron said, "They'll get a shower and a clean bed for the night, plus some food. And Lord knows they need to talk to a shrink. I think I even need to talk to a shrink."

"Me, three." I took a half-dozen steps back toward the ladder and smiled. Sending witnesses to the hospital wasn't standard police procedure. "You're a good guy, you know that?"

His eyes crinkled at the corners with the ghost of a smile as he laid one finger across his lips. "Shhh. We'll keep that between us."

"Can I get a room number?"

"I'll text it to you as soon as I have it. And I'll let the nurses know you're an approved visitor. I put them in the locked ward." His eyes strayed back to the bloody scene. "Just in case whoever did this was watching."

I shuddered, shooting a glance at every dark corner. "I'll call you if I get anything useful."

"And I won't share what you give me until you print it."

"Fair enough."

Aaron gave me the specifics of the discovery and early forensic findings before he walked me out. I scribbled down every word, my mind racing ahead through a lead and wondering if there'd still be anyone in the news-room when I got the story written. With this kind of a jump on everyone, I wanted it on the web five minutes ago.

"Thanks, Aaron," I said. "I owe you one."

"I think we're even. It only took me a year." He grinned. "All access, right?"

"You do know me," I said. "This is worth playing my favor card."

"Have fun pissing Charlie off. I'm sure I'll hear all about it tomorrow."

Charlotte Lewis from Channel Four was my biggest competition in Richmond. Pissed didn't cover how angry she'd be when this story went up. More reason to rush.

"Sorry." I wrinkled my nose at Aaron.

He waved a hand. "I can handle it. I can't let anyone film this. I don't have to say I trust you to leave out the gory details?"

"I don't want to write them, much less make people read them over their oatmeal," I said.

"And if anyone saw or heard anything—"

"Complete anonymity. You want your number instead of Crimestoppers?"

"Please." He nodded.

"Thanks, Aaron." I put one foot on the ladder.

"Thank you. We need all the leads we can get, and time is not our friend. The chief called in every detective we have. We're all running on donuts and Red Bull until further notice."

He flagged down a uniformed officer who escorted me through the trees to a splintered footbridge that probably dated to Belle Isle's days as a Confederate POW camp. I was almost as thankful for the bridge as the story access. I'd call crossing the boulders after dark a small miracle—espe-cially given the stilettos on my feet. No way I could do it again with my knees still jelly from the crime scene.

Thanking the officer for his help, I ducked out of another ring of yellow tape, far enough down from the tangle of reporters waiting for a comment that no one noticed me. Not that any of them would have recognized me.

Back in my car, I locked the doors and peeled out of the park's tiny lot, my hands gripping the wheel to keep from shaking.

* * *

My heart stopped pounding before I made it to St. Vincent's, but the blood-splashed walls and spent candles flashed on the backs of my eyelids with every blink.

I checked my cell phone for the room number Aaron had promised and found it, plus two texts from my closest friend, Jenna, and one from my ex-boyfriend/still favorite ATF agent, Kyle. I replied to both with a promise to return to the party if I could, cringing at the thought of him alone in a roomful of strangers. Probably not what he had in mind when he accepted Jenna's invitation. Which she sent him without asking me. But I didn't have time to worry about her not-so-subtle matchmaking attempts at the moment. I stowed the phone in my bag and stepped into the elevator, pushing the button for the eighth-floor psychiatric ward.

It had been a while since a story brought me to this part of the hospital. Stark white and gray walls greeted me as I stepped off the elevator, a jarring departure from the high-end home decor in the rest of the building.

I half-shouted my name into an intercom just as the buzzer sounded and one door clicked open to reveal Chris Landers, a homicide detective I'd met only a few times since he joined the department last summer. He blanched at my outfit, but straightened his face into an all-business look in a blink.

"Aaron said he'd send you," he said, shaking my outstretched hand.

"How are they doing?" I asked, stepping through the doors when he waved me inside.

"The guy is a mess. Malnourished, psych issues, maybe drugs. No idea how long he's been on the streets."

"He won't tell you?"

"I'm not sure he remembers." Landers ran one hand through his curly brown hair. "He keeps babbling about his 'safe place.' I feel bad for him, but I can't get a damned thing out of him, and right now what I need is information."

"Age?"

"Early to mid twenties if I had to guess," he said.

Aw, jeez. "That's young."

Landers shrugged. "We've seen an uptick in the twenty-something homeless population in the past couple years," he said. "People graduate college with a mountain of debt and no job prospects—the ones who can't go home to mom and dad end up on the streets."

I nodded understanding and reached for a notebook and pen, arching a brow at him. "Do I get any of this on the record?"

"I'd rather the rest of the local media not spend the next three days hounding me for statistics on vagrants."

He had a point—his work had to come first. I could find the same thing in twenty places online, anyway.

"Aaron said there were two callers," I said.

"White female, about the same age. Practically catatonic. Can't say anything. Or won't. She just stares."

"Well, these should be fun and productive interviews." I sighed. Not that I could blame them. I'd seen some nasty stuff in almost eight years at the crime desk, and I was more than a little freaked if I let images of the scene into my thoughts.

The scene. "You have an age estimate on the victim?"

He shook his head. "From looking? Early to mid twenties. But I'm sure we'll have an ID tomorrow. We got clean prints."

I nodded.

He gestured to the nurse's station and turned for the door. "I've gotten all I can here for the moment, so I'm going to see if I can run down any more leads." He paused, staring hard at me for a moment. "Aaron trusts you."

I smiled. He also owed me a very large favor. "I have a good handle on what folks need to know and what they don't. I won't compromise your case. Maybe I can even help."

"I hope so." He put a hand on the crash bar and closed his eyes. "I've never seen anything like that. Not in real life."

"They walked me in. It's...utterly horrific. Go. Find him."

"Him?"

"Statistically speaking, you're looking for a thirty-something white guy, right? She was...on display. That's Ted-Bundy-type stuff."

"You know your serial killers." He nodded approval. "First rule of police work, by Christopher Landers: follow the easy trail. Rule number two: never discount anything."

"Noted. I think we're going to get along, Detective."

"Thanks for coming, Miss Clarke."

"It's Nichelle. And I should be thanking you." I smiled, wishing I could see Charlie's face when she read my story.

He disappeared to the foyer, and a stoic nurse with a gray bun tight enough to double as a face lift directed me to two rooms at the end of the hall. "They won't be here more than eight hours," she said. "State law says we keep them at least that long, but I'm going to need those beds in the morning."

I bit my tongue, thanking her and turning for the end of the hallway. It wasn't her fault there weren't enough beds in any psych ward in the state. But letting myself wonder how much easier Landers's job would be with a better mental healthcare system wouldn't get me anywhere but pissed off.

Information. These folks had it, Landers needed it. And if I could pull it out of them, I'd help the investigation, and win a bigger headline than everyone else had as a bonus.

I tapped on the first door and poked my head in when no one answered. A skinny guy with sun-ravaged skin and shaggy, greasy hair sat in the floor in one corner, his long arms trying to pull his knees through his chest.

"Hey there," I said gently.

"Safe. Safe. Bloodeverywherenotsafeanymore," he muttered into his thighs.

I stepped into the room and shut the door with a click that might as well have been a gunshot. He jumped three feet, a small scream escaping his lips.

I turned mine up into a friendly smile. "I'm so sorry. I didn't mean to startle you."

"Who are you?" He flattened himself against the wall. "Hookers part of the treatment here now?"

I swallowed a laugh, widening my smile and shaking my head. "Fair question. I'm a reporter. Who was at a costume party when this call came in. One of the interesting things about my job is I don't get to say when news breaks. I think this is officially the most ridiculous outfit I've ever come to work in, though." I inched closer. "I'm Nichelle."

"I'm not." His gaze stayed focused over my shoulder, interest playing around the corners of his mouth. "What do you want? How'd you even get in here?" He scrubbed at his nose with the dingy cuff of his faded Yankees windbreaker.

"A cop who owed me a favor got me in," I said. "I just want to talk to you about what happened tonight."

My words contorted his face into a mask of terror and he sank back to the floor, hugging his knees again. Same response Landers got.

New tactic.

"Or not," I said hurriedly, scooting toward a drab gray armchair and perching on it. "We can talk about whatever you want. What's your favorite food? Place to hang out? Time of year?" Questions popped through my lips on auto-fire, my words tripping over themselves trying to get him back.

His head raised slowly. He blinked and looked around the room, finally settling his hazy blue eyes on my cheekbone. "I like pizza."

"Me, too." I said, pulling out a notebook and pen. "You ever been to Bottoms Up?"

"Best pies in town." He nodded. "One of the cooks there gives us leftovers on Friday nights. Nice guy. He says they even make the cheese fresh. Like, make it."

I scribbled as he talked. My brain sped forward, hunting a way to bring up the dead girl without sending him back into his hidey-hole.

"That explains why it's so amazing," I said. "You have friends, huh? I imagine sticking together is safer than being alone."

"Sure. There's me and Fl—" he stopped. "No names."

I raised both hands, doubting any of them went by their real names, anyway. "Sure. Whatever you feel comfortable with."

He toyed with the laces on one of his worn green combat boots. "There's four of us. Or, there were. Three now, I guess."

I caught a deep breath. Hot damn. Were they so flipped out because they knew the victim? That could be a huge lead for Landers. And a giant exclusive for the *Telegraph*. I gripped my pen tighter. He had to say it.

Baby steps. Easy questions.

"Where's the guy who isn't here?"

He pulled at the shoelace again. "Shelter. Wanted a shower."

"Why didn't you go with him?"

"I was working," he said.

I jotted that down. Worth coming back to, but I didn't want to shut him up by asking what he meant. Clearly, he didn't have a nine-to-five.

"They said you sleep down on Belle Isle sometimes?"

He nodded. "It used to be a switch house for the power plant. No one's ever there at night. Cops patrol the park pretty good after dark, watching for drug dealers. But if you know the way through the woods, you can get in there without crossing the rocks, and they don't see you. It's a safe place to sleep. Cool in the summer, with the breeze from the river and all the concrete."

My hand flew across the page. I was afraid to even breathe too loud, not wanting him to stop talking now that he'd started.

"How did you get up into the loft?"

"Rope ladder. I made it. It was like our own private clubhouse. Safe. No one could get up there unless we let them up. She liked that."

I underlined those words. I didn't remember noticing any rope, which made it worth mentioning to Aaron.

"But there was so much blood. Not a safe place anymore." His head dropped to his knees, his hunched back rising and falling with hitching breaths. "She was all cut up. And her eyes were still open. Still so pretty. Greener than the oak leaves."

He sobbed, resuming his rocking.

I reached for his shoulder, my hand stalling in midair. I wanted to comfort him, but folks who live on the streets aren't generally too touchy-feely. I also wanted the girl's name. He knew her as well as I knew my favorite Jimmy Choos. Flat-out asking wouldn't get me anywhere, though.

I watched, staying quiet. He'd forgotten he wasn't alone in the room.

"Don't you think her family might want to know?" I kept my tone soft when I finally spoke. Chances were, the fingerprints would ID her within twenty-four hours. But I wanted it first.

He stopped rocking, raising his head slowly. "They know. Of course they know. They killed her."

2

I tried to get him to elaborate for a half-hour. More rocking and several muttered refrains of "stupid, stupid, stupid, big mouth, stupid" were all he offered before I thanked him and let myself out, crossing the hallway to the girl's room.

I stopped short when the door opened to reveal a harried-looking doctor.

"Are you a relative of this patient?" he asked, his eyes widening when he saw me.

I smoothed my skirt and hoped my hair had fallen at least a little. "Not exactly," I said. Damn. Having permission from Aaron to talk to a patient worked on nurses, but I was pretty sure a doctor wouldn't let me in there if the President himself said it was okay.

He put an arm across the doorway. "Family only," he said.

Double damn.

"I really need to talk to her."

"She's not going to be talking to anyone for about six hours," he said. "Shock. She's been sedated. Maybe sleep will put her in a good enough frame of mind to avoid getting herself killed when we have to kick her out in the morning."

My eyebrows went up.

He sighed. "As much as I wish I had enough beds to keep every derelict in the city who could use some therapy," he began, and I raised one hand.

"Preaching to the choir, doc."

Well, shit.

If they'd drugged her, I wouldn't get anything else at the hospital tonight. Since the call came in so close to the eleven o'clock broadcasts, I knew without looking the TV stations didn't have anything but a breaking report about a body discovery and a short live feed from the river. So I had until morning to put something more together and get it to my editor for the website.

Journalism in the age of the Internet ion deadline is five minutes before someone else might have it.

The doctor rushed past me when a sharp shrieking echoed down the hall. I threw a last glance at the closed doors and checked my watch, hoping Kyle hadn't bored with the party and bailed early.

Maybe Captain SuperCop could help me figure another angle to work.

"On my way back," I tapped in a text to him as I stepped into the elevator, "Wait for me?"

He didn't reply before I got to my car. I turned toward the suburbs, laying on the accelerator. My thoughts raced faster than my little red SUV through what I knew, and what Charlie could possibly come up with before morning. If the prints came back before dawn, she could have the victim's identity before the early show.

Considering that, I shot past who the woman was to how she ended up on the street. The guy I left muttering in the psych ward knew her, and more than in passing. But why did he think her family was responsible for the horror scene in the old switch house? I was pretty far from assuming he meant they took a knife to her, because—well, mostly because I wasn't ready to think someone could do that to their own kin. The first step to that kind of murder is dehumanizing the victim, which would be harder for relatives. I hoped.

I turned into Jenna's driveway still pondering and spotted Kyle's black Stetson in the far corner of the wraparound porch. He claimed Wyatt Earp from Tombstone—loosely eighties attire at best—was the only thing he'd had time to come up with on short notice. Since he knew good and well I had a serious Texas-girl weakness for sexy cowboys, I didn't buy it for half a second.

He did look good, though. Hanging back in the shadows, I admired the way his lightweight duster hugged his broad shoulders, falling into folds at his narrow waist and hitting his starched jeans just above the heels of his Justin ostrich dress boots. My relationship with my ex, who also happened to be my favorite hotshot ATF agent, was nothing if not complicated. More so lately, thanks to my friendship with a certain Mafia boss.

Fortunately, I thought fast enough on my feet to avoid giving up that Joey was anything more than a source. Unfortunately, Kyle didn't care for the idea of me knowing Joey at all. But he was getting over it. I hadn't decided if that was a good thing.

Our friendship was easy. But Kyle wanted more than friendship. I wasn't sure I did.

Sure, my knees still went to jello at the sight of his profile under the Stetson when he turned his head, and my pulse sped at the memory of knocking said hat to my porch during a pretty amazing kiss. The sticking point: in the two months since, I'd been unable to replicate the chemistry.

Possibly because Joey was a damned fine kisser, too. When he was around, anyway.

I sighed, putting one hand on the porch rail and raising the other as Kyle turned toward me. My greeting faltered when Tanya Murphy, an angst-ridden poet who helped out at the bookshop Jenna ran, stepped forward with him, one goth-manicured hand clamped around his bicep.

Complicated. Everything had to be so complicated.

"Nicey!" He grinned when he spotted me, then followed my gaze to Tanya. His ice blue eyes skipped between us for a moment and the grin settled into a confident smile. "Anything interesting? Or did you run off and leave me here all by myself for nothing?"

"Wait till you hear," I said, my eyes stuck on the fingers wrapped around his arm. I raised my gaze to Tanya's face and found a tight smile pasted there, her hazel eyes pitching daggers my way.

I grabbed Kyle's other hand, lacing my fingers with his and offering him my warmest smile. "I could use your expertise, if you're interested in cutting out of here early." The memory of the murder scene shook off the guilt following the territorial feeling. I did need to talk to him. And if it kept him out of Tanya's bed—well, that was her problem.

He tipped the corners of his lips up in a sexy smile, his eyes skimming my form-fitting costume before they returned to my face. "Which expertise are you in need of? I have many."

Tanya's hand fell away from his other arm, and she spun on the heel of one black stiletto biker boot and stalked into the house.

Kyle didn't look sorry to see her go. "I know better than to get my hopes up," he said, pulling me to him and wrapping an arm around my shoulder. "But one of these days, we have to get the timing right."

"One of these days," I echoed, breathing in the light, summery scent of his favorite cologne and fighting through memories of some lovely, long-ago evenings when the timing was more than right.

"Just let me tell Jenna goodnight," I said, turning for the front door. "And don't pick up another ingénue while I'm gone."

"I can't make any promises." He chuckled. "How about I come with you and thank her for the hospitality? It was nice of them to invite me. I haven't been to a non-business function since I moved here."

Jenna's eyes popped wide when I hugged her and whispered I was leaving with Kyle. From the overly loud "have fun, doll," and sloppy chortle that followed, she'd had several more margaritas after I left for the river.

I squeezed her hand and promised to call her the next day. Not that she'd remember.

Settled in my passenger seat with the Stetson across his knees and a six pack under his belt, Kyle leaned back and turned to me. "What's up?"

I took a deep breath, my hands trembling again at the memory of the bloodbath down by the James.

"Murder. And not your garden variety." I started the car and backed into the cul-de-sac. "I've never seen anything like this, Kyle. Not even on paper. It was... God." I shook my head as I pointed the car downtown, searching for words. "Evil. How could a human being do such a thing?"

The tension in my voice made quick work of his Dos Equis. He sat up straighter, running one hand over his close-cropped hair as he tried to clear the beer fog from his brain.

"What did you see?"

I stopped at a light and put the blinker on to signal a turn toward the freeway.

"A woman." I closed my eyes. "She was...it was—there was so much blood, Kyle." I sniffled, blinking impatiently over the tears pricking at the backs of my eyes. "Horror-movie-type stuff. They made an altar. There were candles. She was laid out. Carefully. Like a museum piece."

He reached over and squeezed my hand. "I'm so sorry, honey." Annoyance crept over the sincerity in his tone. "What the hell possessed White to let you into a scene like that?"

"Me." I shook my head. "He owed me a favor. I think I need to re-examine my reward structure." I kept quiet about Aaron asking for my help, because I wasn't altogether sure he was supposed to. Kyle might get pissed enough to call and yell at someone if he thought Aaron was putting me in harm's way.

Driving on autopilot, I answered his tight questions as fast as he could ask them. He was particularly interested in the scene and the method of entry. "If they had a rope ladder they pulled up behind them, then she let someone up, or they brought their own ladder." He tapped his index finger on his knee.

I nodded. Something else to ask Aaron about. Continuing my story, I paused when I got to the bit about the victim's family. I didn't want anyone else to have a shot at that angle before I could dig deeper. But I had to tell Aaron, so I might as well pick Kyle's ATF-agent brain about it while I could.

I slowed to a stop in front of his apartment building, turning in the seat to face him.

"When I was at the hospital, the guy who found the body said something. But I'm not sure what to make of it."

"I'm listening."

"He knew the vic, Kyle. That's part of the reason they're so freaked."

"You think he did it?"

I shook my head hard enough to budge my shellacked halo of frizz. "Nope. Tom Hanks couldn't have pulled off the performance that dude put up tonight. But when I asked about her family—I was trying to get a name. You know how street people are about names."

He nodded.

"So I asked him if someone should let her family know. And he said, 'They know. They killed her.'"

Kyle sat back. "Huh."

"That's what I said."

"Literally, killed her? Because they'd have to be pretty sick."

"Exactly." I felt the corners of my lips turn up in a smile, which seemed all kinds of wrong, given our subject matter. "I had the same thought. That makes me oddly proud of myself, Captain Bigshot."

He winked. "You're learning." His eyes flicked toward the building's front door and his voice dropped half an octave. "You want to come in? I could teach you some other stuff, too."

I swallowed hard. That sounded way more tempting than I wanted to admit, especially with him looking like he'd walked off the cover of a western romance novel.

It also sounded complicated.

I twisted my mouth to one side. "I don't know."

He dropped his eyelids half-shut and leaned toward me. "Need convincing?"

What I needed was to find the stomach-cartwheels his kisses used to give me. I traced one finger along his jawline, the slight stubble rough under my touch.

"You do look good in the hat."

I closed my eyes and tipped my head to one side, my hand sliding behind his neck. His lips closed over mine and I sighed as he pushed me back into the seat and deepened the kiss.

Ten years apart had done a lot for Kyle's technique—but his improved skill didn't trigger any fireworks. Maybe I wasn't trying hard enough. I pushed the duster back over his shoulders and attempted to get lost in the moment. Making out with Kyle was way more fun than thinking about the butcher scene Aaron had to analyze.

"Come inside," Kyle whispered, moving his lips to my neck. He paused, taking a deep breath. "Jesus, how do you smell so good?"

"Christian Dior." The words came out in short huffs, like I'd been for a run. My fingers found the top button of his shirt as his mouth explored my collarbone. It could be so easy. I could follow him upstairs and we could be us again.

Joey's sparkling dark eyes and low, sexy voice flashed right on the heels of that thought. But Joey had made himself awfully scarce the past couple of months.

I sighed.

Could I do this? Yep.

Was I sure I wanted to? That was the hundred-thousand-dollar question. And the answer was no, whether I wanted it to be or not

I pushed gently at Kyle's shoulders as his hands moved to unclasp my bra. "Whoa, there, cowboy."

He pulled back half an inch and studied my face, slumping into his own seat after he figured out I wasn't staying.

"That's a 'go home' whoa, not a 'slow down' whoa," he said. "You know, you're making me work harder for this than you did when we were kids, Nicey. I don't get it. Is there someone else?"

Oh, boy.

I pulled in a deep breath. How to explain without hurting his feelings? No freaking clue.

"Kyle, you know I love you. I always will," I began gently.

He retrieved the hat from the dashboard and fiddled with the crease in the front. "That sounds suspiciously like an opener for letting me down easy."

"Nothing about this is easy. I'm trying, but I can't seem to find the old fire, you know?" I laid one hand over his and he nodded. "I'm sorry. I wish it was different. But I think we should try the friend thing. For now, anyway. I wouldn't hurt your feelings for the world, but it's not fair of me to let you keep hoping for something I'm not sure will ever be, either."

He tapped a finger on the hat brim, raising his eyes to mine after twelve hours (or possibly a good three minutes that felt like forever) of contemplation. "I don't suppose I have much of a choice." His voice was soft, and the catch in it told me he was hiding hurt feelings behind his grin. "I can appreciate your honesty. But I won't say I'm not sorry."

I pulled his hand to my lips, brushing them over his knuckles. "I am, too."

He squeezed my hand. "I wish I was the kind of guy who could be mad at you. It'd make my life easier. But I'm not."

"We okay?" I raised hopeful eyebrows.

"Right as rain, Granny B would say." He kicked open the door and stood, turning to lean back into the car. "Goodnight, friend. Don't get yourself in over your head chasing this lead, and be careful with White. He might like you, but he wants this collar more than he wants air right now. You think he's doing you a favor. But there's a lot in this one for him. Watch your back."

I nodded. "Thanks, Kyle."

"Call if you need me." He shut the door and disappeared into the building.

His disappointed half-smile followed me all the way home. I knew I'd done the right thing by telling the truth, but it still kind of sucked. There was a hell of a headline waiting for me, though. Dead chick and psycho killer first. Boys later.

Kicking my Manolos to the kitchen floor, I patted my toy Pomeranian on the head and stretched. I wanted the story on the web before the early news shows, so I grabbed a cup of Colombian Fair Trade and my laptop and settled on the sofa to write.

Richmond Police are combing the boulders of Belle Isle for clues in the early light this morning, following the grisly discovery of a murder scene in an old switch house overlooking the park just after 10 p.m. Saturday.

"Evil. Evil is the only word I've got," RPD Spokesman Aaron White said as he surveyed the scene.

White said the young woman was stabbed

I paused, staring at my blinking cursor. Filleted was the word I would personally use, but I didn't want to include too many details of the scene in the story. Walking the line between "enough to nail the exclusive" and "too little to screw up the investigation" wasn't easy on the best day, and at two in the morning on very little caffeine, it was damn near impossible. Stabbed. I nodded, adding "repeatedly." Good enough.

The scene was discovered by vagrants looking for shelter.

"No one's ever there at night," the man who called police told the Richmond Telegraph *in an exclusive interview. "Cops patrol the park pretty good after dark, watching for drug dealers. It's a safe place to sleep. Cool in the summer, with the breeze from the river and all the concrete."*

I added a few more comments from Aaron, tiptoeing around the forensic jargon, but hinting that this murder was anything but standard issue. I put his number in the last paragraph with a plea for information. That would bring the nut jobs out of the woodwork and give him some sorting to do, but chasing wild geese was often the only road to someone who could actually help.

I emailed the story to my editor a little before three, adding an "urgent" flag and a note that I'd be in the newsroom as soon as I got a few hours' sleep.

Standing under the super-bright security light I'd recently added to my backyard, I watched Darcy run a lap around the fence line, still wondering what kind of person could do something so unspeakable.

The puzzle invaded my sleep, dreams peppered with flashes of blood-soaked walls and glassy green eyes, a voice from nowhere repeating a refrain of "they killed her."

They who?

3

I kicked the tangled covers the rest of the way to the floor around eight-thirty, giving up on sleep the third time I woke with blankets strangling my legs. I never rest well when there's a big story in the works—it's nearly impossible to get my brain to shut down—but a potential psycho on the loose added a whole new level of fitful to my slumber.

Darcy didn't move when I plunked my feet to the scarred 1920s hardwood and shuffled to the bathroom. A ponytail and a little concealer later, I found two texts on my cell phone from my editor. Charlie didn't have close to what I did, which always put Bob in an excellent mood. Score one for the crime reporter.

Juggling a latte and my notebook, I stepped off the elevator into the newsroom at nine-fifteen and nearly walked into Shelby Taylor. Her eyes narrowed, her full lips twisting into a sneer before I could get the "excuse me" out of my mouth.

Beating Charlie made Bob happy. It also pissed Shelby off. Not that our copy chief wanted the TV station to scoop us. She just wanted my job, so anything that got me a brownie point or two with the bosses stuck in her craw. And now that she was no longer sleeping with the managing editor, she was more irritable than usual.

"How'd you manage to get more than everyone else in town this morning?" she asked, swiping her spiky black hair off her forehead before she laid her hands on her Barbie-doll-sized hips.

"Why in God's name are you here on Sunday?" I countered, stepping around her and turning toward my desk. "Don't you have a life? Surely Les and his hairplugs moving on hasn't been that devastating. Except when you count the loss of job potential. It must be humiliating, having the guy you were only sleeping with to get my beat dump you."

She gaped at me for a second, recovering with a smirk and a Splenda-coated tone. "I'm sure you wouldn't know anything about that, would you? Because you didn't have an exclusive this morning that's got Charlie Lewis ready to spit nails. How's that ATF agent friend of yours? Still in bed?"

"I don't have to stoop to your tricks to get ahead, Shelby. And it's not an ATF case."

"Mmm-hmm." She widened her eyes and offered a conspiratorial nod. "Whatever gets you through the day, sugar."

The glare I fixed on her retreating back should've burned a hole right through her lacy peach tank top. Her jibe stung more than a little behind the memory of Kyle's lips on mine after I asked him about the murder. I stomped to my desk. If Shelby was half as good at reporting as she was at pushing my buttons, she'd have a column in *The New York Times*.

I dropped my stuff to the tacky brown seventies carpet in my little ivory cubicle, the weekend crew quieter than usual. Settling into my chair, I glanced at Bob's door. Closed. Rare was the story that would get him into the office on a Sunday. Even several years past his wife's death, he honored her wish that his weekends be his own. For the most part, anyway. If he'd seen what I saw last night, he wouldn't leave the newsroom for a month. But given the looming first anniversary of his heart attack, I'd rather keep stress away from him.

I flipped my computer open, laying my notes alongside, and began typing everything I could recall about the murder scene.

An hour later, I had six pages of details I could reference no matter how long the search stretched on. I saved it as "Craven 1," and sent it to the printer. Staring at the *Telegraph*'s home page for a minute, I added a copy of that morning's write-up to the printer queue and stood to go grab them. Retrieving a file folder from the back of my bottom drawer, I named it for my favorite nightmare director, too, and stashed the papers inside.

Checking the clock, I deemed it late enough for normal people to be awake and grabbed the phone, dialing my friend Emily's Dallas cell number.

"Any wedding bells yet?" she drawled by way of hello.

"Oh, go find your own wedding bells, Doctor Sansom," I laughed. Em had been a good friend since forever. Lucky for me, she was also a top-of-her-field criminal psychologist who didn't mind helping me out with a tangled story here and there. As long as I didn't quote her, or ask too much.

"You have to be kidding," she said. "Hasn't it been almost a year since he moved up there? What the heck are you waiting for, doll?"

Em had been there for me when I left Kyle in the terminal at DFW International so many years ago, heading to Syracuse to chase my dreams of covering the White House. Throwing psychology to the wind, she'd told me if it was meant to be, we'd find our way back to each other.

She believed we had. I didn't want to talk about it.

"Just making sure I know what I want," I said. "Isn't the shrink in you proud of me for not jumping into anything serious?"

She sighed. "But the romantic in me wants to live vicariously through you. Forever love, fate—all that drivel I'm not supposed to believe in."

"No Mister Rights in your neck of the woods these days?"

"Girl, I can't even find a Mister Okay For Tonight," she said. "I'm thinking I may have to lower my standards. But I suspect you didn't call to talk about my love life. And since you say you didn't call to talk about yours, what's up?"

"I'm covering a murder this morning," I said, my voice quavering in the middle of the statement. "One unlike anything I've ever seen. I was hoping I could bounce a couple things off you. Just want to know if you think I'm on the right track."

"Hit me."

I gave her the rundown of the scene, a few sharp intakes of breath her only reply until I paused to make sure the coast was clear before I told her about Mr. Brooklyn Baseball. Em cleared her throat as I scanned nearby corners for spiky black hair. Shelby's a good lurker.

. . .

"As your friend, I feel the need to ask if you've talked to anyone about this," Emily said. "Like, a professional anyone. That's a powerful thing to see."

"I'm talking to you," I said.

"Then allow me to put on my shrink hat and ask you how that made you feel, Nicey?"

"Scared shitless. And sick to my stomach. It also made me want to help."

"Help who?"

"The guys at the PD who are trying to catch this nutball." I sighed. "Anyone who loved this woman. What if this is just the beginning? If someone can hack one woman up, what's to keep them from doing it again?"

"That, in my professional opinion, is a perfectly normal response for you," she said. "You are motivated first by your do-gooder instinct, and second by ambition, my friend. Helping your cops with this will fulfill two major needs for you. It sounds like you're dealing fine, but if you find yourself needing to talk, call me. Now, about this crime scene: I've never been called in to help with a bonafide serial killer, but there's a possibility you've got yourself one. There's also a possibility this was a ritual murder."

"Ritual?"

"Candles, display—everything you described? Could have significance for the killer for many reasons," she said. "And your killer could be a single person or a group. If it was a ritual death, there was likely more than one person present for the sacrifice, even if only one killed her. I'm sure your cops are looking at every angle."

"But how many angles are they going to give me?" I wondered aloud.

"As few as they can get away with," she said. "I know you get along well with your guys, but no cop ever fully trusts a reporter."

"So if I want to stay ahead of Charlie, I have to dig up what they're not sharing," I said.

"Bingo."

"Thanks, Em," I said, smiling. "What would I do without you?"

"You'd probably be crazier," she said. "But still just as lovable."

"And short one amazing friend."

"You ought to try the ritual angle first."

I closed my eyes. "There was so much blood, Em."

"Whether or not it was all hers will tell you something."

I cradled the receiver and considered that, wondering if Aaron had time to have blood typing results back. Probably not on the weekend.

What else did I have that Charlie didn't?

The guy from the hospital. I flipped through my notes from his interview.

"There's a cook who gives us leftovers on Fridays."

I shoved my notebook and laptop back into my bag and stood, wondering how early the kitchen staff at Bottoms Up got in on Sundays. And hoping the benevolent cook was chatty.

* * *

I tapped the toe of one strappy emerald Manolo on the slate-and-camel-tiled floor of the entry, waiting for a hostess with a pixie cut and matching smile to return with the manager. It was easier to go through the front door and ask to talk to the kitchen staff than hang out and wait for the back door to open. As long as it worked.

"What can I do for you, Miss?" the manager's dark eyes crinkled at the corners with a grin as he stuck a hand out. I shook it, returning the smile.

"Nichelle Clarke, *Richmond Telegraph*," I said. "I'm working on a story I think some of your staff might be able to help me with, if they have time to chat."

He waved me into the bar and gestured to a black ladderback chair at a small round table, nodding for me to sit as he pulled out the opposite chair. "What kind of story?"

Since the word "murder" would likely get me tossed out on my ass, I smiled and said "the homeless."

"What would my kitchen staff have to do with that?"

"Word is, you have a few people who have developed a reputation for helping. I'm hoping they'll help me, too."

He knit his thick eyebrows together. "I'm not sure if I should get you someone to interview or say no comment and ask you to leave." He spread his hands over the black laminate tabletop. "I can't have it advertised we feed the less fortunate—we're running a business, not a soup kitchen."

"I understand," I said. "I'm happy to leave names out of it." It was an easy trade, especially because it carried the bonus of making it harder for Charlie to follow my tracks.

He stared, not offering a reply for a dozen heartbeats.

I kept my expression neutral. He blinked first, sighing.

"I got four kids. Three boys and a girl, all grown and married," he said. "The people I see on the streets down here—some of them are barely adults. It just about kills me on the daily, ma'am."

I nodded. "I can only imagine."

He pushed the chair back and stood, waving me to my feet. "I read the paper every day. You write about crime. Something bad happen to someone?"

"Do you really want to know?" Not that he wouldn't see it on tomorrow's front page. But I didn't have to be there when he did.

He snapped his dark eyes shut. "Don't think I do. But you think we could help?"

"I hope so."

"You need to talk to Carl." He turned for the swinging door next to the bar. "He should be here by now. Follow me, and don't touch anything."

The dining room was still quiet, but the kitchen bustled with prep for the post-church lunch rush. Mixers whirred, meats sizzled on a long grill, and clouds of steam rose above a stove top covered with huge pots of boiling pasta.

Men and women in black pants and white t-shirts covered by long, sauce-stained aprons shouted conversation over the din. It died when I stepped into the kitchen, curious eyes following every move.

I kept a smile on my face and stayed on the manager's heels until he stopped in the far corner, where a tall man with enormous biceps and a gleaming bald head worked a table-sized clump of white goo I suspected was the fresh mozzarella that covered most of the food in thick, stringy layers.

He nodded to the manager and glanced at me before returning his attention to stretching the mass of cheese to the edges of a large tray. The way the muscles in his arms rippled, it wasn't easy work.

"Carl, this is Miss Clarke. She's a reporter at the *Telegraph*, and she wants to ask you a few questions."

"Making cheese is news, now?" His teeth flashed bright against his dark skin when he grinned at me. "Forgive my manners, but I'm not sure you want to shake my hand right now."

"No worries. Nice to meet you. And while that looks fascinating, food and wine isn't quite my area of expertise. I'm actually looking for information on a group of homeless people. I hear y'all feed them on Friday nights."

Carl glanced at his boss, who nodded an okay.

"There's a lot of folks without a place to stay or food to eat around here," Carl said. "Why throw out pans and pans of stuff at the end of our busiest night of the week when we can do some good with it?"

I pulled out a notebook and pen, jotting his words down. "Absolutely."

"Who are you looking for?" he asked. "And why? Some of those folks got stories that make living on the street seem like a Jimmy Stewart movie."

I put a star by that and looked up.

"The guy I talked to was probably twenty-three, twenty-four. Thin, with shoulder-length hair and a deep voice."

"Picasso." Carl nodded. "Green combat boots, right?"

"That's him. They call him Picasso?"

"He's...different," Carl said, continuing to work on the cheese. "Autism? Maybe slightly slow? I'm not sure. But he can draw like nothing I've ever seen. Makes a little money that way. In the summers, he sells sketches down in the Slip."

I scribbled, underlining as I went. And I thought the guy was in shock. Better than Landers, who thought he was a junkie. "Sketches. Was that what he meant when he said he was working?" I asked.

"Probably. I don't think any of them have regular jobs. Hard to get work when you don't have an address."

"Do you know where they hang out?" I asked.

"I never followed them away from the restaurant or nothing." Carl gathered the edges of a long piece of white muslin around the cheese wheel and cinched them together with a rubber band he pulled off his wrist. Turning, he leaned on the wall. "Why do you care, ma'am?"

"I'm working on a story about a murder," I said, my eyes straying to the manager who didn't want to know. I got that, but I needed a lead on who the victim was—and where she came from. The trick was finding out without giving these men nightmares.

"The one I heard about on the TV this morning? The pretty blonde girl on Channel Four was down at the rocks." Carl ducked his head. "No disrespect, ma'am. We don't get the paper."

I smiled. "I understand. Yes. That one."

"The TV lady said the police weren't saying much. Why do you think we know something about it? I can tell you this: the bunch you're asking about wouldn't hurt anybody. Not unless they didn't have a choice. Picasso —he's a good guy. The girls help him deal with people—he's not great with people—and he takes care of them. Flyboy provides the muscle."

"Flyboy?" I jotted more notes.

"He wouldn't hurt nobody, either, ma'am." Carl paused. "I'm not sure I ought to be telling you all this."

"I don't think they hurt anyone, Carl." Every word true, at least for now. "I think one of them got hurt."

He dropped his head back against the wall. "Lord Jesus. Who?"

"I couldn't get a name out of Picasso."

Carl sighed, pinching his eyes shut.

I leaned on the wall next to him. "I see some pretty crappy stuff in my line of work," I said, dropping my tone to a shade over conspiratorial and leveling a sad gaze at him. "But this is the kind of story that makes me want to trail this sicko all the way to the courthouse. She was pretty. Long, dark hair. Bright green eyes."

"Jasmine." His Adam's apple bobbed with a hard swallow and I scribbled the name. "What happened to her?"

"I'm not entirely sure you want to know. Any idea if that's her real name?"

"I doubt it. The ladies have a thing about flowers, this year. Last year it was singers."

Damn."You're sure you don't know where they call home? There has to be a main place, right?"

He raised his head, studying my face. "You're not looking to get them in trouble?"

"I'm just trying to help."

"I don't know for sure, but there's only so many places around here. And they're always around on the weekends. If I was looking, I'd start walking."

I glanced down at my Manolos. Why not? "Which way?"

"Head under the bridge. Maybe over to the canal. That's the way they leave when Picasso doesn't have his sketchbook."

"Thank you, Carl."

"Let me know if you need any more help." He hefted the cheese wheel and half-turned for the walk-in cooler in the back corner. "What is wrong with people?"

"I wish I knew."

The manager nodded acknowledgement as I thanked him at the front door. I stepped out into the sunshine and turned for the canal, taking the route under the train tracks and keeping my ears open. Picasso and Jasmine. Couldn't find jobs, and didn't have homes. Not much, but more than Charlie had. I wanted to build on it more than I wanted to go home and fetch more practical shoes.

4

Crunch. Crunch. Crunch.

I sped up, not advertising the fact that I was watching the guy as much as he was watching me. I'd trekked clear to the end of the canal and turned back with nothing to show for it except messy shoes, sore toes, and the large man trailing me for the last hundred yards. He wore a threadbare black tank and frayed cargo shorts that probably used to be khaki-colored.

I studied the buildings dotting the street as I neared the bridges. Most of them dated back at least a century, and ten years ago they were probably an abandoned haven for folks with no place else to go. But that was before urban revitalization spread to Shockoe Bottom. Now, structures once left for ghosts sported new windows and trendy condo signage.

My shadow's sneakers whispered over the gravel faster. The guy had three inches and probably thirty pounds of muscle on me. He inched up on my left. I folded my hand into a fist, spinning on my heel.

"Can I help you?" I bit the end of my tongue, the words sharper than I wanted. No need to go looking for a fight.

He jumped back three feet. "I'm sorry, ma'am," he said, raising both hands in mock surrender. "I wasn't trying to scare you. It's just—this isn't really a great place to take a walk alone."

I let a controlled breath out. "It's the middle of the day."

"Even so."

I smiled. "I appreciate the thought," I said.

He eyed my shoes, his eyes traveling slowly up over my tangerine sundress. "Are you the lady from the hospital?"

My eyes widened, Carl's words floating through my thoughts. *"Flyboy provides the muscle."*

I put a hand out. "Nichelle. And you're Flyboy?"

Nodding, he shook my hand, his fingers rough on my palm. "Why are you here?"

I softened my face and my tone. "Y'all called her Jasmine, right?"

His face fell, his eyelids working overtime.

"But that wasn't her real name." I didn't bother to inflect the question mark.

"I don't think so. I don't really know."

"Do you go by your real name?"

He snickered. "Flyboy? No. I used to want to do that. Fly. I was headed for the Air Force Academy, but—" He stopped, shaking his head and dropping his eyes to the dirt.

"But?"

"It didn't work out that way."

I filed that away, afraid to pull out a notebook.

"What can you tell me about her?" I asked gently.

"What do you want?" He narrowed his eyes.

"To help you." I met his gaze head-on.

"How?"

"Well, I thought I might start by helping the PD figure out who killed your friend. Maybe keep them from doing it again."

He tipped his head to one side. "Why?"

"Because it's the biggest story I've seen this year. Maybe ever. And it has the bonus effect of saving lives."

"You think our lives are worth saving?"

I blanched. "Of course."

He stopped blinking, and I shrank from the pain in his dark eyes. His face was younger than mine. His eyes were not.

I stood up straight and arranged my features into a smile. "It's not what gets done to you. It's what you do with it."

He nodded. "Sounds like something my granddad would've said. Hard to remember sometimes, though."

"I'm sorry."

He scuffed a toe in the rocks. "Me, too."

"How long were you and Jasmine friends? Or maybe a little more than friends?" I ducked my head and caught his eye. "Not that I couldn't be reading it wrong."

"You're not." He sniffled, looking around. "We've been together since last summer. We were going to get out of Richmond. Jazz—she kept talking about getting us the cash we needed for a new start. Bus tickets, a car, a cheap apartment for a while."

Solid plan. And finally, something I could work with. Where would a homeless woman get a big chunk of cash?

Probably nowhere good.

"And did she?" I asked. "Get the money you needed?"

"Not yet. She said it was coming."

"But she didn't say from where?"

"No, ma'am."

Of course not.

"Where were you going?"

"Colorado. She loved the mountains. Said they felt like home."

I pulled a notebook and pen from my bag. "Do you mind if I take notes?"

"No cameras."

"Of course." I nodded, scribbling about money and mountains. "Can you tell me what happened last night? When was the last time you saw Jasmine?"

He raised his head, his eyes focusing on something behind me. "Friday afternoon. I got picked up to go on a crew to the Fan. Remodeling job at one of the big houses over there. I get day-labor construction crews sometimes. The pay is shit, but it's cash. Keeps us fed, mostly. She was watching Picasso sketch the rocks. I got back and he said she took off after food about dark and never came back. We looked all over. All night. All day yesterday. Nobody saw her."

"And you were the friend who went to the shelter?" I guessed.

"I wanted a shower." His voice thickened and he cleared his throat. "It's been so warm out. I didn't know she was in trouble. I never would have... She was my girl, you know? It was us against the world."

"Did your friends keep looking?"

"They were tired. Picasso is—when he gets tired, he's no good to anyone. So I told them to go. I said, go to the old switch house. No one is ever there at night. It's quiet and cool and they could sleep."

I sucked in my cheeks, biting them to keep my jaw from falling open. He sent them to the murder scene? I couldn't tell if that was damning or the craziest actual coincidence I'd ever seen.

I scooted back a small step, leaning against the bridge support and scribbling. My thoughts raced ahead. Could desperation and frustration, and not a Charles Manson wannabe, be responsible for that bloodbath? Maybe. I pinched my lips together, looking up. But why not just strangle her and dump her in the river?

I tucked my pen away, wondering how fast I could get back to my car and get a hold of Aaron. Carl the cook didn't think this guy could've done it, and I'd pass that along—but I had to tell my cops about this chat.

"Do you have any idea what happened to her? Anyone who might have had a fight with her? Wanted to hurt her?"

"I can't." His face twisted into a Braque portrait, the features blurring into an olive mask of grief. "Violet said they cut her up. And lit candles. She was the sweetest, smartest girl I ever met."

Well, hell. Thank you, Dr. Jekyll.

"I'm so sorry for your loss." I tucked the notebook away. Aaron had his work cut out for him. And so did I, because these people would trust Landers about as far as they could shotput him.

"Thank you."

I fished a card out of my bag. "If you think of something that might help, or if you see anything, give me a call?"

He shoved it into his shorts. "Picasso said you were nice. He's good at reading people."

I smiled. "I am, too. Or at least I like to think so."

He looked up at the rusted underside of the train trestle, watching the sunlight flash as a string of cargo boxcars roared overhead.

"Wait," he said.

I leaned forward, not sure I'd heard him over the clatter of the train.

He straightened, his gaze searching my face for something I wasn't sure I could offer.

"Wait here. Just for a minute."

I leaned against the track support, hoping I was right to trust him.

* * *

Less than ten minutes later, I heard his voice again. Sort of. He was a touch out of earshot, so I strained to eavesdrop, but only got about every third word. Like listening to an out-of-tune radio.

Flyboy's tone was heated, insistent. The other voice was female, and uncertainty rang from it like the last bell before summer vacation—high, shrill, but full of promise.

It had to be Violet.

I grabbed for my notebook. The men might not know where Jasmine was from, but women talk to each other. I just needed this one to talk to me.

A few long heartbeats later, he dragged her around the train trestle and clamped an arm around her shoulders, pulling her close to his side to hold her in place.

The dewy look that came over her face as she melted into his ribs made my stomach twist.

"This is Vi," he said.

"I'm Nichelle." I put a hand out and smiled over the unease. Other woman. Who appeared off-her-nut infatuated with the dead chick's boyfriend. Oh, boy.

She brushed her fingers against mine, not meeting my gaze.

"I'm very sorry for your loss," I said.

She shrugged.

Flyboy nodded. "We're a family."

The way she gazed up at his jawline, Violet did not want the role of little sister.

Her head bobbed like she'd read my mind. "Jasmine was the closest thing to a sister I've ever had." Violet cast her eyes at the dirt, her voice monotone. Detached. Creepy.

"By all accounts, y'all were very close. I'm trying to figure out who she was. Make the story more about her life than her murder. But I need you to talk to me."

"About what?" She looked up at me, finally, a sparkle missing from her blue eyes.

"How old was she?" I asked.

"A little older than me, I think. Twenty-four? Twenty-five? We don't exactly throw birthday parties."

I glanced to Flyboy and he nodded.

She leaned harder into his chest. He squeezed her shoulder and she smiled. I got very interested in my notes, because I didn't have to be psychic —or even very perceptive—to see he was trying to comfort her, and she was reading way more into it.

"How old are you?" I asked, feeling my brow furrow.

"Why?" her voice found an edge.

"I'm just—I can't figure out how y'all ended up here. You don't have to tell me anything, of course, and I don't have to print everything you tell me, but I'm trying to understand what's going on."

She glanced back at him, but he was drawing a pattern in the dirt with the toe of his sneaker. I knew he didn't want to answer me. I hoped she'd want to talk about herself, and maybe then she'd talk about her friend.

"I've been on my own since I was seventeen," she said. "I put myself through school with scholarships, work study, and student loans."

"You have a degree?" Landers's words from the night before flashed through my thoughts. "In what?"

She snorted. "Economics. Fat lot of good it did me. I graduated and got a job waiting tables. Then I got a second job pushing fast food. Then I started selling makeup."

The pen stopped moving, my eyes pulled up by the pain in her voice. "What happened?"

"It wasn't enough." She shrugged. "My roommates moved away, so my rent tripled. Credit cards. Student loans—most of mine were private, and there were so many bills. I lost my apartment, and then my car broke down and I didn't have a way to get to work."

"Your family? There must be someone?" I forgot to take notes, my heart hurting for her.

She shook her head. "There's not." Something in the tone told me not to push. "This is my family."

"You're all pretty close?" I asked, dropping my gaze back to the paper.

"We are. Were."

"How did she end up here?" I asked. "Do you know?"

"She didn't talk about her past," Violet said. "Like, at all. Ever. She said the present and future were where the good in her life lay."

I got every word of that. Where the hell had this woman come from that living on the streets gave her hope for a better future? My fingers itched to call Aaron. Surely they had an ID by now.

I glanced up to thank them and Flyboy smiled, his eyes welling up.

"Just like Jazz. Always scribbling in her books."

"What books?"

"She kept journals," Violet explained. "Never could be without a book and a pen. Even if it meant she didn't eat."

"I didn't let her go hungry," Flyboy said softly, and Violet stiffened. He didn't appear to notice.

"Do you—" I paused, clearing my throat and fighting to keep the excitement from my voice. "Do y'all have her journals? And could I borrow them, maybe?" I smiled my most earnest smile at the cloud that flitted across Flyboy's face. "I'll take good care of them. And I'll bring them back."

"You think they might help someone find out what happened to her?" he asked.

I nodded.

Violet leaned away from him. "I'm not sure Jazz would like that," she said slowly.

He tipped his head to one side. I held my breath. And my tongue.

"She's not here to tell me that. If the books can help." He shrugged. "What are we going to do with them?"

"There are only two," she said, turning a distrustful stare on me.

"I won't let anything happen to them," I said.

"Vi, will you get them for me?" Flyboy asked. "I can't look..."

She nodded, squeezing his hand, and turned back the way they'd come. I didn't try to follow—they obviously didn't want me to know where they called home.

He resumed scuffing the ground with his toe, tears dripping from his bowed face to the dirt.

"I'm sorry," I said.

"She shouldn't be...it's not fair." The words tore from his throat. "Why? Why her?" He sniffled.

I stood silently, not sure there was a way to comfort him. But I could find him an answer.

Violet returned with two cloth-covered blank books, pain in her eyes when they lit on Flyboy. She looped an arm around his waist and handed me the journals.

"Thank you." I smiled, half-turning for the side street where my car was parked. "Hey, Flyboy?"

He looked up, dragging the back of his hand across his face and pulling Violet to his side. "Yes, ma'am?"

"Who else knew about the power plant?"

He shrugged. "Everybody, I reckon. But we could sleep up there with the ladder pulled up."

"Who would she have let up there with her?"

"Nobody but us." Another tear escaped his left eye and disappeared into the scruff along his jawline. Violet shot me a clear go-to-hell look and reached up to thumb the tear away, murmuring something I couldn't hear.

I felt eyes on my back until I turned the corner.

Money. Romance. Jealous girl. And an unknown, unhappy past.

I started the car and turned onto East Cary, headed for Grace Street. Aaron better be at his desk instead of on his boat, beautiful summer day be damned.

5

The crimson edges of the photo peeping around the file folder in the center of Aaron's desk told me I didn't want to see the pictures. He gestured to a black plastic chair in front of me and sank into his gray one before he spoke.

"What the hell is happening here, Nichelle?" He flipped the folder open and I cringed, but the top sheet, at least, was a detective's narrative. A very long detective's narrative, from the looks of the scrunched-up scribbles covering the page.

"I wish I knew." I perched on the edge of the chair. "I talked to a few folks today. I have a couple of things I think might help you. And a few questions."

"Of course."

"This is a screwy case if I've ever seen one, detective."

"Screwy. Scary. Sadistic. I have lots of S words for it."

I felt my lips turn up in a ghost of a smile. "I take it you don't have any solid leads yet?"

"Not a one. Please tell me you got something." He tapped a finger on the paperwork, nervous energy thrumming in the air around him.

"A few things." I pulled out my notebook and flipped it open, running a finger down the first couple of pages before I looked up. "Those folks who called it in? They knew her. Like, were friends with her. I tried to get a lead on her family, and the guy you saw last night told me they killed her."

Aaron's jaw fell onto his knee, his eyes wide. I gave him a minute to process before I spoke again.

"I'm thinking he doesn't mean literally," I said. "But I couldn't get him to say anything else. And there was another guy who's part of their group. He and the vic—they called her Jasmine—had a thing going."

Aaron snatched up a pen and flipped a piece of paper over, jotting notes.

"You didn't get a name for the boyfriend, did you?"

Not a real one. They call him Flyboy. He said something about the Air Force Academy. Not sure how that'll help you, but it's a teensy lead."

"I'll take it." He sat back. "Everything about this has been like trying to find a needle in a barn during hay harvest season."

"Here's another one for you: Flyboy said they wanted to leave Richmond. There were four of them. Two girls and two guys. They all live on the streets. And they wanted to get the hell out of Dodge and make a fresh start."

"Where?"

"Colorado."

"The Air Force Academy." Aaron made more notes.

I nodded. Aaron was a brilliant detective. But this case had shaken him in a way I'd never seen. "The victim was talking about getting money for them to move. A lot of it. But if he knows from where, he wouldn't say. Oh, and he works off-the-books construction."

He kept writing. "Gives me something to go on." Aaron's chest heaved with a sigh and he sat back and dropped his pen. "I'll take anything right now."

I clicked out a pen. "How is it possible y'all haven't ID'd her yet?" Landers said they had clean prints. The DMV database should have produced a name and former address hours ago.

"She didn't have a driver's license or a criminal record."

"A dental, then?" Those were harder to match, but with a case like this, the command staff would've lit a fire under whoever was working on it.

Aaron shook his head, running one hand over his close-cropped blond hair. "They've been on it since the middle of the night. There are no matching records."

I tapped my pen. "She didn't come from nowhere."

"It looks like she might have. The chief even called in a favor from the damned FBI and got their superbrain people to check it. There's no record of a dental match anywhere in the United States. And the head forensics guy over there says he buys that, because the decay and damage levels in her molars indicate she's never seen a dentist."

What the ever-loving hell?

"How old was she?"

"Early twenties. Between twenty-one and twenty-five."

I nodded. "Her friends said twenty-four or five. How does a person get to be that old and never go to the dentist?"

"It happens in poor families more often than people think," Aaron said. "It's one more question mark hanging over this, and the clock is ticking. Fast."

"Did you find anything else useful at the scene?"

"A whole lot of blood."

"No weapon?" No way the killer had been so careless, given the elaborate nature of the murder scene, but I had to ask.

"Nope."

I stared for a minute at the bluish hollows under his eyes, just a shade darker than his irises. He looked beaten. "It's a hard one to handle," I said gently. "I didn't sleep well last night."

The corners of his mouth turned down and he dropped his chin to his chest. "I sent my girls back to school this morning. They got home for summer a couple weeks ago. I made them call around and find places to stay and go back. They're too close to her age. I can't have them here with a psycho on the loose."

I nodded, unable to imagine how worried Aaron must be to give up vacation time with his daughters. Ticking clock, indeed.

"The guys both said they slept in that loft in the summer," I said. "They had a rope ladder they could pull up behind them to stay safe. Did you find one?"

He grabbed his pen and scribbled that down before he looked up. "We did not."

"So someone took it," I said, writing notes myself. "Who would she have let up there with her?"

Violet.

"There's a girl," I said. "The other one in their group. She seems very interested in the victim's boyfriend."

He shook his head, writing more.

"Name?"

"Goes by Violet."

He nodded a thank-you. "Landers is good. So are the other forty guys we have on this. We'll figure it out," Aaron said. "I just hope it's before anything else happens."

"You really think it could be a serial?"

"Off the record?" His baby blues were serious. And scared.

I nodded.

"The way she was cut up, Nichelle... I think it almost has to be."

Damn, damn, damn. Everything in me shrank into a ball of terror. Covering a serial killer is like walking blindfolded through a minefield in nothing but combat boots. The public has a right to know, but the newspaper has a responsibility to avoid inciting a panic. If they were hunting a psycho, there was precious little I could do to help with the investigation. But I could find out who the victim was, and if anyone she knew had motive. Landers didn't have time to investigate both possibilities. So I'd focus on what he couldn't.

I'd tell him about the journals. After I'd read them.

I tucked my pen away and stood. "Call me if you find anything? I'm going home, at least for a little while. The dog will run away if I don't spend some time on fetch today."

"Thanks for your help, Nichelle," he said. "I owe you one."

"We'll worry about that later."

He smiled.

I paused in the doorway and turned back. Already bent over the case file, Aaron's brow furrowed, his eyes scanning the paper like he could decode the secret message if he just stared hard enough.

* * *

I spotted the sleek black Lincoln as I turned onto my street, and my pulse picked up speed despite my best efforts at control.

"You are not excited to see him," I lied through gritted teeth. "He hasn't even bothered to call in over a month."

Inching the car toward my house, I grasped for composure.

By the time I turned the key on the kitchen door, my face was set to "studiously uninterested," and I hoped for more casual than hurt if I had to talk.

The kitchen was quiet. So was the dog. I ambled toward the living room and peeked around the archway to find Joey settled in one corner of my overstuffed navy jacquard sofa, my toy Pomeranian flopped over in his lap. His long fingers ran absently through Darcy's silky russet fur, his dark eyes staring at nothing.

His broad shoulders and clean-shaven profile were sexy as ever. Dammit. I pulled in a slow breath and managed to keep from jumping into his lap (or flinging a piece of my beach glass collection at his head—it was a toss-up, really) by virtue of the same willpower that had kept me from gobbling the two pound bucket of white fudge almonds in the break room Friday. Giving myself a mental gold star, I cleared my throat.

"If it was dark in here and you were wearing that jacket," I cast a cool gaze at the camel-colored Armani suit coat tossed across my chaise lounge, "I'd have déjà vu, stranger."

My thoughts rewound almost a year, to the first time I'd met Mr. Mystery. Coming home from a long day, I'd found a strange man in an expensive suit sitting on my sofa holding the dog. He'd offered me a story tip and scared the crap out of me—but we'd become...something I didn't have a word for...in the months that followed.

At least, I thought we had.

Joey's eyes snapped to me and the dog's head popped up. She gave me a once-over and dropped her chin back to Joey's knee. He did the same and his lips crept slowly into the sexy grin that played a prominent role in my better dreams.

Must. Resist.

I narrowed my eyes and leaned against the doorframe, folding my arms across my chest. "You forget what I look like? Or maybe you're in the wrong girl's house. Got your keys mixed up?"

He shook his head. "I only have the one key." His voice was low, his eyes serious. "And quite a memory for important things."

My pulse stuttered. Damn him.

"So, you lost it? Your phone, too?"

He locked his dark eyes with my violet ones, shaking his head slowly.

The utter calm pissed me off.

"Then where the hell did you disappear to?" I half-shouted, my resolve cracking. Why try to act like I didn't care? He wasn't stupid, and he was as good or better than me at reading people. "I called, I texted you. You've been ignoring me for almost five weeks, and now here you sit, petting the dog on a random Sunday like you belong here or something."

"I don't." He said it so quietly I almost didn't hear him.

"I'm sorry?" I felt my brow furrow.

His dark eyes lost their playful gleam. "I don't belong here." He cleared his throat, dropping his gaze to Darcy's collar. "I never did. I tried to stay away. Then I saw your article this morning."

My thoughts pinged in a thousand different directions. He didn't want to be here. Or felt like he shouldn't, anyway, and I knew him well enough to know that could end whatever we had going on.

But he was here. Because he saw my story.

About the crazy butcher scene and the dead woman.

Shit.

Was he worried about me?

Or did he know something about her?

I latched onto the latter, pushing emotion to one side and holding it at bay with thoughts of the murder scene. Joey couldn't have had anything to do with it. I'd wear ski socks with my Manolos before I'd believe that.

So why was he in my living room?

I pushed off the wall and perched on the edge of the chaise. "Why exactly would my story make you decide to break this vow of silence?"

He twisted his mouth to one side and hauled in a deep breath. "No comment?"

"I'm so not in the mood for games I'd turn down a round of spin the bottle."

He nodded, a frustrated sigh making Darcy pop to attention. He dropped his head back and stared at the ceiling. "This can't work. I know it, and I know you know it, too. One of us has to be strong enough to back away. So I try. And then I see this." He pulled his iPhone from his pocket, brandishing it. My story was on the screen. "What the hell are you doing, nosing around in this? Do you have any idea how dangerous it could be?"

"Aaron asked me to help."

From the stiff set his jaw took, that was the wrong thing to say.

"I would've chased this story anyway," I added. "It's horrifying. Which sells a shit-ton of newspapers. And helping the cops catch this guy adds the bigger bonus of being a freaking public service. How could I not 'nose around in' this one? It practically has 'Hey, Nichelle, big headline this way' stamped across it in neon."

"At the risk of giving myself some déjà vu, the headline does you how much good if you get yourself killed chasing it?"

"Why does your brain always jump to that?"

"The same reason you always wonder if I'm the culprit when I try to warn you off a story? Just a guess." He grinned, and my insides turned to mush.

It couldn't just be easy.

I ducked my head and caught his gaze. "To be fair, I dismissed that immediately today. There's no way you had a hand in this." Joey had criminal underworld connections that had come in handy for me in the past. The kind that go with being fairly high up in the Mafia. But he wasn't a murderer. Almost eight years at the crime desk had graced me with a fail proof psycho radar, and Joey didn't fit the bill.

"Thanks." His wry smile made my lips curve into an involuntary grin. "But I'm still worried. I'm not saying don't write about it, but what the hell were you doing, interviewing psych patients? And where have you been this morning?"

"Talking to people who won't talk to the cops." I sat back. "They're dealing with street people. And I'm in the very rare position to help Aaron with a criminal investigation, with the bonus that he trusts me enough to let me in on it. I've got stuff no one else can get. It's a helluva lead. I can't walk away."

"Can't is too strong a word. Won't. But I know better than to argue you should put your life ahead of the story. So I figure maybe I can help point you in a safer direction."

"Which is?"

"Your detective friend is right. Whoever did this isn't your garden-variety crime of passion killer." Joey leaned forward, a line creasing his brow. "If I'm reading between the lines right, your murder scene had a setup. Some ceremony to it. It was planned. Maybe even professional. For the record, Miss Clarke, that's not something I want you anywhere near."

"I found myself wondering today if it was her friend." I fidgeted with the hem of my sundress. I hadn't really wanted to be there, either. But I wanted the story almost as badly as I wanted to kiss Joey. "I met a girl who has a crush on the victim's boyfriend."

"It wasn't her."

"How do you know?" My head snapped up.

He chuckled. "Always a little doubt."

"That's not what I meant."

He sat back. Darcy resumed her spot on his thigh, pushing her nose under his hand. I smiled. My dog is an excellent judge of character.

"Did you talk to this woman?" Joey asked, scratching Darcy's ears.

"Yes."

"Of course you did." He rolled his eyes. "Is she a bodybuilder?"

I laughed. "No."

"Think about what you saw. Is she strong enough to have done it?"

"No." I sighed.

Joey nodded. "I don't know who did it—" he paused and shook his head when I raised a brow. "Believe me. If I knew, I'd walk them into the PD myself. Anything to get you out of the middle of this."

"I think it's my turn for the eye roll, but it feels trite," I said. "If you're so ready for me to abandon this, why help me?"

He sighed. "You won't give it up no matter what I say, right?"

"Right."

"So if I play bodyguard and offer opinions, maybe you'll avoid becoming steak tartar."

"Can't hurt." I barely got the words out, my throat closing over a wash of emotion. I missed him. Opinions meant he'd be around. I leaned forward, reaching one hand out. His face softened, the guarded lines disappearing.

"I should have known better," he said softly, setting Darcy on the floor and sliding onto the coffee table. He leaned his cheek into my palm.

"Than to come here?" His skin was baby-soft under my fingertips. And he smelled so good.

"Than to try to avoid you. I can't do it."

I tipped my head to one side when his eyes fell shut. "I'm glad. Because I don't want you to."

Joey's breath warmed my lips, and my pulse jackhammered a staccato beat.

Thwap. Thwap. Thwap.

I opened my eyes, and Joey turned his head. Surely my heart wasn't beating that loud. The kitchen door clicked shut and I muttered, "what now?"

Joey's fingers closed over my hand.

"Hey hot stuff, how was Agent Sexy last night?" Jenna. Her voice was playful, her flip flops slapping her feet with every step.

Her timing sucked.

"Even better than you expected? I've waited for you to dish the details all day and—" the words died on her lips when she rounded the corner, her eyes popping so wide I could see white all round the brown. "Oops."

I turned my head slowly back to Joey. Hurt plain in his dark eyes for a split second, he set his face to "stoic stare" as I sat back, shaking my head at them both. "No."

"Or maybe I was right." Joey dropped my hand, standing and offering Jenna a polite nod before he grabbed his jacket, shot me an unreadable glance, and walked out.

6

"I'm so sorry, doll," Jenna flopped onto the chaise next to me as the front door slammed.

I peeked at her through splayed fingers, my head cradled in my hands.

"I don't know what the hell I'm doing, Jen. Except trying to help Aaron figure out this murder. It's kinda sad, dead people being the only thing in my life that make any sort of sense at the moment, huh?"

She leaned one shoulder against me and giggled. "I'm not sure I'd put it that way. Mostly because it is kinda sad. And I don't believe there's a soul who would feel sorry for you if they got a look at that dude. Was that him?"

I nodded.

"Damn, girl. Talk about a rock and a hard place."

"I'll pass up the suggestive pun opportunity and just agree with the sentiment." I leaned back and closed my eyes, the dog scratching at the front door making me sigh. "Me too, Darce."

"What happened? I thought you said he was in incommunicado."

"He has been. Then he was here when I got home. Claimed he was worried when he saw my story this morning."

"Me, too. But I'll get there in a second," Jenna said. "Y'all looked pretty cozy when I came in."

"We were getting that way."

"And what about the other one?"

"I didn't sleep with Kyle last night. No matter how hard I try, I'm just not getting a spark with him. Of anything other than friendship, anyway. Pretty sure I hurt his feelings, but he was sweet about it. And now Joey's feelings are hurt, too. I give up. Is there a convent around here?"

Jenna laid one hand on my knee. "Could I have worse timing? I didn't know you had company."

"How could you? I haven't heard from him in weeks. I'm kind of pissed at him, with his sexy jawline and magical smell having taken their leave so I can think straight. He just decided he wasn't good for me and bailed without even saying goodbye, or giving me a chance to have an opinion? What kind of ass-backward, Donna Reed crap is that?"

"Maybe he figured you'd talk him out of it?"

"If he really didn't want to be here, I couldn't, could I?"

"Doll, from what I saw just now, the question is not whether he wants to be here. It's whether he feels like he ought to be. And like it or not, those are very different things."

I nodded, leaning my head on her shoulder and focusing on the long, flat box in the center of the coffee table. Inside were five-thousand laser cut pieces of a Manet that would be easier to put together than my personal life.

Joey. Kyle.

Kyle. Joey.

I'd almost swear they were in cahoots, trying to drive me bonkers.

"I have more important things to worry about." I sat up, retrieving my notes from the floor. "You want to talk about a murder?"

"I'm not going to be any help. I gathered it wasn't the typical dead coed. But I got the feeling you were being vague. Though not as vague as Charlie Lewis."

"I was vague on purpose. She was vague because it's all she's got." I grinned. "Mom's perspective: could you see a scenario in which a parent could have someone murder their daughter?"

"I'm not crazy, of course, but I can't imagine being angry enough at one of mine to want them dead." Jenna bent forward and picked Darcy up, rubbing the dog's velvety ears. "Here's what I would want: I'd want to be notified before I saw her picture on TV. It would suck to find out your kid was dead that way."

"I agree. But Aaron can't notify the family until he finds out who she is." I waved the notes. "And based on this, I hope he brings them in for questioning after he notifies them. Assuming there's anyone to notify. She was on the streets, which means she felt like she couldn't go home."

I opened my mouth to ask about the party just as my cell phone chirped a text alert. Bob.

I held one finger up and clicked the message open. "Two seconds."

She shrugged. "I don't have any place to be. The kids are still at my moms, and Chad is running all afternoon. Marathon training."

"'What the hell is this?' in all caps and a web link from Bob are never a good combination," I said, touching the blue words on my screen.

"River City Four-one-one," I read aloud.

I scanned the blog post, words failing me. Most of them, anyway. "Shit."

"What's wrong?" Jenna pressed her cheek to mine and looked at my screen. "What is that?"

"It appears to be a blog. Written by someone who knows way more about this case than they should." I clicked my contacts open. "Can we have a rain check on catching up? Looks like I have something else to investigate."

"Sure, honey. I'll talk to you soon." She let herself out as I flipped my laptop open and punched in the blog address.

"This is the very last thing I need, Darcy." I reached for my cell phone. "Like I don't have enough deadlines breathing down my back already."

* * *

Aaron sounded as flabbergasted as I felt, though there wasn't much he could do about it but be pissed off. He promised to put it on the cyber crimes unit's watch list and hung up.

I clicked back through a dozen entries, all of them recent. All of them detailed. Too detailed. How had I missed this?

The blogger's profile was no help, the name listed as Girl Friday (cute, if

I hadn't been so annoyed) and current city as Richmond. The profile was set up in mid-May, the avatar a notebook and pen.

I called Bob next.

"Is it Shelby?" I asked when he picked up.

He chuckled. "While I wouldn't put it past her, she was in the newsroom until late last night. She emailed me about a feature for tomorrow at nine-fifteen. And I'd can her for leaking stories online. I'll go with 'probably not.'"

"Who the hell is it, then?"

"Not a clue. I know it's not you. You know it's not you. Keeping the publisher on the right side of that once Shelby catches wind of this and stirs it up? Well. I do love a challenge."

"What possible motivation could I have for writing a crime case blog? Like I don't have enough work to do with the eighty-hour weeks I put in for y'all? Ask Andrews that."

"Noted." Bob sighed. "I miss the days when my biggest worry was whether Channel Four could get a piece written and to the anchor before we got the afternoon edition out. Calling in copy from pay phones, drinking Scotch in the newsroom after five."

"Like Mad Men with ink stains?" I smiled. Bob was my hero. The history he'd had a front-row seat for in the seventies and eighties, the difference he'd made with the stories he wrote—it was everything I aspired to do.

"Less makeup, but yeah," he said. "No bloggers, no twitter. I'm showing my age, but it was a simpler time."

"The hashtags get tricky." I laughed. "But I do love my cell phone."

"Ah, but I saw Elvis in concert."

"Now that, I'm jealous of. The Pulitzer? Eh. Elvis? You got me."

I could practically see his eyes crinkle at the corners when he chuckled. "Your story this morning was good, kiddo."

"I have more good stuff. Hopefully it won't wind up on the Internet. Before we put it there, anyhow."

"Can't wait to see it. You'll be in for the meeting tomorrow?"

"Unless there's another dead body."

"Let's hope not."

I clicked off the call and put the phone down, staring at my computer screen. One of the first posts chronicled an ATF bust of a fake medical marijuana ID operation. Kyle wasn't lead on the case, but he had to know something about it. And he might know how this blogger had gotten so much information. The post quoted a lot of "unnamed sources" and had details about the location I didn't get. Neither did Charlie or anyone else. How?

I clicked back to the main page. Our mystery crime writer had only eighty-seven followers, but Jasmine's murder was the kind of case that could put the whole city on edge if more people started reading this. There wasn't an attributed quote from the police department, but Friday out-and-out called the case a possible serial murder in her lead. I agreed, privately —but putting that kind of language online could cause a panic.

Growling a string of swearwords, I looked around for the dog. Nowhere in sight. I set the computer on the coffee table, got up to search, and mulled over calling Kyle.

Darcy lay by the front door. I bent to pet her and she lifted her head, gave me a moony-eyed stare, and sighed.

"Don't I know it, girl." I scooped her up and hugged her. "What a mess."

Kyle was likely still upset.

Because of the way I'd left things the night before.

Left.

Him at his apartment.

"Oh, crap, Darcy!" I put her on her feet and dove for my cell phone.

"Yeah?" Kyle's voice tried for cheer, but I could hear the hurt. I wanted to hide under the coffee table.

"I completely forgot about your car until just now," I said. "I've been working all day. I'm sorry. You want me to come get you and take you to pick it up?"

"One of the guys from the office took me by this morning," he said. "But thanks."

I dropped my voice an octave. "I really am sorry."

He sighed. "I'm not mad at you, Nicey. Hurt? A little. Frustrated? You bet. But I don't think you owe me an apology."

"Stop it," I said.

"Stop what?"

"Being such an amazingly decent guy."

Kyle grunted a half-chuckle. "Habit. Anything new on your dead woman?"

"I talked to a few people this morning. Nothing definite. Except that there're no prints on file. And no missing person's report, either."

"Huh. She had to come from somewhere."

"She'd been on the streets for a year. That's not enough time to be booted from the DMV's system, right?"

He stayed quiet long enough for the silence to tell me I was onto something. "No. I've read some journal cases where people disappear from colleges or prep schools and a report isn't filed. School administration assumes they went home, family thinks they're at school. Early twenties, you said?"

I grabbed a pad and pen and jotted that down. I wasn't sure I bought it, given the timeframes, but it was worth checking.

"Speaking of odd." I bit my lip. "Bob sent me a link this morning. There's a blogger writing about crime in Richmond."

"Someone bigfooting your territory, Lois?"

"If that was all it was I wouldn't be nearly as annoyed. She's got stuff on this murder no one should have. She called it a 'possible serial' in her freaking lead."

"She who? And...wow." He whistled and I pulled the phone away from my ear.

"The writer profile is under 'Girl Friday.' So I'm going with she. It doesn't look like she has too many followers yet, but eighty-seven can become eighty-seven-hundred overnight with the right luck. And as soon as Shelby finds out about this, she'll try to convince anyone who will listen that it's me."

"How did your editor know about it?"

"He—" I stopped. "He didn't say, actually. I don't know."

"So, what can I do for you? I'm no computer hacker."

"No, but there's a post here about y'all's marijuana ID bust," I said, his words giving me another idea. "I was going to ask you how she knew so much about it. But now I'm wondering: do you know any computer hackers?"

"We have a cyber unit, like everyone else these days," he said. "I'm not tight with any of the guys over there, though. As for your other question, that wasn't my case. I might be able to ask around a little. What does she have?"

"I'll send you a link." I stopped and leaned against the archway that led into my living room. "This isn't just about me not wanting to lose a headline. I don't want bad information getting out. Or stuff leaked that could compromise an investigation. I've worked my ass off to earn the trust of every law enforcement agency I deal with, and I don't want all the chiefs and commanders handing down 'no talking to press' edicts because anyone with an Internet connection can play Lois Lane."

More defensive than I would have liked, but Kyle's reply was soft.

"I know all that. I don't want someone leaking my cases all over the Internet, either. If this person is putting sensitive ATF information on the web, I have a vested interest in checking it out," he said. "Thanks for the tip."

"Anytime. Call me if you find anything?"

"I might call you even if I don't."

"I'd like that." I smiled. "You're too good a friend to lose."

"Back at you. We'll figure it out. I hope."

"Me, too." I clicked off the call and wandered to the kitchen, opening a can of tomato soup and spreading butter on bread for a grilled cheese sandwich as I considered the past two days.

What did I need first? To know who the victim was. What did I know? No prints and no dentals.

I spooned a can of Pro Plan into Darcy's dish and carried my lunch to the table, considering reasons for the lack of ID. Small town. Poor family. Remote location.

I set the dishes in the sink as my cell phone twittered the theme from *Peter Pan*.

I frowned at the unfamiliar number. "Clarke," I said, putting the phone to my ear.

"Chris Landers, Richmond homicide." He sounded annoyed. And tired. "White says I need to talk with you. Can we grab coffee this afternoon?"

Is a Louboutin sole red? "Can you be at Thompson's in twenty minutes?" I asked, already striding out the door.

He could.

7

Landers strolled into my favorite coffee shop at two-twenty on the nose.

I rose from an overstuffed armchair in the back corner and waved. He nodded and stepped to the counter to order.

"Thanks for coming to meet me on Sunday," he said, taking the plaid-upholstered chair opposite mine.

"My hours often mirror y'all's." I sipped my white mocha and studied him over the rim of the cup. "I appreciate you calling me. What can I do for you?"

"Aaron told me you spoke to the victim's boyfriend this morning." He set his cup on the table and leaned forward. "I need to know if you're holding anything back. I've hit a wall at every turn so far, and I need something. Any kind of break."

"Aaron told you I might be hiding something?" I raised an eyebrow.

"On the contrary, he insisted you wouldn't. He trusts you. I don't trust any reporter."

I sat back and blinked. "Thank you, detective."

"No offense," he said. "But my dad was a reporter. The story is always first." The bitterness in his voice belied history I didn't want to visit.

"Maybe for your dad," I said gently. "But people come first for me. At least, I like to think so. Maybe that's why Aaron trusts me."

The journals I'd stashed under the loose floorboard in my coat closet bopped through my thoughts. But I'd promised to return them, which I couldn't do if they were in the evidence locker at the PD.

He held my gaze until he seemed satisfied with something he saw in my eyes. "Fair enough. Which people?"

"The victims, usually," I said. "I try very hard not to muck up your investigations. I did talk to her boyfriend. I gave Aaron everything he said that struck me as relevant." I smiled. "Aaron asked me to help because he knew I'd do it."

He nodded, his lips disappearing into a line. "I can respect that."

I pulled my notebook out of my bag. "If you want my honest opinion, y'all should take a look at the woman—the one you couldn't get anything out of last night? She seems pretty lovesick over the victim's boyfriend," I said.

He jotted that down. "Aaron said you told him that, too. I'm not sure a woman could have done what I saw last night."

Same thing Joey said. I tugged at a lock of hair. "Jasmine knew her. She would've let her up there."

He nodded.

I smiled. "I'm happy to share information. If you want to return the favor, I might be able to help more. I have a knack with puzzles."

"You also have a knack for investigating." He grinned. "I've done my homework. Though there's not a badge in this city who doesn't know your reputation for poking around in murder cases."

"I have a decent track record behind that reputation," I clicked the pen in and out.

"I suppose you do," he said. "What do you want to know?"

"Whatever you don't want to tell me will do." I grinned.

"Off the record until I say otherwise?" He dropped his voice. "I'm dead serious about that."

"Of course." My toes tingled at his grave tone. Charlie was going to turn emerald before this was over. Not that it was terribly important. Just a nice bonus.

"The coroner was bothered by the bloodstains at the scene," he said.

"What? Why?"

"Because the girl hadn't lost enough blood to make that much of a mess."

"So either there was a second victim," I began, scribbling every word down.

"Or she laid into the killer."

I nodded, jotting that down. "If she got enough of a piece of the guy to make such a mess, it wasn't the boyfriend. He was pretty scantily-clad when I saw him this morning and didn't appear to be in pain." Thank God. He seemed like a decent person. I wanted to trust him.

Landers nodded. "What's giving me heartburn is the second victim theory. What if there's some sicko with a dead woman in his living room, looking to start a collection?"

"Why not leave the second one in the old switch house, too, though? I mean, why go to all the trouble of setting up the scene and then only leave one masterpiece behind?"

"I couldn't tell you." He sipped his coffee. "But I'm not crazy."

"Sometimes I think your job might be easier if you were."

"You and me both. My background is all in justice and criminal forensics. There are many days I wish I'd gone for a psych degree."

I made a note about his history. "So are the forensics crews back at the scene?" I asked.

He nodded. "Cleanup isn't scheduled 'til tomorrow. We're taking more scrapings."

"If some of the blood belongs to the killer, you could get lucky in the FBI database." I stared at the painting of the state capitol building behind him, something worrying around the back of my brain.

"It's not like they didn't take samples last night. But it was all the same type. All from her. This whole damned thing is weird."

"Maybe they got it all from close to the same place?"

"Maybe. I told them to make sure they checked every corner today."

Every corner. The dark reaches of the room. And the woods outside.

"Hot damn." I mumbled.

"I'm sorry?" Landers furrowed his brow.

"What if there was someone else there last night?" I asked. "Aaron said something about the killer hanging around, and that fits with a serial profile, at least some of the time. But there's this blog that's been bugging me all day. They had stuff about this case they shouldn't have. What if the blogger was lurking last night? Watching you guys?"

"I don't know how anyone could have gotten past all the uniforms we had out there watching the perimeter."

"There are miles of woods and river down there," I said, more to myself than to him, though he nodded.

"Maybe," he said. "What blog? I haven't seen anything but your story and the local TV coverage."

"I'm not sure you want to look." I fished my phone out and pulled it up, handing him my cell phone. "The good news is, it doesn't have too many followers."

"Fan-goddamn-tastic," he grouched, handing it back and running a hand through his curls. "I don't have enough pressure. Now I have to find a way to keep information about an open investigation off the fucking Internet."

"Sorry. Aaron said he has cyber watching it."

"Maybe they'll manage to put a stop to it before it blows up. All I need is the whole city seeing Jack the Ripper on every corner because some blogger hollered 'serial killer.'"

"Understood." The word sounded far away, the shadowy alleys of the Bottom crowding my thoughts. Were any other young women suddenly missing from the streets?

That could tell me if Landers was on the right trail—or if I might be.

I smiled a thank you at Landers, itching to go see if I could find Jasmine's friends.

Something told me they'd be long gone as soon as they scraped up bus fare.

* * *

Ninety minutes and six thousand faces later, I was ready to take my aching feet home when I spotted a familiar jacket moving through the bustling farmer's market on 17th.

I picked my way through watermelon-thumping shoppers and heat-weary farmers, my eyes locked on the Yankees windbreaker. In eighty-seven-degree weather. It had to be the same one I'd seen at the hospital the night before.

I caught up and he turned to look at me. "I saw you," he said, not breaking stride, a sketchpad tucked under one arm.

"Last night," I said. "I'm Nichelle. How are you feeling today?"

"No, you were with Flyboy this morning," he said. "I told him you were nice."

"I appreciate that. I want to ask you a few more questions. Are you going to work?"

"Weekends when the weather's nice are good for sketching," he said. "Money is better, too. People who are here during the week won't pay as much."

Haggling with homeless artists over a drawing? People never cease to amaze me.

"Have you drawn a few today?" I asked.

"Five. Seven is better. I like sevens. I'm going up to the slip. People come to the market in the morning. In the afternoon, they go up there."

I nodded, picking my way across the cobblestones beside him for a half block before I spoke again.

"Are there any other girls who haven't been around lately?" I asked, reaching back through my memory to my abnormal psych class for typical timeframes. "If you think about the past month or two, have you noticed anyone disappearing?"

He twisted his mouth to one side and slowed his pace slightly. "I don't think so," he said. "We don't see as many other people as we used to. Before Jazz came."

Oh, really? "Why is that?"

He shook his head, dropping his eyes to his shoes and mumbling. "Better before." Turning abruptly, he crossed East Cary to take a seat on an empty bench bolted into a crumbling section of the brick sidewalk. He pulled half a pencil from a box, and set the empty container on the seat next to him. Flipping his pad open, he stared at me without blinking for so long my eyes had sympathy pains.

I smiled.

He bent his head, moving the pencil across the paper lightning-fast. And mumbling. If I hadn't been so focused on his face, I'd have missed the words entirely. As it was, I couldn't testify in court I'd heard right. "Everyone goes to the church shelter. Except us. She cried if we went to the church shelter."

Huh. I didn't want to risk reaching for a notebook, and there was little chance I'd forget that.

My eyes dropped to his lap, and my jaw followed suit. My face popped off the paper, my hair falling around it in soft waves. He shaded the hollow at my throat and looked up, then added a couple of light lines next to my eyes.

"You're pretty." He pulled the paper off and handed it to me.

I smiled a thank you, digging a twenty from my bag and putting it in his box. I looked around and added another.

"That's too much," he said.

"You're very talented," I replied. "Thank you for the picture."

"Jazz said people would come. She told me they would ask questions about her. I wasn't supposed to answer them. She was afraid. But you're not scary."

"I like to think I'm not," I said. "I have a feeling she wasn't talking about me, though." I perched on the bench next to him. "Did she ever tell you where she was from? How she ended up down here?"

He studied his shoes.

"I'm trying to help find out who hurt her," I said. "You told me last night her family killed her. But I'm not sure what you meant. Did she talk about her parents?"

"People were mean to her," he said, scuffing the toe of one worn-out Reebok along the seam between the cobblestones. "We don't talk about it, not really. It's all so far away. Better not to think about it." He shook his head.

"How did you end up here?" I asked.

"Don't remember." He sniffled.

I wanted to pat his arm or put a reassuring hand on his slumped shoulder, but I didn't want to startle him. He wasn't nearly old enough for the level of exhaustion in his eyes. I folded my hands together and nodded.

Marveling at the exquisite artwork in my hand, I shook my head. Such skill. Grace and heart oozed from every line.

I looked up. "Did you ever sketch Jasmine?"

He nodded, laying a finger across his lips and flipping back in the book. "See? Pretty. She didn't like for me to draw her."

There were three different portraits, two profiles and one of her sleeping face.

I pulled out my cell phone and clicked into the camera. "May I?" I asked. Aaron might already have one of the department's artists working on a sketch, with the difficulty they'd had getting a name. But this guy was beyond talented. And he'd drawn a living, breathing woman who was his friend. There's something more recognizable about that than a PD rendition of a corpse.

He nodded. I snapped photos of his artwork.

"Thanks." I tucked my phone away. He focused his gaze behind my shoulder, trying to smile. I turned to find a woman pushing a cherub-cheeked toddler in a hip pink stroller. Her eyes locked on the sketch resting across my knees.

"How much?" she asked, turning to Picasso.

"Only fifty bucks," I said before he could, pushing off the bench and grinning at the baby. "She's adorable. I think I'm going to come back and get my best friend sketches of her kids for her birthday."

"Really?" Picasso smiled as the woman hunted through her Coach tote for cash.

"Thanks for talking to me," I said, extending a hand. "I'll see you again soon."

"Don't wait," he said as he shook my hand. "Things are weird. Weirder every day."

I nodded, turning south when the woman laid the cash in the box and spun back to wipe the little girl's face. A block down, I ducked into an open-air coffeehouse and clicked out a pen, scribbling everything he'd told me as fast as I could. By the time I put the pen down, my eyelids sagged. A hot bath and food didn't sound terrible.

First, I needed to file a follow-up story and do some research on the four-one-one blog. Then maybe some rest would help me find the puzzle pieces to pull this corner of the picture together.

8

The sun sank into the trees, goldenrod and coral deepening to violet at the horizon as I turned onto my street.

Three hours at my desk produced a day two story with a sidebar featuring the sketches and pleading for help identifying the victim, but netted me less than nothing else. I went back seven years in the *Telegraph* archives, but didn't find anything on a missing autistic kid (I'd done a story on the program for autistic children at Syracuse in college, and it fit) with a flair for art. Something about Picasso told me he'd been on the streets since before he was old enough to vote, and that made me sad.

I grabbed a yogurt and a Diet Dr Pepper and settled on the couch with Jasmine's journals. Two hours later, I was convinced there was something horrible—maybe horrible enough to be important—in her past. She loved Flyboy, she loved her friends, they were going to Colorado. Life on the streets was all sunshine and roses. She doodled in the margins—hearts, daisy chains, and boxy "T"s with halos of stripes. I jotted a note to check missing persons reports for the first initial T.

I also flagged four repetitions of "Mr. B was right. I'm free," but found nothing to indicate who that was, or what he was right about. I paged back through, turning carefully to make sure the magical key I'd hoped to find wasn't on a stuck-together page. Nope. Not one word about anything that happened more than a year ago. No mention of jealousy, money, or why the Methodist shelter was worthy of tears. Strike one.

I took Darcy out to play and fell into bed.

Sunrise didn't bring me any closer to an answer, nor did the fitful dreams that came between Sunday's round of fetch and Monday morning's body combat class. Maddening. Something was there, but it danced around the edges of my brain, vaporizing every time I got close. I gave up trying to catch it and made a mental grocery list as I squatted, sidestepped, and ap-chagi'ed to the pounding dance music.

Rinsing conditioner out of my hair with twenty minutes to get to the news budget meeting, my eyes snapped open.

Jasmine didn't want to go to the shelter. The church shelter. She'd made Picasso afraid of people who might ask questions about her.

Every story I'd ever read about crazy religious sects spun through my brain on fast forward.

Holy Manolos.

I toweled off and threw my gym gear into my duffel bag, climbing into my car with nothing but mascara and lipstick on my face. My still-damp feet slid in my Jimmy Choo wedges as I rushed for the newsroom.

I flew off the elevator, barely returning my friend Melanie's grumpy "good morning." The fat folder tucked under her arm told me she was headed to City Hall for a budget work session. Summer money season made me excessively thankful I didn't cover the council. Numbers make my eyes cross.

I plopped my black leather tote down in my cube and pulled out my computer and notebook, scribbling my thoughts before I hurried to Bob's office for the meeting. Lost in my suspicions, I almost walked into Grant Parker as I rounded the corner.

"In your own little world of dead folks this morning, huh?" My friend's emerald eyes crinkled at the corners when he flashed his famous megawatt grin. He waved a copy of the city final. "You had exactly no fun this weekend."

"I wouldn't say that." I matched the grin with one of my own, sinking into my usual Virginia-Tech-Orange upholstered armchair and smoothing my linen pants. "Kicking Charlie's ass is always fun."

"And watching it never gets old," Bob said. "Nice work, getting the inside track at the PD. Though I've seen Charlie Lewis in action enough times to know I wouldn't want to be Aaron White this week. Or maybe you, either. She's got to be good and pissed at losing to you two days in a row."

"I'm sure," I said. "But she'll live. It's not my fault they trust me more."

"Sure it is." Parker feigned outrage. "Damn you for being honest and upstanding."

"Pesky morals aside, I also don't come with a cameraman."

"That could change before too long," Rick Andrews's voice came from the doorway, and I turned my head to see Shelby's spiky black hair poking over one of our publisher's charcoal-suited shoulders.

I tossed a WTF glance at Bob and he shrugged a reply.

"Good morning, Rick," he said, dropping his copy notes to the desktop. "To what do I owe the honor today?"

"There's a blogger who's taken it upon himself to add to Nichelle and Charlie's competition," Andrews said, stepping to the center of the room. Shelby scurried inside and shut the door behind her. I steeled myself for an ass-chewing, glaring at Shelby. She twisted her full lips into the smirk that always made me want to smack her and I turned my attention back to Andrews.

"This morning, he has video of the murder scene from Saturday night," he said. "It could be time to step up our game. Our website can feed video, too."

The half-spent candles flashed on the backs of my eyelids, my stomach doing a slow somersault. "What kind of video?" The words were somewhere between a rasp and a croak. I cleared my throat. "That is, what's in the video you saw on the four-one-one page?"

"A pan of the murder scene, complete with police tape," Andrews said.

"But not the body?" I asked, the edges of my notebook biting into my fingers as I tightened my grip on it.

The look that crossed his face made me glad he didn't know what I'd seen Saturday night. Andrews didn't care much about anything but selling papers, and I refused to describe the scene in detail for a variety of reasons. I made a mental note to tell Bob to keep my knowledge of it to himself.

Andrews shook his head, drumming his fingers on his thigh. "I noticed the page doesn't have too many followers yet, but that could change. I don't want to lose out on this story." He glanced at Shelby. "Thank you for bringing it to my attention, Sandy."

I bit blood out of the inside of my cheek trying to hide a grin. Parker coughed over a laugh. Shelby stared daggers at us both as she stepped forward. "Anything for the good of the paper." She flashed a put-upon smile at Andrews. "You know, if Nichelle needs to concentrate on this murder coverage, I'm happy to pitch in and help with the courthouse. Or anything else."

"I'm perfectly capable of doing my job, thanks, Sandy," I chirped, hitting the last word hard and drawing a soft chuckle from Bob.

Andrews just nodded when I turned back to him. "I'm afraid the PD won't give me the kind of access they have so far if I'm toting a camcorder." I smiled my most earnest smile. I had less than no interest in a cameraman sidekick, and juggling my notebook and a palmcorder didn't sound appealing.

Andrews twisted his mouth to one side, folding his hands behind his back. Parker made an exaggerated version of the same face at me over the publisher's shoulder. I swallowed a giggle and looked away. When I glanced back, he stuck his tongue out at me. I winked and clicked out a pen.

"Let's see what happens with this," Andrews said finally. "You do good work, Miss Clarke. Most of the time."

He meant I did work that was good for occasional national wire pickup and ad revenue. I bet he didn't read my stories without one of those things attached. Lucky for me, his odd fear/respect/jealousy relationship with Bob meant he stayed out of our hair for the most part. Especially since Les Simpson, the managing editor, had gone back to bean counting and sucking up to Andrews full time, pulling back on weaseling himself and Shelby into the newsroom. That had made for a lovely few months.

The last thing I needed was for Andrews to get a burr under his designer saddle in the middle of such a big story.

"The PD's cyber unit is working on finding the blogger. Just for their own informational purposes, though she's going to get herself way on their shit list if she's posting video of crime scenes. I hear the ATF has an interest in talking to her, too."

"Her? How in creation would you happen to know the blogger is a woman, Nichelle?" Splenda dripped from Shelby's words.

"Girl Friday? Call it intuition. You might have lost yours after so many years at the copy desk, but mine works just fine."

"You wouldn't happen to know who she is, now would you?" She spoke to me, but looked at Andrews, who raised an eyebrow.

"You're not working with anyone outside the newsroom, Miss Clarke? I don't suppose we have a specific policy on that, but I—"

"I wouldn't. Even if I had the time," I said, turning to Bob.

"Nichelle is nothing if not loyal," he said. "I'd stake my reputation on that."

Andrews nodded. "Good enough. For now. Let Sandy here know if you need any help." He spun on the heel of one wingtip and walked out.

Shelby flounced behind him. The section editors filed in when the room cleared.

"What's he doing slumming down here?" Eunice Blakely asked, lowering herself slowly into the chair opposite mine and straightening her bad leg. She had a half-dozen screws in one hip as a souvenir of her war correspondent years, which ended with a helicopter crash during Desert Storm. These days, she ran a tight ship in our features section and kept everyone fed. "It's not even noon."

She pulled a large Ziploc baggie from her coral canvas tote and laid it on Bob's desk. I leaned forward, peering at the contents. Bars, speckled with oats and bitsy chocolate chips. The peanut butter smell that hit me in the face when I opened the bag made my stomach gurgle.

"Eunice, you're a magician," I said, swallowing the first bite. "Tell me these are part of your healthy cooking jag, and I might kiss you."

"Pucker up, buttercup." She grinned. "Figured I needed to make up for the almonds from Friday. My sister sent me this powdered peanut butter stuff that's my new miracle food. Tastes great, bakes well, almost no fat. Those won't cost you more than five minutes in the gym."

I helped myself to another one, snatching my hand out of the way as the rest of the staff descended. Bob dropped the empty bag into his trash can and grinned. "Now that we've eaten, can we talk about the news?"

"Aw, why not?" Parker said. "We're all here and everything. Might as well."

I glanced around and noticed our sports editor was missing, which explained Parker's presence. Normally, I'd ask where Spencer was—curiosity is an occupational hazard—but after Andrews's blog-and-pony show, I took it as a bonus from the universe to brighten my Monday and focused on Bob. Spence had proven himself to be a bitter jackass during a big story I'd covered in the spring, and we still weren't speaking.

"The story of the week—month, whatever—is going to be Nichelle's coverage of this murder," Bob said, looking around. He fiddled with a paperclip, blowing out a frustrated sigh. "I'd trust anyone in this room with my life. Here's the thing: Andrews was here because there's a blog that's popped up lately about crime in Richmond. I don't think it's professional enough to be written by anyone in our newsroom, but just in case, I want y'all to keep anything you hear in this room to yourselves for the duration of this story. Understood?"

Nods and murmurs from the crowd faded into awkward silence.

"You've got the inside track, right, doll?" Eunice asked finally.

"So far," I said. "The problem I see is our online friend either doesn't understand she's pissing the cops off, or she doesn't care. I've got a decent chance of staying ahead of Charlie because Aaron and I are helping each other out, but it's harder with someone who doesn't play by the rules."

Bob nodded. "I have utter faith in your snooping abilities," he said.

"You always know how to make a girl blush, chief." I batted my lashes.

"It's a gift." Bob dropped the paperclip and looked at Parker. "Sports? The Generals look good this year."

"They do," Parker said. "We've got coverage of tonight's divisional face-off leading, and I have a column on the kid who won the Nate DeLuca scholarship. The first anniversary of his death is coming up." He glanced at me and I dropped my eyes to my notes. A year ago, DeLuca was the Generals' golden arm, a starting pitcher whose death got mixed up in a crazy story that nearly resulted in mine.

"I can't wait to read it," I said.

Parker smiled. "I guess I'd better bring my A game, then."

"You always do." I grinned.

Bob moved on to features and Eunice outlined a summer family fun section while I checked email on my cell phone. It was Monday, all right. Ninety-seven messages before nine a.m. I scrolled down the screen, Aaron's name catching my eye.

Call me when you can get away.

I bounced in my seat until Bob dismissed the meeting, hoping Aaron had good news.

* * *

Bolting for my desk, I made it four steps before Parker's voice froze my Jimmy Choo in midair.

"Can we talk?" he asked, falling into step beside me.

The uncertain tone from our resident Captain Charisma was enough to make me forget Aaron for a minute.

"Never too busy for you. What's up?" I stopped and turned to face him, leaning against a long row of filing cabinets.

His full lips disappeared into a thin white line, and he tipped his perfectly-tousled blond head. "It's Mel."

Uh oh. "I saw her going out to a budget session." I kept my voice even. "Everything okay?"

"I dunno." Parker shoved his hands into the pockets of his khakis. "We're just—she's not—" He sighed. "Let me try that again. Nothing's really up. It's just not as much fun as it was. Not as easy. I've never been in a relationship before, really. Is this normal?"

"Boy, are you asking the wrong girl." I laughed. "That sounds like a Bob question. But I'll say that from talking to my friend Jenna, who's been married for, like, ever, it seems good relationships go through phases."

"Yeah?" He nodded, more to himself than to me if I read his face right. "When did it start?"

"Right around when TJ died," Parker said.

I nodded. I'd noticed some tension in paradise when Parker's friend lost his teenage son in April. I smiled and channeled Emily. "Have you talked to her about it?"

"Not really."

"Maybe you should try. If there's something weird between the two of you, letting it fester is only going to make it worse."

He nodded. "We're supposed to have dinner tomorrow night. I'll ask her."

"Holler if you need to talk." I patted his arm. "It'll be okay. Maybe she doesn't handle dead people well. Not everyone sees them on such a regular basis." I glanced at the big silver-and-glass clock on the wall between the elevators. "I have to run, but really. I'm around if you need me."

"Thanks."

I strode to my cube, grabbing the phone and punching in Aaron's cell.

"Happy Monday, Sunshine," he said.

"I bet mine's happier than yours, unless you've got something Earth-shattering for me." I leaned one hip on my desk, reaching for a pen.

"I think I might. Landers asked me to find you. He's up to his ass in alligators this morning and didn't have time, but he said he promised."

More work to keep my voice even. "Oh, yeah?" I clicked the pen out and flipped an old press release over. "What's up?"

"We sent forensics back out there to take more blood samples," Aaron said. "Turns out, all that show was made with two different kinds of blood."

"So Jasmine got a piece of the killer? Or there's another victim?" I scribbled as I fired questions at him.

"Or the killer knows someone who works on a ranch. It was cow's blood."

I almost dropped my pen. "What?" I forced my lips around the word. All they wanted to do was gape open.

"Beats the shit out of me. Everything we've come up with here is screwier than the last thing." Aaron sighed. "I don't suppose you want to offer one of your crazy hunches?"

"No one ever listens to them," I said.

"Try me."

"I did have a thought this morning, but I haven't had time to check it out." I twisted the phone cord around one index finger. "It's kind of nuts, though."

"Any goose chase is better than sitting here scratching our b—never mind," Aaron said.

I laughed. "Frustrated, detective?"

"Oh, you can quote me on that, Miss Clarke."

"But not the part about scratching things?"

"Please don't."

I snorted. "So, I went back down to the Bottom yesterday afternoon and I found the guy who called this in the other night. He is a really, really talented sketch artist. Seriously good."

I heard Aaron's computer keys clicking as he noted that. "That's where you got the sketches you ran this morning," he said. "Do me a favor and email Charlie that info? She's convinced you got them from me. Thanks for putting them out there, though. We're circulating them through law enforcement."

"If I get Charlie off your ass, do I get dibs on anything the sketches bring in?"

"Sounds fair to me. So, about your hunch?"

"I asked if any other girls were missing," I said. "Because of what Landers said about the bloodstains. But artist guy told me he didn't know because they couldn't go to the church shelters anymore. He said Jasmine cried if they tried to. Then he told me she said people might come around asking about her, and he should be afraid of them." I paused for a breath.

"A cult." Aaron clicked his tongue. "Son of a bitch."

"It took me twelve hours to get there, but that's where I landed, too," I said. "Why do you sound like I just made your day worse?"

"You're from Texas, right? Cops and crazy religion don't mix well. Ever been to Waco?"

"Ah. I was in elementary school when that happened, but I remember my mom having the news on nonstop for all of that spring." A flash of her sobbing into the telephone skated through my brain, and I flinched. My mom never cried, and the memory unsettled me.

"So many things went wrong down there that no one will ever even know about," Aaron sighed. "The thing is, it's almost always the same. People resent intrusion and don't trust the government, and to them, my badge represents the government. Jesus. I'd rather deal with a serial. Good old fashioned psychopaths are logical. People who think God's telling them to murder young women, I can't figure."

"Just a theory. And no one ever listens to my theories."

"Your gut has a good track record." Aaron chuckled and I grinned. "But this is going to get very complicated. If you're right, who knows where she was from, how many people there are, who owns the land, if it's in another state? My haystack just got a whole lot bigger. And wrapped in a big, fat spool of red tape. That could be federal territory."

"Could still be a serial. Or a random nutjob. Or someone she knew. Even if she ran away from a religious sect, it doesn't mean they killed her. What if our psycho was trying to set his scene and didn't get enough blood out of her?" I paused. "Speaking of blood, you didn't happen to catch today's post by our Girl Friday, did you?"

"I haven't had time to catch if the sun came up," he said. More computer clicking. "Cyber is on that. Why?"

I waited four beats and bit back a grin at the string of swearwords in my ear when he found the video. "Because there's that," I said.

"What the hell is the matter with people? Is this person—and I'm using the term loosely this morning—trying to incite a riot?"

"I'm betting she's trying to increase her readership," I said. "But I thought you should know."

"Thanks. I don't have time for an amateur Lois Lane right now, Nichelle."

"I'm keeping an ear out," I said. "Because neither do I."

I twisted around and looked at the clock. "Crap, Aaron, I have a trial starting in three minutes." I hung up, my mental puzzle shifting to include cults and cows.

But how to find a link?

Waco.

Maybe Kyle knew where to look.

9

Downtown blurred past my windows in a mishmash of art-deco building fronts that usually topped my list of favorite Richmond features—but I didn't even notice them. Stopping at a light, I punched Kyle's number up on my screen and typed a text to him. "Wondering if you can help with my new theory. Give me a call when you have a few?"

I dropped my cell phone in the cup holder and laid on the gas, the chatter from the police scanner in my passenger seat noticeably lighter than usual. The whole department seemed on edge.

I ticked off a mental to-do list that started with the trial and the day's police reports, and ended with a fat question mark over the next day's murder follow up. Even if I got somewhere with cult research, I wasn't tipping my hand to Charlie and the rest of the country without having the story nailed down, and that wouldn't happen in a day.

I rushed through security and into the courtroom, a drug lord who'd run half the Southside two years ago already seated at the defendant's table.

I focused on the opening arguments, keenly aware of the Ginsu swords Charlie stared at me for half the morning. Ducking out before she could corner me, I sped back to the office, checking my cell phone as I turned into the garage. Nothing from Kyle.

My police reports were lighter than usual, a fatal car accident in the pre-dawn hours the only one interesting enough to warrant space. I wrote a short piece from the report and left a message for the victim's husband. Thirty-four year-old woman, driving to work when she'd run across a pickup full of drunk teenagers speeding down a dark country road with no headlights on. "Such a stupid waste," I murmured, shaking my head as I typed.

The kids all tested through the roof for blood alcohol at the St. Vincent's ER, more than an hour after the crash. The driver was in juvenile custody, but I knew the Commonwealth Attorney's stance on DUI— Jonathan Corry lost a girlfriend to a drunk driver once upon a time, so he'd push to try the driver as an adult. The kid was likely headed for actual prison, and vehicular manslaughter carries six to ten in Virginia.

I sent that story to Bob with a note that it might get a couple of inches longer if the husband called me back. Which wasn't likely, but I was okay with that particular "no comment." Asking people to talk to me in the middle of tragedy is my least favorite thing about my job.

It took forty minutes to find attorneys from both sides of the drug dealer's trial and write up the day one, and I smiled as I attached it to an email. Two down. As snarled as my bigger story was, I'd take my gold stars wherever I could get them.

I checked the next day's court docket and pulled notes for two trials I'd need to pop into. After I'd read the first file four times and still couldn't have told a mad bomber what the defendant had (allegedly) done if it meant saving all of downtown Richmond, I dropped the folder and wandered to the break room in search of some caffeine.

I plunked quarters into the Coke machine and twisted the top off a bottle of diet, checking my cell phone for the hundred and seventieth time since I'd texted Kyle. Still nothing.

"You all right, sugar?" Eunice pulled a plate of club sandwiches on homemade bread out of the fridge and offered me one. I bit into it and contemplated as I chewed. On one hand, I was free and healthy and had a job I loved and a nice place to live. On the other, I was insanely frustrated with something I'd always thought I wanted.

"In the grand scheme? I'm fabulous," I said after I swallowed. "In the right-this-minute, I'm annoyed. How about you?"

"I remember those days." She nodded. "Want to talk about it?"

"Eh. It won't do either of us any good. But thank you." I smiled.

"Anytime." She shuffled toward the door and I grabbed a paper towel for my sandwich and followed. "You do good work, Nichelle," Eunice said, turning back toward me. "Don't worry about the whole big mess they have going on at the PD. Don't worry about this Internet crap. Just go get the story. Do your thing, and you'll figure it out."

"You should charge for your advice." I smiled. "Thanks."

Her words followed me back to my desk. She was right: I was so focused on helping Aaron and beating Girl Friday, I felt like I was on deadline every second. The stress had eaten my mojo.

"Time to get my groove back," I said, flipping my computer open.

"Can you find mine, too?" Melanie's voice came from the other side of the cube wall. "This has been a sucky summer so far."

I bit my lip. I didn't want to tell her what Parker had said that morning, because he hadn't given me permission to.

Plus, there was my whole murder-investigation mission.

But I didn't want to be a bad friend, either.

"I'll keep an eye out for it," I said. "Want to see if yours is drinking with mine? We could grab a cocktail after work and talk."

"That sounds great. Five-thirty?"

"Provided I get through the day with no more dead people."

Cell phone check number one-seventy-one. Nada.

Men. I'd just have to find out for myself.

I opened my browser and searched "religious sects, Richmond VA." My screen flooded with hits, most of them from conspiracy theory websites. I scrolled, but nothing jumped out.

"The church shelter." Picasso's words pinged through my thoughts. Maybe I was looking in the wrong place.

A new search told me there were a lot of churches in Central Virginia. I narrowed it to addresses more than thirty miles from Richmond, figuring Jasmine wouldn't go just up the street if she fled something she was afraid of.

The list was still three miles long. Was there something about Virginia that made people seek Jesus so readily? My finger hovered over the mouse, an hour of reading giving me nothing but a headache.

Scrolling to the top of the page, I clicked to images. And found seven million thumbnails of church buildings. Scrolling, I hovered over a few to pop them up, too frustrated to even admire the beautiful architecture.

On page forty-six, I found something.

A tri-color, multi-angle image of a boxy T.

Except it wasn't a T—it was a cross. With rays of light shooting in every direction.

Rays of light that would look like stripes if doodled with a ballpoint.

I followed a link trail from the PDF to the United States Patent and Trademark Office website.

And almost fell off my chair.

Not just any church. The symbol my murder victim had doodled in her journal a hundred times was trademarked by an international Televangelist.

"Hot damn," I breathed, clicking to the ministry's website.

The light-haloed cross was the logo centerpiece for Way of Life Ministries. Religion via satellite, complete with on-site studios and a residential education arm.

Kyle's theory about college whispered through my thoughts. I clicked to the page about the school. Smiling coeds in button-down oxfords dutifully studying The Good Book.

I kept clicking. Way of Life was headquartered northwest of Richmond near the foothills of the Blue Ridge.

"She loved the mountains. Said they felt like home," Flyboy had said.

Leaping Louboutins.

I'd never watched TV church, but I'd read enough news stories to know the folks who ran them could be pretty far from garden-variety worshippers. They had privacy. Plenty of land.

And cows.

A postcard shot of a wide green field—spreading toward the mountains at the horizon, a red barn to one side and a herd of black angus cattle dotting the landscape—filled my screen.

In Texas, ranches are so common you could drive past sixty longhorns on your way to the grocery store if you went the right way.

But I seldom saw cows around Richmond.

And Aaron said "cow's blood."

"Organic on-site farming keeps the body healthy to serve the creator," the caption read. So, cows they slaughtered?

Could this be what Jasmine fled?

My gut said it was at least as possible as Landers's fear of Jack the Ripper lurking in Shockoe Bottom.

A brief read of some of the staff bios told me it'd take months for Aaron or Kyle to get a search warrant for the compound. Way of Life employed more lawyers than the tobacco company up the road.

"Why all the legal savvy, pastor?" I stared at the perfect pompadour and toothpaste-ad smile of Simon Golightly, airwave savior to millions. I didn't trust the guy on sight, mostly because people who surround themselves with an army of attorneys usually have something to hide, be it from the cops or the IRS.

Opening a new window, I ran another search and copied the reverend's bio into a blank file. Saving it, I closed my laptop and headed for Bob's office. Eunice might have helped me find my mojo, but getting Bob to let me go snoop around Golightly's fortress would take some fancy footwork.

10

A half-hour of arguing later, all I had to show for it was an aching throat and Bob's blessing to see what the Internet and Kyle could dig up on Golightly.

"Cows? You want me to let you go see if a TV preacher is mixed up in this woman's death based on cows?" Eyes wide, he sat back in his chair and shook his head. "That's tenuous if I'm being generous. Maybe cattle aren't a common sight downtown, but we have plenty of dairies in Virginia. Slaughterhouses, too. Cow's blood could have come from a hundred places."

I fidgeted in my seat, my eyes on the carpet. He wasn't wrong. "But Bob —" I began, then paused. I hadn't told him about the journals. On purpose. He'd tell me to give them to Aaron, and I wasn't ready to. I'd promised to return them. I also didn't want to distract Landers until I was sure I had something worth distracting him with.

Bob raised one hand. "You think there's a story out there? I'm willing to trust your hunch enough to say there might be. Whether it has anything to do with your corpse, I couldn't begin to guess. Do your research. Talk to your friend at the ATF. But you can't charge around accusing people of murder because they run a school and raise their own beef. Nail it down. Then come talk to me."

"Going out there would help."

"A guy with that many lawyers will have no qualms about hauling the newspaper into court, Nichelle," he said. "And I guarantee you, he has the money to tie us up in legal bullshit 'til we go bankrupt. Stay away from him."

I stomped back to my desk at five-fifteen, grumbling about my editor, and found Mel waiting, computer bag slung over one shoulder and tired eyes in need of some fun.

"Me too, sister," I said, turning to pack up my stuff.

Twenty minutes later, seated across from her in a cushy leather booth with a glass of Moscato in front of me and a burger on its way from the kitchen, I smiled. "What's up?" I asked in my best I-know-nothing voice.

Mel toyed with the straw in her amaretto sour and sighed. "Grant's being weird. And I'm not sure what to do about it. I don't want to pressure him, but it feels like he's drifting away."

How did I get myself appointed relationship therapist? By playing matchmaker, I guessed, since I certainly didn't have the romance resume for it.

"You guys seemed really happy for a long time," I said, smiling at the waitress as she set a colossal burger and a pile of shoestring fries in front of me. "Maybe this is the normal cycle of a relationship?"

"I guess," Mel sighed. "I just don't know how to put it back on the upswing, and I'm afraid he's going to get tired of it and bail before it goes that way. He has to feel the same thing."

"Have you tried talking to him about it?"

"And give him a reason to dump me?"

I spent the next hour demolishing the burger and growing annoyed with Melanie's lack of confidence. Where was my intelligent, sassy friend? Maybe I hadn't done her a favor, setting her up with Parker. To hear her tell it, he was pity-dating her, and I wasn't sure which one of them I should be aggravated with about that. My last-ditch was to appeal to the logical side that made her so good at seeing through the city council's BS budget numbers.

"When did it start?" I drained the last of my water, contemplating ordering another Moscato if we were going to be a while.

She dropped her eyes to the table. "When TJ Okerson died."

I feigned surprise. Lucky for my lousy acting skills, she wasn't looking. "Being there through the good and bad is part of being together, right?"

"But I wasn't there for him. You were. You went to the funeral with him, even."

"He said you were busy."

"I don't do funerals. The last one I went to was my dad's and I swore I'd never attend another."

Ah-ha. Parker's words from earlier rolled around my head, and I glanced at the clock on my cell phone, the file I'd started on Reverend Golightly singing a siren song from inside my laptop. I dropped my balled-up napkin in the middle of my empty plate and put a twenty under the corner of it for the waitress before I stood and smiled at Mel. "I have a long, coffee-driven night of research coming, but here's my Earth-shattering idea: tell him that. He's been mushy over you for months. You two ought to talk. Nothing good comes from keeping secrets in a relationship."

Hello there, Pot. I'm Kettle. But you can call me Black. Or just Nichelle.

I pushed thoughts of Kyle and Joey aside and patted Mel's shoulder. "Communication. Don't all the books say it's the cornerstone of a successful relationship? Talk to him. It'll work out."

"Thanks." She looked up and smiled. "We spent the whole time talking about my problem. Where's your mojo?"

"On a ranch out near the mountains, I think," I said. "But I'm going after it. Don't worry."

She furrowed her brow over her tortoiseshell glasses and I grinned. "Really. I'm good."

"If you say so. Don't get caught in a stampede. Or whatever they do on ranches."

"That's the least of my worries."

I buckled my seatbelt and started the car, and my cell phone burst into *Second Star to the Right*.

I dug it out of my bag and smiled.

"Hey there, stranger," I said.

"Sorry, I've been swamped today," Kyle replied. "What can I do for you?"

"I have a theory."

"Hooray."

I laughed. "You have no idea how much I appreciate your vote of confidence."

"It's less that I lack confidence in you, and more that your theories usually cause trouble for one or both of us," he said.

"I suppose that's fair."

"So what's up?"

"I'm wondering what the feds might know about a TV preacher named Simon Golightly. Runs his operation from a compound out in the foothills of the Blue Ridge. Has a boatload of lawyers on his staff."

"Hmm. I'd say there's a good chance we know something. Off the record?"

"Absolutely."

"I'll poke around. Why?"

"The guy I talked to yesterday said the dead chick was afraid to go to the church shelter, and afraid someone might come after her. Aaron said the lab results showed some of the gross at the murder scene was cow's blood. These folks raise their own cattle and have the potential to be scary church people."

"Lots of people raise cows." Amusement dripped through the speaker and I scrunched my nose in reply. "Plus, not all religious people are fanatics."

"I know that, Captain Devil's Advocate. It's not like I've never been to Sunday School. My mom used to teach it, for crying out loud. But TV religion is at least sometimes more about power and money than God."

"True enough. Jim Bakker, anyone?"

"Exactly. So I want to know what goes on out there."

"Here we go again. Please watch yourself," Kyle said.

"Technically, you have no reason to worry. Bob told me to stay away from Golightly. He's afraid I'll get the paper sued."

"I didn't think your editor cared about anything more than the story. And I did not miss your creative use of the word 'technically.'"

"The paper. He cares about having a paper to put the story in. Golightly's kind of money and influence could put the *Telegraph* out of business if he got mad enough. So I have clearance to talk to you and peruse Google to my heart's content."

"I'm not sure how much good that will do you, but your tone tells me you're not exactly planning to follow this edict to the letter."

"I would never deliberately defy Bob." I smiled as I turned into my driveway and shut off the engine. "But a Sunday morning drive to the country might be nice. We could even take in a church service, if you're up for it."

"There's my Nichelle."

"Bob said not to go near Golightly. The balcony in that sanctuary is at least a quarter mile from the pulpit. That's not near."

Kyle laughed. "What time are you picking me up?"

* * *

Six days later I'd read every article I could find about Golightly and Way of Life, requested copies of the church's tax returns (Yay: non-profit returns are public information. Boo: it takes six to eight weeks to get them), watched two dozen sermon videos online, and compared the doodles in Jasmine's journal to the ministry logo under a microscope.

She'd been there. My gut rarely fails me. But why—and why she left—I needed those puzzle pieces before anyone would listen to me. My cops were still hunting a serial, and Aaron was frustrated enough that a week had passed since I borrowed Picasso's sketches, and still no one had come forward to identify the victim. He didn't need another theory from me until I had more to offer.

Hoping I would by lunchtime, I pulled up in front of Kyle's building Sunday morning. And blinked twice when he stepped outside. His ice-blue shirt color matched his eyes and molded to his muscular shoulders in a way that made my stomach flip.

"Good morning." He settled into the passenger seat of my little red SUV and smiled.

"Morning. Thanks for coming with me."

"I've been covered up with a new case this week, but I snuck a peek at your preacher's file yesterday." Kyle flipped the radio off as I turned the car onto I-95 North and laid on the gas. "He's not exactly the stand-up guy he'd have his followers think he is."

I nodded. "I found a little bit of a trail online, but a lot of things have been deleted. And not well, either. It was like wading through the electronic version of a redacted court transcript. Weird. I did manage to find out his brother did time for an online credit card scam, but I even had to get that from the wayback."

Journalism in the age of the Internet 102: not much can be permanently deleted online. There's a nifty website that stores caches of random pages on different days—and has a searchable database. Yet it had nothing on Golightly, which popped my shady-character radar higher.

I'd contemplated emailing the site's administrator to see if he'd paid them to remove anything, but figured if he had, they might tell him I asked. Maybe he was just lucky.

"Our files have not been redacted," Kyle said.

"So, what is he into?"

"A little bit of everything."

"Does the ATF have an active investigation on him?" Because that would be a dozen different kinds of fabulous.

"No. He's more like a person of interest in several other investigations right now."

Damn. "Why is that?"

"Money. Politics. Who knows? I found some iffy stuff, but nothing I'm convinced would get me a warrant this morning. With folks like this, it can take years to build a case. But you asked me if the guy was above-board, and my answer is a resounding 'no.'"

"But y'all don't have enough on him to do any good." I pressed harder on the gas, the trees blurring into a color wheel of green in my peripheral vision. The peace of a clear summer day and a long stretch of nearly-empty highway, usually comforting, only frustrated me. I had just enough to know something was up. There's nothing more irritating than a crook with enough money to stay out of jail. Add the brutal murder, and I was more than curious about the good reverend.

"If you're going after a guy with this much money and influence, you need a rock-solid case before you step foot on his land. The whole place might as well be layered in red tape, with all the different statutes they can hide behind. With the right kind of lawyers, people can get away with almost anything in the name of religious freedom."

Except murder. I hoped.

"What about the IRS? Tax evasion? It worked on Capone."

"I'm sure there's grounds for jail time there, but again: churches are tax exempt, right? And so are a large part of the earnings you make as an employee of one. I'd lay even odds this guy is not reporting all his income on the right lines. But do they want to fight his legal team in court over an audit? It depends on whether they think the tax penalty would outweigh the cost to the agency."

"Everything is always about money."

"It seems to make the world go 'round."

"But what if they did kill someone?"

"'They' is a vague term. They who? His followers? We haven't even set eyes on the place. I think you're jumping the gun."

"Noted." I put the blinker on and steered onto the ramp for Highway 117. "But let's say there was reason to think someone in this outfit had to do with a murder. Could you get a warrant then?"

"With compelling enough evidence, sure. But how to get the evidence without the warrant? It's a catch-twenty-two. They're in the middle of nowhere. There's no staking them out, because where do you hide? And if they know we're watching, they'll straighten up whatever they're doing real quick."

I huffed out a short breath. "Undercover?"

"Costs money. I'd have to have way more to go on than your gut and a few head of cattle at a Bible academy."

"Of course."

I clicked the radio back on, trying to untangle part of this mess as the highway wound through small towns and large farms.

Kyle made it sound like it would be nearly impossible to get anywhere on this particular rabbit trail. But nearly impossible had never stopped me from trying.

Janis Joplin blared through the speakers as I took the left my GPS told me would take us to the compound. For the first time since we'd left Richmond, there was traffic. A lot of it. Sunday-suited men with neon orange vests stood at intervals, directing cars to the turn off.

"It's another fifteen miles from here," I said, staring at the timer on my GPS screen. "This is a lot of people. Where do they all come from?"

"Miles around, probably." Kyle looked out the windows, interest clear in his tone. "How do I let you talk me into this stuff?"

"I'm charming?"

"There's that."

Janis and Bobby McGee were making better time than we were. I drummed my fingers on the wheel to the rhythm of the song and glanced at the clock again as the orderly line of cars marched toward Golightly's Way of Life church. Which we couldn't even see yet. I squinted at a speck on the horizon, my thoughts returning to the tangled web this murder had become.

If Landers was right, the PD had it covered. If he was wrong, I had two scenarios: either someone from the streets killed Jasmine (Violet, maybe, or someone else nobody had mentioned), or her past caught up with her. A past that had something to do with this ministry outfit.

We followed the waving of more orange-vested men to a parking spot in a concrete sea of cars and hiked a half-mile to the entrance. I stopped twice to dump pebbles out of my coral Stuart Weitzman slingbacks. "It didn't occur to me I was in for a workout when I got dressed," I grouched, hanging on Kyle's arm and sliding my shoe back onto my foot.

I noticed several other women wearing sneakers or flats with their dresses and made a mental note for next time.

Pausing under the grand stone archway, I stared at the thirty-foot 3D version of the cross from Jasmine's doodles. There was no way people could be eyeballing me because they knew why I was there, but I couldn't shake the feeling we were getting the once-over from every direction. I shot Kyle a glance from the corner of my eye. "Let's go see what all the mystery is about?" I murmured.

"Following you, Lois," he whispered, laying a hand on the small of my back.

I stepped into a whoosh of conditioned air, barely registering the metal logo crosses dotting the walls and doors before a woman in a long pink dress and plain ivory ballet flats rushed to my side.

"Welcome to Way of Life." She smiled through at least three layers of peach lipstick. "We're so happy you chose to worship with us today! If you'll come right this way, there's just a few things we need to go over with you before the service starts."

11

Another woman appeared at my other elbow. They hustled me into a side room, leaving Kyle with his jaw slightly loose.

The one in pink shut the door and turned to me with the same smile still pasted in place. Her cohort, in a pale blue dress with cap sleeves and no shape to speak of, chirped a welcome from behind me.

Did I give off some sort of reporter pheromone? Had we driven into Stepford? My brain whirled through possibilities, each more insane than the last.

The welcome wagon faced me, still grinning.

Or maybe not so insane.

"Good morning, ladies." I tried to keep my voice even. Body combat, five days a week for six years. A highly-trained federal agent outside the door. We could take them if we had to. I was almost sure.

"Good morning," the pink one said. "I'm Jenny Sue."

"And I'm Mary Lynn," the blue one chimed in.

"And you are?" they asked me in unison, widening their eyes and their smiles to slightly less than maniacal.

"Leigh." My middle name popped through my lips before I had time to close my mind around the intention. The subconscious is a funny thing. "And thank you. Nice to meet you."

"We're so glad you've chosen to worship with us this morning," pink Jenny repeated.

"But we need to talk with you for just a moment." Blue Mary turned for a row of cabinets that lined the far wall.

I backed a casual step toward the door, endless horror-movie-brain-sucking possibilities for what could be behind doors one, two, and three dancing through my head as I watched their vacant smiles.

Mary turned back with a pair of lemon yellow Havianas that matched the soft summer cardigan I wore over my knee-length turquoise sundress. Her smile hadn't budged. "If you'll just leave your shoes in the cabinet and put these on, we can show you and your," she glanced at my left hand, "gentleman friend to your seats."

Um. "You—you want my shoes?" Of all the things I would have guessed were in those cabinets, flip flops hovered just above Leprechauns on my list.

Blue Mary held out the flip flops. "Insurance, you understand. Carpeted stairs and shoes like those don't mix well."

I smiled. "I appreciate the concern, but I'm the least sue-happy person in Virginia. And I've climbed less stable things than stairs in higher heels than these." I turned for the door and Jenny's hand closed around my wrist.

"I'm afraid it's policy," she said, her voice just a scoche tighter. "Yours will be waiting for you after service is over."

What. The. Ever-loving. Hell?

I focused a laser stare on her hand. She removed it. When I raised my eyes back to hers, I held her gaze for a four count.

This craziness (insurance, my ass) before I'd made it three feet in the door had my bullshit radar on high alert. No way I was getting thrown out over footwear.

I smiled. "I'm holding you to your word, now," I said, keeping my tone impressively airy. I slipped off my shoes and watched as Mary I-couldn't-recall-her-second-name picked my babies up like they had cooties and settled them on a high shelf behind the second set of doors.

I slid my feet into the Havianas, and nearly fell on my face turning back for the door. "Are they coated in Vaseline?" I muttered, shooting a hand out for the wall. Louder and brighter: "I appreciate the welcome, ladies. I do think I can find my own seat. Is the balcony safe?"

They smiled, a glad-to-be-rid-of-me glint in their eyes.

The feeling was totally mutual.

Curling my toes and stepping carefully, I picked my way back to Kyle, who pushed off the wall and put a hand under my elbow. "You still in there? Who was Scarlett O'Hara's oldest child? What was Aikman's career passing record?"

"Wade Hampton Hamilton." I grinned, grabbing his arm. "And twenty-eight ninety-eight of forty-seven fifteen for almost thirty-three-thousand yards."

"What the hell was that about?" Kyle flinched when I poked him.

"Church. Watch your language," I hissed, looking up. "Notice anything different about me?"

The bridge of his nose wrinkled. "You're shorter." He looked at my feet. "What happened to your shoes?"

"They took them. Said I couldn't go into the sanctuary in them." I tugged on his elbow. "How's this for irony? I can't walk in these flip flops they forced on me. Slow down."

"What? Why?"

"I wear heels too much? I dunno. I can't remember the last time I had a pair of these on. My feet are sliding all over creation."

"No, why did they take your heels?"

"They said it was an insurance liability. If I fall down the steps or some nonsense."

"It looks like that's more likely to happen with the ones they gave you." He turned for the stairs.

Pausing at the bottom, I stepped out of the Havianas and picked them up. "If they didn't want my bare feet on their floors, they shouldn't have taken my shoes," I grouched, taking the steps two at a time when organ music started on the other side of the wall.

A cursory glance told me the other women all knew about the footwear rule. I saw an impressive array of flats in every color of the rainbow, but not a single shoe with a hint of a heel. Why?

We found seats in the upper nosebleed, staying on our feet and singing along with three hymns before a man-shaped speck walked to a podium in the middle of a stage that was bigger than my house. And backed by a Mack-Truck-sized gold cross. With silver and copper rays shooting from it to the edges of the wall. These folks got some mileage out of that trademark.

A jumbotron flashed on and showed a young, handsome man with thick bronze hair and violet eyes. He flashed a row of perfectly-bonded teeth and welcomed the thousands of people in the room to the Way of Life.

He raised his arms and everyone stood, turning to say good morning and shake hands. I scanned the room surreptitiously, thanking ten people for blessing me and wishing them a blessed day in return.

Half a football field from us, on the far side of the balcony, I spotted a three-row section of people dressed in identical white Oxfords, heads bowed in prayer while everyone around them blessed their neighbor.

Huh.

When the hymns began again, I poked Kyle. "What do you think is up with the prayer warriors over there? They didn't get up and do the welcome thing."

So far, that and the jumbotron—and the shoe police—were the only things that didn't seem like normal church.

"There's a school here. Like a private Bible college. Except, you know, not accredited by anyone," Kyle whispered.

I nodded. I knew that. I also knew there were more students enrolled in it than three rows would hold. I started to whisper back to him when I noticed the blue-haired woman on his other side, feigning disinterest in our conversation. Stepford fresh in my mind, I decided to leave the analysis for the ride back to Richmond.

Golightly took the lectern to thunderous applause about halfway through the hour. He spoke eloquently and passionately about evil, forgiveness, and loyalty for twenty or so minutes, my eyebrows going up by degrees. I could've sworn some of his words were about Jasmine. "The Good Book tells us he who brings trouble on his family will inherit only wind, and the fool will play servant to the wise," he intoned.

More applause followed his closing prayer, which begged for generous hearts. Subtle.

He took a seat that too closely resembled a throne for me to keep an entirely straight face when it came up on the screens and I coughed over a laugh. Mrs. I'm-not-really-watching-you cut her eyes to me.

A small army of suits filed to the front of each seating section, offering plates in hand. By the time one made it to us, it held a pile of twenties that would keep me in shoes for a year or more. Kyle dropped another one in and got an approving nod from blue hair when he passed her the plate.

I let my eyes roam while everyone else bowed their heads for the offering prayer. Better than a hundred collection plates filed out through the side doors, each tottering high with bills and checks. And that didn't count what the TV audience phoned or wire-transferred in. Philosophers all the way back to Jesus believed money corrupted.

There was a lot of it going backstage at Way of Life.

Everyone stood to sing a last song, then turned for the exits. As Kyle and I shuffled toward the stairs with the crowd, I turned back to the knot of people praying on the other side of the balcony.

They hadn't moved—except for one guy in the front row. The only one in the group not wearing the academy uniform, he had a shock of cropped dark hair and a twill blazer that had seen better days. His head was turned at an odd angle, his eyes wide behind his square glasses.

I'd swear he was looking straight at me.

* * *

Kyle and I rehashed every blip the entire drive back to civilization, with nothing but questions to show for our musing when I dropped him off.

Yes, the group of people praying as though no one else existed was different, but who knew why they were doing it? Maybe someone was sick. Maybe it was an assignment.

Yes, it was a lot of money. A lot lot of money. But taking in cash isn't a crime. Kyle said he'd ask around about tax records, but it would take time.

Yes, Golightly was too smooth. He sailed past charming and into used-car-salesman-with-a-better-smile territory. Was he a criminal mastermind?

Kyle said he'd put money on me learning how to walk in the flip flops before we could find proof.

Pink Jenny had returned my shoes with a smile and a halfhearted invitation to come back soon. Did they dislike all outsiders, or was I special? No way to tell.

And then there were the crosses. Way of Life was covered up with the logo Jasmine had doodled in her journal. Like, indoctrinated-to-the-point-of-scribbling-it-mindlessly covered up. And the trademark meant she hadn't seen it elsewhere. Since I didn't want to tell anyone (even Kyle) about the journals yet, I kept it to myself. But any uncertainty I might have had about Jasmine and Way of Life being connected washed away like a sand castle at high tide. The key to her identity was there. I just had some digging to do.

Playing fetch with Darcy, I was so lost in thought I didn't hear the engine shut off behind me. Or the gate open.

"Are you on some kind of mission to see how many dangerous leads you can chase in a week?" Joey's voice behind me was such a shock I didn't consider his words until I spun around—and almost fell, thanks to an ill-placed Elm root.

His arm shot out to steady me, and I caught myself by bracing both forearms against his chest. I raised quizzical eyes to his and he held my gaze for five hammering heartbeats before he sighed something that sounded like "dammit" and lowered his lips to mine.

Oh. My.

I froze, my brain failing to process his presence, let alone his tongue tracing the seam of my mouth. He pulled me closer, one arm winding around my lower back. I fell against him, parting my lips.

His mouth moved urgently over mine, searching for an answer I wasn't sure I had. At first, anyway. I slid my hands up over his broad shoulders as his moved up my back, thrills skating across my skin and fireworks in my brain obliterating even a hint of anything else.

He laid a trail of tiny kisses across my jaw to my ear and whispered, "Why are you so stubborn?"

"Natural talent?" I wasn't sure how I got enough air to breathe the reply with my pulse racing. I didn't want to admit, especially to myself, how much I'd missed him. He smelled so good. Cologne, sure, but not overdone and floating around something else that was positively magical. Months of dreaming about that smell, and I still couldn't put a finger on exactly what it was.

Right then, I could put my whole hands on him. I took full advantage, curling my fingers into his hair as his mouth moved over my collarbone.

Minutes (hours?) later, I noticed Darcy's plaintive bark, her tiny claws clacking on the back door. I came up for air (and sanity), standing up straight. Someone had loosened Joey's tie. And half-unbuttoned his shirt. A deep breath told me my bra was unhooked and his hands had traveled south.

He let go of me and ran one hand through his hair, which porcupined out in every direction from all my groping.

"Hey there." He grinned and my pulse galloped a few more beats.

"Hey, yourself." I shook my head, stepping out of his arms and leading him into the house. "That's a heck of a greeting."

He cleared his throat, buttoning his shirt and stooping to scratch the dog's ears. "Sorry about that."

"No need for apologies." I winked as I shut the door. "For the kiss, anyhow."

Grabbing two Diet Dr Peppers from my fridge, I followed him into the living room. My pulse finally slowed when I took a seat across from him and put his soda on the table.

"Mixed signals, much?" I asked, sloughing off the romance fog and leveling a serious gaze at him. "You sounded annoyed before we—well. Care to tell me what brought you here?"

He sat back and raised an eyebrow. "Me, mixed signals? Your friend said you spent the night with your ex last weekend."

"I did not."

"But you spent the morning with him today."

"I was wor—" I stopped, tilting my head and narrowing my eyes at him. "How the hell do you know that? Are you having me followed?"

For the first time since I'd set eyes on Joey a year ago, I felt uneasy in his presence. I threaded my clammy fingers together and tried to look more mad than scared.

He rolled his eyes. "You say that like I don't know you at all. I'm not stupid. I just have friends."

"Why on Earth would any of your friends notice who I spent my morning with unless you asked them to?"

"Because you took an ATF agent into Simon Golightly's church."

12

Joey could've slapped me and shocked me less.

"Who? Why? How?" I tripped over the words, my thoughts firing too fast.

"People know I know you. I'd rather some of them not have that information, but there it is. I do not 'have you followed,' but I get occasional calls when you're poking your nose into something other people would prefer you keep it out of. Since I'd prefer you keep breathing through it, I'm asking you nicely to back off whatever you think you're doing with Golightly. If your friend is running an investigation, let him run it. You stay away."

Damn. My brain ran through a long list of other expletives before I managed to make my lips work.

"He's not running anything. He was doing me a favor. But your presence here means I'm onto something." Something bigger than tax fraud.

Joey's full lips disappeared into a thin white line.

I held his eyes until mine hurt from not blinking.

"No. Comment," he said finally. "I've tried before to warn you off chasing headlines. This time I'm telling you: if you value your life, stay away."

"You realize you're just making me more curious."

"There's that whole saying about curiosity and cats."

"Lucky for me, I'm a dog person." I crossed my legs.

He dropped his head back and heaved the biggest sigh I'd ever heard. "You are infuriating sometimes, you know that? Why are you even interested in Golightly? He's way out in the middle of nowhere."

"I got interested in him because I think the Jane Doe from last week ran away from his outfit. But after what I saw this morning, I'm interested in lots of things about him. Where does all that money go? How much of it does the IRS know about? Who goes to his Bible academy, and where do they come from? What kind of stuff do they teach? Why did the Stepford brigade accost me and steal my shoes on the way into the church?"

"Why did what? Your shoes?" Joey raised his head and his brows.

"I stepped through the door and these two women with Easter egg dresses and plastic smiles nabbed me and made me take my heels off before they'd let us into the sanctuary."

"Why?"

"They said it was an insurance thing. I almost fell down the steps in the freaking flip flops they gave me and I can walk fine in my heels. I don't buy it. That place is gift wrapped in seven-hundred and ninety different kinds of weird."

"They're unusual." He folded his arms over his chest, his muscles straining the seams on his azure button-down.

"Did they kill this woman?" He wouldn't tell me, even if he knew. But I had to ask. It's like inquisitive Tourette's.

"I have no idea. Stay far away, Nichelle. I'm serious."

"You're always serious. And mysterious. But the Richmond PD thinks they're looking for Jack the Ripper, and I think they're looking under the wrong rocks."

"Why?"

"She told her friends someone might come looking for her. Richmond is the closest 'get lost in the crowd' big city to Golightly's place unless you want to live on the streets of D.C., and who would choose that? She was afraid to go to church. Oh, and cows. Golightly has cows."

"So?"

"There was cow's blood. At the murder scene."

"What? Why?"

I shrugged a how-the-hell-should-I-know.

He drummed his fingers across his thigh. "No other people in Virginia raise cattle?"

"No other churches. That I could find, anyway."

"So you thought you'd go to church and find a 'have you seen this girl?' ad in the Sunday Bulletin?"

No, I thought the funky symbol they own the rights to being all over her diary was weird. Still not sharing that, though.

"I went to get a feel for the place. Which Kyle thought was off, too. And I didn't go alone." I rolled the last bit around my head for a few beats before I said it, knowing Joey didn't like the idea of me doing much of anything with Kyle. But maybe if I could show him I was playing it safe (safer, anyhow), he'd tell me why he knew anything at all about Golightly. Which I wasn't entirely sure I wanted to know.

And there was the central problem with our crazy relationship: he was sexy as hell, and so sweet to me. But there was this whole other part of his life I knew very little about. By choice, really. It had been a year. I could've dug up a dossier on him. But part of me didn't want to violate his privacy, and the other part was terrified of what I might find.

"I appreciate that." Joey's tight smile said he wasn't sure he did. "But that was the dumbest thing you could have done. Don't you remember Waco?"

"Does anyone know any other case file? Unless the reverend is stockpiling guns, Kyle's guys have no bone to pick with him."

Joey flinched, but kept quiet.

Holy shit.

I studied his face, which he tried to keep stony and blank.

"They're stockpiling guns?"

"No comment."

Translation: maybe.

My thoughts ran to other reasons Golightly might not want the ATF in his cheap seats. I needed a pen for that list. "Whatever. If they don't want Kyle around, there's something fishy going on. Something no other reporter in the state has a lead on."

"Why do I bother?" he huffed.

I smiled. His cryptic routine irritated me, but his heart was in the right place. As was his everything else.

"I appreciate the concern," I said, softening my voice and my face. "But this murder is a big deal. And the air around Golightly's place thrums with shady vibes. I'll be careful. Kyle is interested in this, too."

"I'm not sure how to take that."

"I wish I knew what to tell you. He's an old friend." Every word true.

He leaned forward, resting his elbows on his knees, and studied my face like it held the key to a dead language. I smiled. Sort of. It was hard to avoid squirming under that gaze.

He finally smiled. "Whatever I'm doing here, steering clear doesn't appear to be an option. So I suppose I'll do my best to keep you safe."

"Starting tonight?" Did I really say that? It sounded like my voice.

That magical smell. I could still breathe it with him leaning in like that. Better than a drug, hand to God.

He grinned. "I have no other plans."

"Want to hang out a while? Watch a movie? Have some dinner?"

"I'd like that."

Me, too.

* * *

Joey knew the characters' names in *Breakfast at Tiffany's*, which I found way more charming than I probably should have. By the time Paul proposed, Joey had leaned back into the corner of the sofa and wrapped an arm around me. My head fit perfectly into the curve of his shoulder. The credits rolled before I knew it, and his arm tightened around me like he didn't want me to move any more than I wanted to. I closed my eyes and took a deep breath. Utter. Magic.

He cleared his throat. "That was fun."

I nodded. Happy. Normal. Date-like, even. "Dinner?" I asked.

He followed me to the kitchen, and I wondered how we could be not speaking one day and so cozy the next as I pulled the ingredients for pasta pomodoro from my pantry and fridge. Joey found a bottle of summer red in my wine rack and opened it, pouring two glasses and setting one on the counter for me.

"What can I do?" he asked, laying his cufflinks on the yellow tiled countertop and rolling his sleeves up a bit.

I peeked at him through my lashes as I ran water into a stockpot. He fit so easily into my kitchen. Into my life. It was hard to be annoyed with his disappearing act when I had a feeling I understood his reasoning. Not that I agreed with it. But I got it.

I pointed him to the cutting board and a pile of vegetables. "You want to chop those?"

"Sure." He slid the board onto the counter next to the sink and picked up a tomato and a serrated knife like he made dinner here every night. "How do you want them cut?"

"Just diced. Not huge." I shut off the water and put the pot on the back burner, then pulled out a skillet and sprayed it with olive oil.

Eleven kinds of awkward silence ensued. I sipped my wine.

"So, how have you been?" I asked.

He cut his dark eyes to me and grinned. "Frustrated. You?"

"About the same."

He nodded slowly. "This is so..."

"Complicated?"

"I was shooting more for 'impossible.' But complicated works."

I sighed and took the cutting board from him, pushing the veggies into the hot skillet with a wooden spoon and stirring. "Why can't things be easy?" I wasn't even sure who I was talking to.

"Where's the fun in that?" he asked.

I arched an eyebrow. "I can think of some fun to be had with it."

He chuckled. "Me, too. That's the problem."

"Why is it a problem?" I pulled off an Oscar-worthy job of sounding like I didn't know.

"Why did I come here today?" He picked up his glass and rolled the wine around in it, then set it down again and shoved his hands in his pockets. "I don't want you to get hurt. And if I'm really honest with myself, being close to me could get you hurt. Maybe in more ways than one." He dropped his chin to his chest.

I laid the spoon on the stovetop and stepped toward him. "My general reply to your concern for my safety is 'I don't care,'" I said, running one hand up his arm and catching his gaze. "What if I say it again?"

His mouth edged up into the sexy smile that threaded through my better dreams. "Impossible. You are impossible. Believe me, I get it. When I'm here, I don't care, either." He shook his head. "That's not true. I do, but not enough to go. When I get far enough away from you to get my head clear—that's when I care. I know I'm putting you in danger. And I feel like a selfish jackass for wanting to call you. To kiss you. To be with you." He whispered the last words as I stretched up on tiptoe to cover his lips with mine.

Damn the pomodoro. (And everything else but Joey's lips—and hands, which were behind me, turning off the stove.)

Full. Speed. Ahead.

* * *

Years of repressed hormones can do a number on a girl when they all go flying around at once.

To wit: the jangled nerves I got whenever I considered the possibility of this moment were nowhere to be found when it was actually happening.

I ran a light touch over his earlobe with my index finger and smiled at his sharp intake of breath. His mouth seared mine, the kiss equal in pent-up urgency from both sides.

Joey's strong, sure hands slid up and down my back as he dropped tiny kisses across the bridge of my nose and on each eyelid, a soft laugh rumbling through his chest when I reached behind his head to pull his lips back to mine.

This kiss was different: he wound one hand into my hair and cupped my jaw with the other, exploring every millimeter of my mouth with his tongue at window-shopping speed. I worked his tie off, dropping it to the floor and moving my fingers to the buttons on his shirt. He caught both of my hands in one of his and pulled his head back a fraction of an inch, crooking a finger under my chin.

"Where's the fire, Miss Clarke?"

Um, it sure looked like it was in his eyes, pitch-black and smoldering. There are never smelling salts around when you need them.

"You're not serious." I tried to ratchet my breathing back from chased-by-Freddy-Kreuger to decent-workout, but gave up after three seconds. "We don't have the best track record with this."

"You're expecting company?"

"I wasn't last time, either." Huff-huff-pant. "Or the time before that."

He backed up half a step, pulling me with him, and shot a glance at the front door. "It's locked. As long as we leave it that way, we have all," he kissed my forehead, "the time," my nose, "in the world." My lips.

My knees dissolved. He fit one elbow behind my legs, scooping me into his arms, and pressed his forehead to mine.

"You told me a story once about a fantasy that started this way." He turned for the bedroom.

"I have about a thousand fantasies that start this way." Wow, my censor switch had flipped clean over to "off."

"Pick one." He covered my mouth with his.

Oh. My. God.

I opened my eyes when I felt the soft chill of my down comforter against my back. Joey leaned over me, both elbows locked, triceps standing out under the cotton of his shirt.

"You are so beautiful," he said with such a serious face I had no reply, save for a nod and a whispered "back at you."

He smiled, and I pushed the spaghetti strap of my sundress off one shoulder. "You waiting for more of an invitation? Because I'm fresh out of stationery."

Shaking his head slowly, he lowered himself to the bed next to me. My heart threatened to slam right through my ribcage. He smiled, tracing my cheekbone with a feather touch. "I believe this is all the invitation I need."

And then he kissed me. Everywhere. I never knew a human being could withstand that much electricity and not go into heart failure. Somewhere in there, all the clothes came off, flung to the corners of the room.

Propping himself on one elbow, Joey stared into my eyes like he could see into my heart. Maybe he could. Nothing registered except the heat radiating from his skin, and how badly I wanted him.

"What are we getting ourselves into?" He brushed my hair out of my face. The way the muscles in his shoulders flexed with the simple motion was all it took to speed my breath again.

"Let's figure that out tomorrow." I pushed myself up and kissed him, pulling him back down with me.

He never broke eye contact.

Fireworks flashed. Bells rang. A choir sang. Maybe just in my head, but I couldn't swear to it.

Lying next to him later, our arms and legs braided easily together, I ran my fingers over his chiseled chest. I wanted to say something, but words—for possibly the first time in my nearly thirty years—failed me.

"I'm kinda glad you went snooping around Golightly's church this morning," Joey said, folding one arm behind his head.

"That was the secret? I could've gone out there months ago." I giggled.

"Timing. Absence makes the heart grow fonder, they say."

I shook my head, tipping my chin up to look at him. "No more running away."

"I don't want you to get hurt, Nichelle." He sighed. "Selfish jackass, party of one."

"Two. Party of two." I snuggled into his arms and resumed tracing nonsense patterns across his skin. He took a hitching breath and pulled me closer.

I knew good and well there were special obstacles to being with Joey. But something that felt so right couldn't be impossible. "We can be selfish together," I murmured.

I looked at him again when he didn't reply. His eyes were locked on the ceiling fan.

I laid a hand on his cheek and turned his face to mine.

"We. Will. Figure. It. Out." I punctuated the words with kisses, hoping I was telling the truth.

He smiled. "We're smart, right?" His voice was tight. I knew why, but didn't have a good answer, so I just nodded. This moment was too perfect to let the what-if monster trash it.

Returning my head to the spot between his shoulder and collarbone that seemed tailor-made for it, I closed my eyes. That smell was a thousand times more magical from where I lay.

"I might never move." I'm pretty sure I said that out loud. "What a way to end a rough week."

He ran his fingers lightly up and down my arm and over my back. "Dinner will wait. You feel like a nap?"

I nodded ever so slightly and he hummed softly. His voice was exactly as I'd imagined: deep and safe, vibrating through his chest under my ear. It took me until sleep crept in from all sides to place the song: "It's Impossible."

Maybe. But maybe not.

13

Peter Pan. Crowing over my head with Tinkerbell hot on his heels as Joey kissed me. From the heat in the kiss, Joey and I were headed straight for R-rated, non-Disney-sanctioned action. Tink pulled my hair. I swatted at her and returned my attention to Joey.

"Is that your phone?" Joey's voice sounded thick with sleep, a one-eighty from the urgent kisses.

Damn. My phone.

I shook myself out of the dream, still in Joey's arms. Night had seeped through my roman shades while we dozed.

I reached for the charger where I'd put my cell phone after Kyle and I returned from Way of Life three centuries ago. My fumbling fingers got it unplugged on the second try, and I cracked one eye at the glowing display.

"My mother, master of timing." I grabbed for a blanket like she could see us.

Raising the phone to my ear, I pasted on a grin. "I miss you," I said brightly. I did, craptastic timing and all. "What's going on with you?"

"I just got off the phone with Rhonda Miller." She'd been crying and sounded half-hysterical. My breath stopped, thoughts of Kyle's big teddy bear of a police officer father—and then Kyle himself—blasting the sleep right out of my head.

My mom doesn't cry.

"Deep breaths, mom. What's wrong?" Joey sat up and laid a hand on my shoulder. I laced the fingers of my free hand with his.

"She talked to Kyle earlier and he told her he tagged along with you to church this morning. The one that Golightly guy on TV runs." She sobbed harder. "You can't go back there, Nicey. Promise me right now you'll stay away."

I dropped my jaw. And the phone. Scrambling to pick it up, I shooed Darcy back to her fluffy pink bed. "Mom, are you there? What the hell is the matter? And why do you care about Simon Golightly?"

"What?" Joey's fingers tightened on mine with his murmur of surprise and I threw him a WTF look and a shrug.

"Stay away. Please." I could barely make out mom's words.

My brain refused to process it. I'd watched her endure years of chemo and radiation, losing the man she loved, and everything in between, and I'd never heard her bawl like that.

"Okay mom." I made soothing noises until her gulps of air quieted slightly. "You going to tell me why?"

"Just promise me."

Crossing my fingers like a child, I felt guilty anyway as the lie slid through my lips. She was in Texas. What she didn't know wouldn't hurt her.

I plugged the phone back into the charger after I swore twenty more times to stay away from Golightly and ran mentally through thirty ways I could kill Kyle.

Hugging my knees, I tried to shake the memory of my mom's wails out of my head. "What is this guy into?" I wondered aloud. "And what could my mother possibly care?"

Joey massaged my suddenly tight shoulders. "If I knew anything about your mother, I'd tell you. Is she really religious?"

I shook my head. "We went to a bitty little church up the road from our house for most of my childhood, but she's not super devout. And she's never shown even a passing interest in TV Jesus. This is the weirdest thing ever. And I've seen some crazy stuff."

Darcy barked. I stood, pulling the blanket around me, and padded to the doorway. "I need to let her outside. You hungry?" I threw a glance over my shoulder at him.

"Starving." He flashed a wicked grin and stretched one hand toward me. I smiled, admiring his bare torso because...damn.

"Pasta." I leaned against the doorframe and tried for serious. Not sure it worked. Joey was in my bed. I sucked my cheeks in and bit them to keep from squealing like a schoolgirl at an Elvis concert. "I'll turn the sauce back on."

He raised one eyebrow. "I'll get your laptop?"

"I left it in the car." I smiled. "I wouldn't have walked away, anyway."

"I know. Can you hand me my pants?" He waved a hand toward the top corner of my third-hand antique armoire.

"Do I have to?" My turn for the wicked grin.

"If you want your computer, it'd help."

"Do I really want it that bad?" I tipped my head and feigned indecision before I grabbed his trousers and tossed them to him.

Yes, I did. With my mom's raw voice and Golightly's oily grin gnawing at my gut, I needed some answers.

* * *

Joey left his collar unbuttoned and his tie off. I sat across my little bistro table from him in yoga pants and a *Telegraph* t-shirt, sipping wine and laughing between bites of pasta. Fork forgotten, he recounted how his grandmother blew up half her kitchen making lasagna one Christmas.

"Half the side wall of their house gaping open, freezing air and snow rushing in—and my grandfather's only worry was the food," Joey grinned, spearing a tomato. "All that is to say, I come from a long line of men who take their pasta seriously. And my grandmother would approve of this."

I raised my glass. "I'm honored."

He said goodnight a half-hour later with a couple of long kisses and a promise to call the next day.

"I'd stay if you'd let me." He cradled my cheek in his palm. "Just so we're clear."

Happy tears pricked the backs of my eyes, sending my lids into southern-belle flutter mode. "And I would love to let you." Lord, would I. I cleared the lump out of my throat and kissed him again. "But if you stay, I won't work. And I have at least one ginormous story that needs my attention. Very possibly two."

He pulled his thumb across my cheekbone. "Be careful. Please."

I closed my eyes for a long blink, biting my tongue to keep from asking him back in. Damn this mess of a story. "I will."

"Call me if you need me." He dropped his hand to his side and stared, concern and reluctance warring across his face. "And call your church buddy at the ATF if you need him."

"He's an old friend."

"But he wants to be more."

Lacking a good reply, I squeezed his hand. "Today was..."

He smiled and turned for the steps, pulling his fingers slowly from mine.

"It was," he said softly before he disappeared into the night.

I settled myself on the sofa with the rest of my wine, Darcy, and my laptop, and tried every search engine anyone ever thought of, hunting a lead on Golightly. Nothing.

Tapping my index finger on the keyboard, I looked around, hoping a fresh idea would pop out of the air. I flopped back into the corner of the sofa when it did not. Ideas are persnickety that way. Leaning my head back, I closed my eyes and hauled in a deep breath. The magical smell that fit Joey like one of his tailored suits clung to the upholstery.

What. A. Day.

I let my thoughts roam back over the better parts of it until my fingers itched to grab my cell phone and tell him to turn right the hell around.

Boy, was I glad Joey's friend had tattled on me.

"Joey's friend!" I bolted upright, reaching for the computer. Darcy yipped, prancing toward the front door.

"He's not here, girl," I called, my fingers flying over the keyboard.

Slow on the uptake, party of one.

I found the list of staff members at Way of Life and copied it into a new file, then started searching the Internet for information on them, one by one.

Joey hadn't said his friend worked at the church, and I knew if I called to ask him, he wouldn't tell me. To be honest, I wanted no part of getting his "business connections" pissed at him. I'd seen plenty of news stories (and movies) about what happened when you jacked with the wrong guy in the mob. I liked Joey's kneecaps just the way they were, thank you very much.

But who was new on the ministry's staff? That could give me a lead. The number of hits in the Google results told me the reverend wasn't interested in redacting his employees' online history.

I looked over the long list of links, then back at my docket of better than forty names. Then at the clock. Oy.

I should trade the wine for some coffee. But if there was a needle to be had in this scarecrow factory, I would find it.

* * *

Two ticks past three, I came across something. Blinking my bleary eyes to make sure I was reading right, I scrolled back to the top of the police blotter from the *Redway* (California) *Register*, looking for a date.

Nine years ago, one of Golightly's top muckety-mucks had been about as far from the fold as a guy could get, picked up on indecency and weapons charges. Or at least, someone with his fairly unusual name had been.

"Indecency with a minor and assault with a deadly weapon, Darce," I raked my fingers through her fur, "is often code for 'armed child molester.'" In some places, word choice saves the paper from being responsible for a lynching.

But was this Edwin Z. Wolterhall Golightly's Edwin Z. Wolterhall? How many of them could there be?

I clicked to the newspaper's complete archives. Nothing but the obits and crime blotter went back that far.

Damn. It was midnight on the west coast. No one would be in the newsroom at a bi-weekly that called a town of twelve-hundred home. I punched the number on the header into my cell phone for morning.

Back on the Way of Life site, I saved Wolterhall's grinning, coiffed-and-Sunday-suited staff photo to my growing WOL folder. I re-read his bio. An accountant. My gut said I was on the right trail, my physically-exhausted self satisfied enough to head to bed.

I took Darcy out and halfheartedly tossed her squirrel a couple of times. She didn't care. She was tired, too.

Drying my freshly-scrubbed face, I stared into the violet eyes in the mirror. Golightly was into something shady. Jasmine had abandoned Golightly's ship.

What else did I know? Money—truckloads of it.

Holy cow.

Jasmine talked about getting moving money.

Was she trying to blackmail the reverend?

14

Skipping body combat in favor of sleep, I still dragged ass into the news budget meeting five minutes late. Bob alternated disapproving glances with a rundown of the day's copy. When all the section editors had rattled off their lists, he turned to me. "You have anything to add this morning, Nichelle?"

"I'm sure I will, but I don't know yet," I said through a yawn that probably showed off the pop tarts in my stomach.

"Late night?" Eunice's tone was one of genuine sympathy, but Spence's derisive snort narrowed my eyes.

"Some of us don't mind going above and beyond, Eunice," I said. "I know you understand."

Spencer rolled his eyes, but stayed quiet. Thank God. On four hours of sleep and less than two cups of coffee, one sarcastic retort was all I could muster.

"Hang out, Nichelle," Bob said. "The rest of you, go find me something to print."

I was too beat to care that his abbreviated dismissal of the staff meant he was annoyed.

And entirely unprepared for him to close the door and hand me his iPad when Spencer finished glaring at me and strolled out.

"He should see someone about his grudge issues," I said before I looked down at the screen.

"Richmond PD close to arrest in gruesome murder case," the latest blog headline screamed.

"The hell they are," I said, scrolling down. Girl Friday had more "unnamed police sources" saying the detectives had honed in on a lone suspect and were tearing the Bottom apart looking for Jasmine's killer.

"What is this? I thought you were inside this police investigation, so how could this blogger have an arrest when you don't?"

Telling him I'd spent the day before on Golightly wouldn't get me anywhere but chewed out, so I skipped over that. "First of all, since when do we run 'impending arrest' stories? I don't write them, because they strike me as stupid. Criminals read the paper. Especially ones looking to stroke their own egos. Why tell him the cops are coming for him before they get him?"

I took a breath and kept talking. "Second, they are not. Aaron would have called me." I said it with utter conviction. I better be right. I was lying to my mother and risking my neck chasing leads for Aaron — if anyone had a headline before me, I'd be pissed on my own. Bob was just frosting.

Bob sank into his chair and took the iPad back.

"I'm sorry," he said. "I'm not mad at you." His chin dropped to his chest and I leaned forward.

"What's up, chief?"

"Eh. My birthday's coming up," he said.

"A big one this year?" I tried to remember how old Bob was.

"Sixty-five." He grinned. "I don't feel a day over fifty."

Birthday. Blogger. Barking at me.

"Andrews." I sat back in my chair.

"He wants me to retire. He's dropping not-very-subtle hints."

"He wouldn't know tact if it bit him in the bottom line," I smiled at Bob's chuckle. "Do you want to retire? Please say no."

"No."

"Then don't. The staff will mutiny if he tries to force you out."

"You think?"

"You always have our back, chief. Let us get yours."

He smiled. "Thanks, Nicey."

"Let me see what Detective White has to say for himself."

"I'm looking forward to reading all about it."

"I'll have it to you as soon as I can get it." I stood.

"I'll watch for it. This Girl Friday has sent our deadline structure out the proverbial window," he said.

"Indeed. It's damned annoying."

He winked.

I opened the door and nearly walked smack into Shelby Taylor.

"Eavesdropping is tacky, Shelby."

"I just wanted to see if you were in there." Her voice was weird. Like, normal. Absent the Splenda-coated bitchy edge she reserved for me, I barely recognized it.

"Um. Do I want to know why?"

"We need to talk," she said in the creepy-nice tone. "Can I buy you a cup of coffee?"

I glanced around, but Ashton Kutcher and his camera crew were nowhere to be seen.

"Why not?" I needed some caffeine. And if something serious enough for Shelby to be nice to me was going down, I wanted in the loop.

I dug my keys out of my bag and followed her to the elevator.

* * *

Shelby sat across a round teak table from me stirring her latte, her face betraying some seriously conflicting emotions.

"If you're waiting for me to die of curiosity, I'll admit to wondering, but you've got stiff competition for my attention this week, Shelby," I said.

She looked up. "I want to help."

I blinked. "With what?"

"The blogger. It's not you. I know it's not you. I only tried to make Andrews think it was you because I want your job."

"Are we playing true confessions? Because I knew all that already. I also know it's not you. You'd rather run naked down Monument Avenue than climb across Belle Isle to sneak into a bloody murder scene for video."

"Indeed." She smiled.

I sipped my white mocha, waiting for her to elaborate.

"This whole thing is making me feel wretched," she said. "It took me days to figure out why. But I'm pretty sure it's guilt. I've never been very nice to you, but I love the *Telegraph*."

I raised one eyebrow and she nodded. "I do. I've let my opinion of you cloud my better judgment, and I regret that. But I'll be damned if an amateur is going to beat us to a story this big. So how can I help you?"

I left the eyebrow up, staring at her. She looked and sounded perfectly sincere. But Shelby had knifed me in the back (thigh, arm, chest—she's not picky) so many times in almost eight years working together that I didn't trust my eyes. Or my ears.

"You don't believe me," she said, returning the stare without blinking.

"I'd like to, Shelby, but I don't know."

"I suppose I deserve that," she said. "I'll prove it to you. Really. Give me something to do."

"I'm not sure what to tell you. Aaron's got the PD's cyber crimes unit on it. They'll find her. I'm sort of surprised they haven't already."

"They can't arrest her."

"No, but they'll haul her in for questioning and probably scare the shit out of her. If she doesn't have a j-school or legal background, she won't know what she—or they—can and can't do."

I hadn't really stopped to consider until I said those words out loud what would happen if the PD caught up with Girl Friday. Somehow, championing Aaron putting the smackdown on someone who was reporting—sort of—made me feel squicky.

"What if I can figure out who she is?" Shelby asked.

"And do what? Us catching up with her likely won't do much but piss her off. And turning her in to the cops feels childish."

"She's putting information out that's irresponsible and wrong," Shelby said. "She's going to incite a panic."

"True." I fiddled with a sugar packet.

"What if we could explain in a way that keeps her out of hot water with the cops but also keeps her from doing it?" Shelby's wide eyes looked downright earnest. It was creepy. I dropped my gaze to my coffee, considering.

"That would be the best thing all around, I suppose," I said slowly. "I don't have time to hunt for a Lois Lane wannabe this week, though."

"I'll do it," she said. "I don't have a life anymore, anyway."

Her last words were so glum, I felt sorry for her in spite of myself.

"All right," I said, smiling. "See what you can dig up. And let me know if you want me to talk to her."

"I want to come with you if you do," she said. "Is that okay?"

I checked the corners for Ashton Kutcher again. No cameras. So weird.

"Sure, Shelby."

"Thanks, Nichelle." She stood. "I know you have work to do."

"Tons of it. Thank you for the latte."

"It was the least I could do."

I followed her out into the sunshine, still waiting for someone to jump out and tell me I'd been punk'd. Talk about a day I never thought I'd see—Shelby Taylor seemed to actually want to help me.

* * *

Aaron was my first call when I got into the car.

"It is definitely Monday," he said when I wished him good morning.

"That doesn't sound good," I said. "What's up?"

"You see that blog this morning?"

"I did. I'd like to know what's going on there, as a matter of fact."

"I don't know who this person is, but someone's ass is about to hit the door for leaking classified information about an open murder investigation." He sounded both pissed off and resigned.

I swerved into a parking lot on Grace, drawing irate honks from the two cars I cut off, and dug a notebook and pen out of my bag.

"I think you should start talking, Aaron." I fought to keep the edge out of my voice. We got along well. We'd worked together for years. But Emily was right: they wanted all access to what I'd been able to find out, and it looked like I wasn't getting what he'd promised in return. Yelling at him wouldn't fix it, though. And there were those journals, even if they weren't any help.

"I'm sorry, Nichelle," he said. "I know it won't make you feel any better, but my orders come from pretty far up the chain. I told them I'd promised you. Hell, Landers even spoke up on your behalf, flashing the notes you sent him last week. They said no media leaks until we'd made an arrest."

"Why?"

He sighed. "No comment."

I tapped a finger on the steering wheel, trying to get a handle on my temper.

"You're mad," he said.

"I'm disappointed," I countered, impressed with the softness of my voice.

"I'm sorry."

"How did Girl Friday get it if you weren't allowed to give it to me?"

"As soon as I find out, you'll be the first to know. I've never enjoyed watching someone get fired before," he said.

"You really think this is a cop?"

"Or someone who knows a cop pretty well." He said. "It has to be."

"I haven't looked at today's reports," I said. "Anything good?"

"Something horrifying, at any rate," he said.

"I'm listening." I clicked my pen back out.

"About eleven-thirty last night, we got a call on an abandoned car."

"I heard that one." I'd been up to my ears in Golightly research, but I remembered my scanner bleeping around that time. And I remembered something else, too. "They were awfully quiet about it, come to think of it."

"Call came from a retired Chesterfield cop. A nineteen ninety-four Buick sat abandoned in front of his house for two days. He recognized the smell coming from the trunk when he was cutting his grass last night. Picked the lock."

"Oh, shit. Description?"

"Caucasian female, between twenty and twenty-four years old. Dark hair. Green eyes. Advanced decomp thanks to the heat. They're working on the dental."

I scribbled all that down, the description I'd typed ten times in eight days making my stomach twist. "Is Landers on this?"

"Strictly speaking, there's little reason to think the two are related. But I'd be lying if I said he wasn't watching."

"Does anyone else have it yet?"

"Charlie hasn't called me, but she will. I imagine everyone else will when they have time to go through the reports, too."

But I could still get it on the web first. Unless Girl Friday's "unnamed source" helped her beat me to the punch again.

My whole life was turning into one big deadline.

"How did the car check out?"

"As stolen."

Of course it did.

"Thanks, Aaron. I'll call you if I have any more questions when I find the report."

"I really am sorry," he said. "About the other thing."

"We're not through talking about that yet," I warned him. "But we can table it for now."

I sped back toward the office, questions flashing through my head. A second body, same race and age range as Jasmine. Same hair color. Landers might have a serial, after all. Where did that leave me with Golightly?

I threw my car into park and jumped out, racing to the elevator. Bob would be happy with being first to a body dump. Though who dumps a body by leaving it in the trunk of a car in the middle of summer, in front of a cop's house? Either this was the unluckiest criminal alive or they wanted the girl found.

I tapped my foot as the elevator climbed toward the newsroom. So many questions, Monday. If I had one answer by Tuesday, I'd call it a win.

Plopping into my chair, I flipped up my laptop screen. The report was close to the top of the list in the PD's online database. The officer's narrative gave a bit more detail to the picture Aaron had painted for me—but the contact information for the caller had been redacted.

Not. Amused.

I snatched up the phone and dialed Aaron's cell again.

"Are you serious?" I said in place of hello. "Why did y'all black out the contact info for the cop who found the body?"

"I need more coffee if I'm going to keep getting my ass chewed for other people's decisions," he said. "As far as I know, it was professional courtesy, because he asked us to. Nothing more interesting than that."

"I want the name, Aaron."

The line fell silent.

"You owe me one, and you know it."

"You'll stop being pissed about the other thing?" he asked finally.

"Deal." If no other reporter had the contact info, my story would be first and better. There are worse ways to start the week.

"You didn't get it from me," he warned before he rattled off the guy's name and phone number.

"I'll just play psychic."

"Whatever works."

I thanked him and hung up, dialing the number he'd given me from my cell phone. If the guy wanted his name held out of the report, he wouldn't pick up a caller-ID from the *Telegraph* office.

It worked, in the sense that he answered the phone. It didn't, in the sense that he promptly barked "no comment," followed by "goodbye."

"Wait! Sir, I know most police officers have a kind of adversarial relationship with the press," I blurted before he could hang up. "But I think if you ask around, you'll find I've worked hard to build a reputation for fairness I'm pretty proud of."

The pause on his end of the line was pregnant enough to gestate an elephant.

He sighed. "I had more than one run-in with the fella who used to cover crime up there."

"I understand you're retired," I said. "For how long?"

"Eight years," he said. "How did you find me, anyway? They promised to leave me out of this."

"I have a little experience with detective work," I said.

"Wait. Are you the gal who—"

"Yes," I interrupted.

More silence. "He was methodical," he said, so low I had to strain to catch it over the hubub of the newsroom.

"He?"

"Somebody strong cut that young lady up. But the blood was drained and gone. And the trunk was lined with plastic."

My hand whipped across the page. "Any markings? Clothing?" Unwelcome images of the murder scene in the old switch house flashed through my head.

"No clothes. The level of decomp was—" He paused. "I didn't touch or move her."

"Why park her in front of your house?" I wasn't really expecting an answer, but I had to ask, anyway.

"My guess? He wanted someone who would appreciate his work."

I scribbled. Sweet cartwheeling Jesus.

"But how did this person know you were that guy? What division did you work in?"

I knew before he spoke.

"Homicide. Twenty-three years."

I thanked him profusely, promising to leave his name out of my story, and dropped the phone back into its cradle. Turning to my computer, I opened a new document, hoping I could avoid inciting a panic myself.

Richmond detectives are searching for clues in the second apparent murder in the city this month, after the body of a young woman was discovered in historic Church Hill Sunday night.

"A nineteen ninety-four Buick sat in front of [the complainant's] house for two days," RPD Spokesman Aaron White said. "He recognized the smell coming from the trunk when he was cutting his grass last night and picked the lock."

The man who made the discovery is a retired homicide detective.

In an exclusive interview with the Telegraph *Monday morning, the complainant, who asked that his name not be used, said what he saw of the scene looked nothing like an accidental death.*

I drummed my fingers on the desk, staring at my notes and trying to decide what to leave out. I wanted the big scoop. But I didn't want to come off like

Girl Friday, with no regard for how my story would affect people who lived in that part of town. If I was honest with myself, her stories were irritating me more than a little—losing to Charlie on occasion was part of the game. But to a faceless rival who didn't have to stick to convention? That pissed me off. Not badly enough to go scaring the crap out of hundreds of people without better reason, though.

"I didn't touch or move her," the retired police officer said, noting that the car trunk where the victim was found had been lined with plastic.

The car was reported stolen from a Burger King parking lot in Ashland on Thursday.

I added a few lines from the detective's narrative, plus the car's license plate info and a plea for anyone with information to call Crimestoppers. Finishing up with a stock quote from Aaron warning residents to be aware of their surroundings and stay safe, I scrolled back to the top and read through the story. Not too detailed, but enough to win this headline for the day. As long as Girl Friday's secret source wasn't in on the investigation, anyway.

I clicked open my file on Jasmine and noted things I wanted to watch: who was the second victim? Who reported the car stolen (and was it actually stolen)? Was there video footage from the Burger King? I knew Aaron would have people checking all that out, and odds were better than even I could guilt him into giving me at least some of the answers. I scanned the day's court docket. Nothing a few phone calls wouldn't take care of.

All that added up to a Monday afternoon I could spend digging for dirt on Golightly and Way of Life.

I emailed the body dump to Bob and packed my bag. Striding to the elevator, I pulled up the phone number for the paper in California where I'd found Wolterhall's name the night before. It was finally after nine a.m. on the west coast. Maybe my lucky streak would stretch a teeny bit further.

Like, through this phone call and out to the Blue Ridge.

15

Journalism Even Before the Age of the Internet 101: if the mention of a story from nine years ago leaves another reporter gasping and speechless, you're following a good trail.

The sweet news editor at the *Register* sucked in a sharp breath at Wolterhall's name. When she found her voice, she told me his was the most horrifying trial she'd covered in her eighteen years at the paper. The public outcry when the guy walked out of the courthouse a free man because of a hung jury kept them buried in letters to the editor for weeks.

Distraught at the (glossed-over) description I relayed of Jasmine's death, she promised to email me a photo of Wolterhall as soon as she could dig one up.

I tossed a quick thank you for the break Heavenward and laid my Louboutin slingback on the accelerator, the foothills of the mountains peeping blue-purple on the horizon.

The sea of concrete that passed for Way of Life's parking lot was largely empty on Monday afternoon. Shutting off the engine, I checked my email. Nothing from California. I tucked my cell phone into the pocket of my cream linen slacks and strolled to the front doors, examining the premises through lowered lashes.

The church building was a massive brick and concrete structure, with wings shooting off in three directions from the central sanctuary (itself easily as big as a professional basketball arena). To the left sat a stately antebellum-style white brick building made to look like an oversized house. A huge veranda wrapped down two sides of the building, covered with climbing roses and jasmine vines I could smell from where I stood. I marked it as the dormitory by the bike rack out front.

Past the dorm were a pair of boxy brick buildings, probably classrooms or offices (or both) and the pasture and barns.

To the right of the church building, I spotted the TV studio—gray concrete with a ten-foot satellite dish on the roof.

I saw probably twenty folks in the academy's painfully plain uniforms, and one guy about my age, dressed in khakis and a blue polo. He paused halfway across the lawn, turning to stare at me before he waved and walked over.

"Can I help you?" He asked, offering a grin almost as wide as his shoulders.

"I'm just visiting," I said. "It's such a lovely day."

"Visiting who?" he asked, his brow creasing for a split second.

"The Lord," I said, hoping I didn't sound too crazy.

He nodded, putting a hand out. His grip was solid, and my eyes traveled up well-muscled arms. "I also like to pray outside. I'm Ben Mathers. I teach at the academy."

"Leigh," I repeated my middle name, since I'd used it the day before. "I'm new to the church."

He leaned against a tree. "Welcome."

I studied his easy smile, something tickling the back of my brain. He hadn't been on stage Sunday. But his picture had to be on the website.

"How long have you worked here?" I asked. A teacher would surely remember Jasmine if she'd been a student here. But I couldn't exactly blurt out that question.

"Six years," he said. "Secular pursuits weren't for me. There's no faith in science."

"What do you teach?" I asked.

"Philosophy, music—a little of everything. Our classes are different from your typical course catalog."

"How does the school work, exactly?" I added an extra dose of naiveté to the words. "How would I enroll?"

"Anyone can apply, but most of our students are college age or maybe a bit older. It's a very close group."

"And what would I do after graduation?"

"There are many churches across the country that hire our graduates as ministers or administrators," he said. "Including this one."

"Does anyone ever leave? Like get here and not find what they wanted?"

He shrugged. "Not often. The students come here seeking a closer relationship with the creator and a more Godly life. We put them on that path."

Not often. But not never, either. His earnest tone said asking him about Jasmine could lead to trouble, though.

"That's very...Christian of y'all," I said.

He shoved his hands into the pockets of his shorts and straightened, his gaze holding mine. The smile on his lips didn't reach his eyes, the almost black irises sweeping down my frame. And lingering on my shoes. "I'm afraid I have a class to run to. It was nice to meet you. I hope you find what you're looking for with us."

Me, too. I watched him walk toward the red brick buildings before I spun for the front of the church. I had a feeling what I was looking for was in there.

I perused the quiet foyer, something I hadn't had a chance to do the day before, thanks to the shoe police.

The doors to the sanctuary stood straight ahead, five sets of twelve-foot heavy wood doubles. Closed. To my right was the weird shoe locker room the Easter egg twins had hustled me into, and the staircase to the balcony where we'd sat for the service.

To the left, a hallway stretched as far as I could see. I stepped toward it, the clicking of my heels on the marble echoing off the paneled walls.

I found a bookstore with Golightly's fifteen titles displayed in the windows and a slight boy with bad acne behind the register, his head bent over a book.

I picked up a copy of Golightly's latest hardcover and flipped it open. Signed. "The way and the life, Simon Golightly." Uh-huh.

Tucking it under one arm, I turned to a rack of CDs. Sermons, of course, and music recorded by the church's house band. I picked a random one of each and carried the stack to the counter.

The young man looked up from his book and smiled. "Good afternoon."

"Hey," I said. "How are you?"

"Blessed and favored of the Lord," he said, punching buttons on the register.

My eyebrows went up, the specificity of the phrase rankling. Like a restaurant that trains servers to reply to "thank you" with "my pleasure" instead of "you're welcome."

"How lovely," I said, at a loss for a reply.

A sixty-dollar charge to my MasterCard later, I took a bag of research material from him and wished him a good day.

"Go with God, washed in the blood," he replied.

Um. "You, too?"

Between there and the office, I passed a food court, a coffee shop, and a florist, all dark and closed up. I also counted nine of the logo crosses adorning the walls.

A honey-colored door with checkerboard windows and a tiny sign that read "administration" sat about halfway between the bookshop and the end of the hall. I opened it and peeked inside.

"You." The word was a cross between shock and disdain, quickly covered by a sugary "what can we do for y'all today?" in a thick drawl. I turned toward it, my eyes lighting on the woman who'd been wearing pink the day before. Today she wore lavender, her dress a similar potato-sack mass of shapeless fabric. Did she make them herself?

I pasted on my best slightly-confused smile. "I so enjoyed the service yesterday morning, I want to get more information on the church. How to get involved, how to donate to the reverend's work. Is there someone I could talk to?" I stepped into the office and shut the door. The walls were paneled in dark cherry, with forest green carpets and deep red furnishings. Like the set from a boys' club in a Spencer Tracy film, minus the scotch and cigars. "Could I talk to one of the ministers?"

She gave me a once over, her brow creasing when she got to my shoes. Raising her eyes to my face, she offered a tight smile. "I'm afraid they're in a meeting."

"I can wait," I practically singsonged.

"They'll be in there a while. Prayer meetings on Mondays take most of the day. We get extensive prayer requests from our congregation on Sundays, you see."

I nodded. "I don't suppose you could help me?"

Her face told me she'd rather kiss a frog's foot. "There's some free literature there on the counter that will tell you about our mission and services."

"What about membership and getting involved?" I asked. "I'd like to know about the educational opportunities y'all offer, in particular."

Her eyes narrowed. "Aren't you a little old for school?"

Ouch. I kept my smile and sunny voice. "I think Reverend Golightly would say no one is too old to find the Lord."

Her smile imitation improved. "Of course, we welcome everyone to the Way of Life family." She eyed my shoes again. What did she have against Christian Louboutin? Was he a closet Satanist or something?

I waited for her to elaborate, but she fell silent and turned back to her computer.

Alrighty then.

I picked up a handful of brochures, wished her a good day, and turned back for the door.

"You'll find the exit to the right," she said without looking up. "Go with God, washed in the blood."

Wow. God bless you, but don't let the door hit you in the ass on your way out. The more time I spent at Way of Life, the weirder it got.

I pulled my cell phone from my pocket and tried to check my email. No signal. I walked a few steps down the hallway to a window. Still nothing.

"They scramble it," a soft, sweet soprano came from behind me and nearly made me jump out of my skin. I turned on my heel, a quizzical eyebrow raised.

A short, plump girl with frizzy red hair and large, black-rimmed glasses smiled from behind the coffee counter across the hall. She dropped the rag she was wiping the counter with and offered a hand. "Good morning. I'm Elise. You're new."

I smiled, crossing the hall to shake her hand.

"I'm Leigh," I said. "I enjoyed the service yesterday and wanted to talk to someone about the church. But the lady in the office said there's no one around to help me."

Her lips tipped up slightly and she shook her head.

"I'm sure they're all in a meeting," she said.

"She said they have long prayer meetings on Mondays."

"Uh-huh." It didn't sound like an affirmation at all. I smiled and leaned closer.

"She didn't seem too fond of me," I said, tipping my head to one side like I didn't get it. "I kind of got the same vibe yesterday, which is making me self-conscious. Thank you for being nice."

"She doesn't like your clothes. Or your shoes," she said.

Again with the shoes.

"What's wrong with them?" I glanced down at my sapphire silk tank, with its perfectly respectable neckline, and cream capris. My Louboutins were the same shade as the top.

"I can see your boobs," she whispered. "And your ankles. The shoes are too," she looked around and leaned in closer, dropping her voice to a bare whisper, "sexy."

My hand flew to my solidly b-cup, no-cleavage-in-sight chest. "I beg your pardon?"

"Your clothes. They fit. You can see your body underneath them. And the shoes." She shook her head and resumed scrubbing. "Not allowed. Shoes like that make men have lustful thoughts."

My jaw loosened, and I fumbled for words. "Not an insurance issue?" I managed.

"No."

I peered over the counter at her outfit. Loose navy slacks, a two-sizes-too-big white oxford button down tucked into them, and white sneakers. The website photos from the classrooms flashed through my thoughts.

I sagged against the counter. "You work here?"

"Work study. I'm a student at the academy."

I nodded.

She flipped on a faucet and rinsed out the rag.

"For how long?"

"Three years." The ghost of a pretty smile almost reached her eyes before they fell on my cell phone. "They scramble the signals so we can't have cell phones."

"Do they?" I had close to seven thousand questions about that, but wasn't sure I could ask any of them without scaring her off.

She kept talking. "No TV. Except the ministry's channel. No phones. All Jesus, all the time." She glanced at her wristwatch. "Speaking of, I have class."

Wow. I watched her jerky, frustrated movements as she grabbed her backpack and flipped off the lights.

"Nice meeting you," she said. "If you're coming back, ditch the shoes."

"Thank you." I paused, then figured one couldn't hurt. "Hey, are y'all ever allowed to leave?"

She shook her head. "I haven't seen my parents in two and a half years."

* * *

I made it back to Richmond before my thoughts stopped spinning.

Stepford meets hostage crisis meets cult was one hell of a sexy headline. My chances of staying off Bob's shit list if I took it to him today were less than that of Golightly's face being a hundred percent natural, though.

I turned into the parking garage at the office and checked the clock. Almost five. Which meant it was after lunch in California. Maybe the sweet woman at the paper there had found the photo I needed.

I rushed off the elevator and almost walked into Eunice. She stepped to one side and laughed. "Breaking news?"

"Something like that."

"Have anything to do with your secret admirer?"

"Um. No?" I scrunched my brow into an explain-please look.

She smiled. "Go see. You got a present."

Huh?

She shuffled onto the elevator and waved as the door closed. I whirled for my cube, stopping short when I turned the corner.

A large crystal vase barely contained what looked like too many dozen red roses to count. I could smell them from ten feet away, and the arrangement covered most of my desk. I dropped my bag, my face stretching into a goofy grin, and reached for the card.

"We will indeed figure something out," it read. I flopped into my chair and kicked off with one foot, spinning and rereading the words several times.

Day. Made.

Tucking the little white rectangle into my top drawer, I fished my cell phone out of my bag and punched the speed dial.

"Hello, beautiful." On the first ring, too. I clamped my lips down on a squeal.

"Hello yourself. I'll tell you what's beautiful—these flowers. They have brightened this crazy Monday considerably. Thank you."

"Always happy to make your days better." Joey chuckled.

I sat back in the chair and sighed, butterflies flapping around my middle. "I wish you could have stayed, you know." I dropped my voice a full octave.

"Me, too. You get any work done?"

"I think I might have found something interesting, but it's too soon to tell for sure," I said. "I'm waiting for a photo."

"You're also being careful, right?"

I rolled my eyes. "Cross my heart. I still didn't give them my real name when I went by Way of Life today."

"Went by? Like it's not fifty miles out of the way?"

"I met a girl who goes to the Bible school." I breezed past his accusatory tone. "And a teacher, too. Got some interesting stuff."

"When can I see you again?" he switched the subject smoothly, an urgency in his voice that set those butterflies in motion again.

"Do you have plans for the weekend?" I asked.

"Sounds like I do now. If I have to wait that long."

Holy. Crap.

"Might save you some driving to bring a bag with you." My voice shook on the last word.

"I don't want to be presumptuous."

"I think I'm inviting you." My very own audacity cocktail: one part lack of sleep and two parts frustration, shaken well and served over Joey's warm voice. I felt positively brazen.

"You think?"

"I am."

"I'll see you Friday. Don't get shot before then."

"I'll do my best."

He hung up.

I dropped the phone, staring at the roses. What was I getting myself into? It wasn't like I could settle down and raise a pack of little Armani addicts with great hair and chiseled jawlines.

Could I?

I shook off the fantasy and lifted the flowers to the shelf above my desk before I flipped my laptop open and clicked into my email.

Fifty-eight new messages. One from my prosecutor friend DonnaJo, three from other lawyers, and one from California were all I cared about.

I held my breath as I clicked the line for "news@redwayregister.com."

Dear Nichelle,

So lovely to talk to you this morning. I wish you the best of luck with your story and your career. The only photo I was able to locate of Edwin Wolterhall was this shot taken as he left the courthouse. It's a profile, but I hope it helps you.

All best,
Dina

I pulled the image up on the screen. Oh, jeez. A digital shot of an old newspaper page. A yellowed black and white page, at that. I could sort of see the lines of the guy's face, but not really. "Of course," I mumbled, my shoulders slumping.

"Of course what? Please tell me our blogger friend isn't back at it," Bob's voice came from behind me. I smacked the laptop shut and spun my chair to face him.

"Just another dead end, chief," I said. "They seem to like me."

"You'll figure it out," he said. "Your track record is hard to argue with."

"I didn't have Girl Friday to chase after last time around this track," I said.

"I keep hoping the PD will figure that out."

"So does the PD." I grinned. "Here's an interesting twist for you: Shelby bought me a latte this morning and begged me to let her help. She says she doesn't care for me, but she loves the paper."

He raised one bushy white brow. "We're sure it's not her? Not that you'd mind if I fired her, but she's the best copy chief in three states. I don't like the idea of having to replace her. It'd take at least two newbies, and Andrews will bitch about the money."

I laughed. "While that would be an excessively clever cover, I don't think so. You said she had an alibi, right? And I can't see Shelby crawling around that switch house taking video of gore. Not her thing."

Bob nodded. "You're right about that. I never thought I'd see the day you and Shelby teamed up. But have at it. You have anything else for me tonight? I'm thinking of going home if you're done. Metro is finished, barring something breaking."

"I have a couple of emails I haven't read. Give me five minutes and I'll let you know."

He glanced at the flowers and offered a softer smile. "Those are nice."

I nodded, unable to keep the grin off my face. "He's nice."

"Glad to hear it."

He wouldn't be glad to hear any more of it, wearing his Pa Ingalls face. The memory of his horrified gasp the last time we'd discussed Joey was fresh even a year later. I turned back to my computer.

"You work too much," Bob said. "Don't you know it's after five?"

"Funny how the news doesn't care about clocks." I didn't turn around. "And I don't see you going home yet."

His chuckle drifted in the direction of his office.

* * *

My thoughts back on Wolterhall, I shot quick replies to a few emails and copied the grainy photograph onto a flash drive before I went hunting for our photo editor. I found Larry in the break room, leaning against the orange laminate countertop while the aging Mr. Coffee burbled.

"Just the man I need to see tonight." I grinned, grabbing my cup from the cabinet.

He tipped the Richmond Generals ball cap I'd never seen him without and smiled, the lines in his face deepening. "You only want me for my brains. But helping you is always interesting. Is it this blog everyone's trying to not talk about? I'm not much good for tracing online, but I might have had a peek or two at her photos and video. Just for grins."

"Actually, not what I was going to ask." I laughed. "But let's come back to it. I have a picture that's not really discernible." I pulled the flash drive from my pocket. "I'm hoping there's some magical enhancer thingy that can help me make out this guy's face."

He took the drive and turned it over in his thick, callused fingers. Larry had started taking pictures for the *Telegraph* as a real-life Jimmy Olsen, freelancing with his Canon on the weekends from the time he was fourteen. In almost fifty years since, he'd stayed on top of photo technology better than a lot of guys half his age.

"Who are we trying to ID?" He winked. "Anyone I should watch for around dark corners?"

"I'd rather not say what I'm trying to find just yet."

"So, Bob told you to stay out of it." Larry nodded.

I laughed. "Something like that."

He turned for the photo cave. "Let's see what we can do."

Twenty minutes of magnifying and filter application later, Larry leaned his bulk back in his chair and sighed. Lacing his fingers behind his head, he looked up at me. "You're lucky I like you. You can be a pain in the ass."

"You love a challenge," I said.

"True. But this is more of one than I have time for at five-thirty on Monday. When do you have to know something?"

"The sooner the better, but whenever you have time to get to it, of course." I managed to keep the frustration from bleeding into my voice. It was sweet of Larry to help, and no one's fault the photo quality sucked.

"Good luck," he called when I spun for the door.

"Thanks. I think I'm going to need it."

16

Journalism in the age of the Internet 103: the answer to almost anything can be found online. But only if you know where to look. And the guy you're stalking isn't crafty enough to cover his cyber-tracks.

Golightly had filled in his so well it had the opposite of his intended effect—the swiss-cheese history had me way more convinced he was shady than I would've been if I'd turned up an arrest record. When I hit a third dead end on the reverend, I focused on Wolterhall. Was Way of Life's accountant really an almost-convicted armed sex criminal?

Another search engine and fifteen dollars to a private records service got me one teensy tidbit: he was born in Montecito, California in March of 1970.

Google Maps said Montecito was twelve miles from Redway.

I noted that as promising and closed my laptop at six-thirty. My back and neck popped loud enough to make me flinch when I stretched my arms over my head.

"Long Monday?" Mel's voice came from the other side of the cube wall.

"You can say that again." I stood, peering over. She smiled up at me and pushed her hair out of her face.

"Hey, that's happier than you've looked in a while," I said.

She nodded. "Grant and I talked for—God, hours. About everything.

Then we did other stuff for hours." The grin threatened to crack her face open.

I laughed in spite of the TMI factor. Her giddiness was infectious. "I'm very happy for you two."

"I owe you big time," she said. "Funny how words are my life, but I didn't want to talk to the man I love about important shit, isn't it?"

My left eyebrow shot up. "The man you what?"

Her grin softened to a serious, non-fangirly smile. "I do. He's perfect. Well. As close to perfect as I've ever seen. Thank you, Nicey."

Aw. I stood up straighter. Having a hand in making someone as happy as Mel looked was pretty cool. "Anytime, doll."

"Anything I can do for you? I can't afford those shoes you wear, but if you need dirt on City Hall, I'm your girl. No holds barred."

I chuckled. "City Hall would be easier to crack than what I need dirt on right now," I said.

"Try me."

"I'm not—" I paused. "Wait. Didn't you tell me once your college roommate works in DC?" I left the question deliberately vague, crossing my fingers.

"She's a case investigator at the IRS," Melanie said. "Something about the look on your face tells me you remembered that, too."

"Guilty. I was going for subtle."

"Not your strong suit. What's up?"

"How close are you?" The collection plates filing back into the inner chambers at Way of Life and Elise's dismissive snort when I'd mentioned the prayer meeting collided in my thoughts and I sagged against the cube wall. They were counting money. All day on Monday. I'd bet my prized newsprint Louboutins they were hiding some of it, too.

"She's like the sister I never had." Mel put a hand on the phone. "You're off the record?"

I nodded. "I won't get her in trouble. But part of what I'm looking for isn't covered by Freedom of Information."

"Of course not. Why would it be easy?" She snatched the handset up and dialed. "S'ok. This way I feel like I'm helping."

She rattled off a quick introduction to her friend Amy, who sounded sweetly guarded when Mel handed me the phone as Parker walked up and asked if she was ready to leave.

Melanie gestured to her chair and handed me a pen, winking and waving as she kissed Parker and they headed for the elevator. I looked around the newsroom. Section and copy editors discussing space and material. They didn't give a flying flip what I was doing. I scooched down in the seat and lowered my voice anyway.

"I need to know what Reverend Simon Golightly and Way of Life Ministries report as income to the IRS," I said, figuring someone who crunched numbers for a living would deal best with straightforward. "I know the church records are public, but I'd rather not wait the six weeks. And I'd like his personal information, too."

"Spell the last name," she said. I obliged. Clicking of computer keys ensued, followed by a low whistle.

"Not your garden-variety struggling man of God, is he?" she asked.

"Nope." The plastic edges of the pen bit into my fingers.

"There's a ton of stuff here," she said. "Last year, the church reported two point three million dollars in other business income, and nine hundred seventy six thousand and change in donations."

I scribbled the amounts. "And the reverend?"

"Just shy of six hundred grand in income. Plus housing. That's another two hundred thousand. Nontaxable." She read me the exact amounts, and I jotted them down.

"Anything flagged in his tax returns?" I asked, wondering if my big break was about to turn into a dead end. It was a lot of money. But I knew that already. And it sounded like he was reporting it all to the government. Dammit.

"Not flagged for an audit," she said. "But there are several returns linked here, which means someone is watching for signs of fraud."

"What's linked?"

"His wife reported three hundred thousand in income from the church and speaking engagements last year," she said. "They file separately, which keeps their income from being classified as uncommon for churches of that size."

"Huh?"

"If a pastor makes significantly more money than most of his peers at similar-size churches, he loses his tax exemptions." More clicking. "These folks have been very careful to skirt that. Meticulous, even. I don't think my tax law profs could have put this return together better."

I jotted that down, Golightly's army of lawyers making more sense with every word.

She was quiet for a minute. "Hang on." Still more clicking. "Clever dude. Or clever accountant," she muttered.

"What?"

"There's a crapton of money coming in from book and video sales," she said. "But it's coming into an LLC that's a subsidiary of the church. Click clickety click. "And going to a charity that looks like it supports the church's Bible college."

"I'm afraid my tax law knowledge begins and ends with the ten-forty EZ," I said.

She giggled. "You and ninety-five percent of the population. The only people who care about tax law work in this building, or have a lot of money they want to keep. This Golightly dude is the latter.

"So, when a pastor writes a sermon, he does so in the course of his employment for the church," she continued. "Just like you write stories for the newspaper."

Light bulb. "The church owns his sermons."

"Exactly. And if he wants to sell them as a book..."

"The church gets the royalty money."

"In theory. Ministers often don't understand that, and have a tendency to get upset if a lawyer points it out. This guy gets it. Really gets it. Not only does it appear, at least on paper, that he's not profiting from the book sales, but the church is putting the cash into a nonprofit ministry."

"No taxes?"

"No taxes."

"How much money?"

"Last year? Three point four million dollars. Their students must be eating lobster and steak every night and driving to class in Ferraris. Sign me up."

I scribbled that down, the drab uniforms and pretty-but-not-fancy dorm dancing around my thoughts. "Huh. Thank you, Amy."

"No one knows where you got this?"

"Not a peep, I swear."

"Then you're welcome. Anything else?"

"You don't happen to see anything illegal that would make a great headline?" I asked.

She laughed. "I see why Mel likes you. Not dancing on my screen, but your guy is interesting reading. I'll take him home with me and let Mel know if I find anything."

"Thanks." I hung up, staring at the numbers. She'd as good as said the guy was shady. But being crafty with a tax form and cutting up young women aren't exactly the same thing.

I shoved every note I had on Jasmine or Golightly into my bag and turned for the elevator. Leaning on the rail across the back wall, I let my thoughts wander. Halfway to the garage, I bolted straight up.

Nine hundred thousand. Golightly reported nine hundred thousand in donations to Way of Life.

No way all those trays full of cash times fifty-two weeks was less than a million dollars.

Secret Monday meetings. Behind closed doors.

A gruesome story I'd done about a tanning salon owner's murder—and the drug money he was laundering—floated to the surface of my thoughts as I charged through the elevator doors toward my car. Businesses that deal in large amounts of cash are perfect for cleaning dirty money, because the intake is almost impossible to spot.

And Joey had a "friend" who'd seen me the day before. A friend who could ID Kyle on sight.

Was it the kind of friend who needed millions of dollars laundered?

That sounded like a big "maybe." And maybe was better than a dead end.

The money had to be the key to what was going on at Way of Life.

I turned out of the garage and fished my cell phone out of my bag.

"You have time to talk?" I tapped in a text to Kyle. "On my way home. I have a new theory."

* * *

The deli down the street from the office made the best club sandwiches in town, and amazing twisty fresh potato chips. The scent from the bag taunted me all the way home, my stomach burbling as I turned into my driveway. To find Kyle sitting on my porch swing.

"Evening," he called, crossing the lawn to take my computer bag. "I got your text. You want to tell me about your theory?"

"After I get through picking a small bone with you."

"Bone? I thought we had a good time yesterday."

"We did. Until you got me in trouble with my mom." I unlocked the door and bent to scratch Darcy's ears. She ignored me and pawed at the bag of food.

"Mine, sweet girl," I said, setting it on the counter and glancing at Kyle. "If I'd known you were coming by I might have brought you dinner. Maybe."

"I'm so confused." He snagged a chip from the bag and flipped one of my little bistro chairs around, taking a seat. "I haven't talked to your mother since Christmas."

"You told your mom we went to Golightly's place yesterday," I said.

"She's always on my case about needing a church family because I'm so far away from my real one," he said. "I was trying to get myself out of trouble, not get you in it."

The picture of Kyle's petite, blond momma scolding her six-three ATF agent son shattered my scowl. "They don't get that we're grown-ups, do they?" I laughed, pulling two Dr Peppers from the fridge and offering him a glass of ice.

"Are we? I don't feel like it most of the time."

"Amen to that." Watching him from the corner of my eye, I split my sandwich onto two plates and grabbed some Fritos from the pantry. "I know you didn't do it on purpose." I smiled, setting the plates on the table. "But I'm not sharing my chips. You get store-bought."

"Fair enough." He bit into the sandwich. "And sorry. Damn, this is good. Where'd you get it? And why is your mom upset?"

"Little deli by the office." I crunched on a chip. "Your mother called mine and told her we went to Way of Life yesterday morning. Here's the weird part: she lost. Her. Shit. Called me bawling her eyes out and ordered me to stay away."

Kyle sat back, his face telling me he would've sooner pegged Buffalo to win the Super Bowl.

"You have the same WTF look I did," I said.

"Why would she give a damn?"

"No idea. It's not like she's super religious, but she's not opposed to religion. I'm stumped."

"But you're not backing off." He didn't bother to inflect a question mark.

"She's in Texas. How's she going to know?"

"What if you break a story out there?" he asked.

I paused, his Captain Supercop brow furrow throwing a heavy feeling into the pit of my stomach. "You know something," I spaced the words out, trying to keep the excitement out of my voice.

"Let's hear your theory first."

"Money laundering. How much do you figure they took in yesterday? Not counting the mail and online donations?"

"Thirty grand?" He shrugged. "I'm guessing, but it's an educated guess."

"They reported less than a million in donations on last year's tax return. So either they're lying and you've got tax evasion, or they're not and the rest of that money isn't theirs." Joey's flinch at the mention of guns bubbled back to the surface. "Or they're buying something illegal with it. But which one?"

"How do you know that? About the taxes?" Kyle asked, skirting my question.

"I have connections of my own, Special Agent Miller."

Kyle nodded, taking another bite of his sandwich.

"What do you have?" I asked when he swallowed.

"Something I wasn't sure I wanted to tell you. I talked to a couple of guys who are interested in that outfit." He bobbed his head from side to side. "Nothing official. But if you insist on pursuing this, it might keep you out of trouble." He grinned. "If you're speaking to me and you still want my help."

I rolled my eyes. "Yeah, yeah. You're forgiven. What've you got?"

"In a minute. I want to go back to this thing with your mother."

"Why?"

"You said yourself, she doesn't freak out. Can I ask you something without getting myself invited to leave?"

"Probably."

"Have you thought about calling your grandmother?" His eyes softened as mine filled with tears. I blinked them away, shaking my head.

My grandparents disowned my mom for embarrassing them by keeping me. And then tried to make up for it by paying for my Syracuse education, no strings. I'd taken them up on the last part—I sent a thank you note, but I hadn't tried to contact them beyond that. I wondered if that was the right choice so often, the letter with their phone number was taped together and worn to tissue. I could recite it in my sleep.

"About seven million times." The words strangled around the lump in my throat.

"This week?"

"No." I shook my head, dropping my chin to my chest. "I can't do it. I always chicken out."

"I think you might have found a reason to face your fear, Nicey. Something's not right about this. I don't need detective experience to tell you that." Kyle's face was somber when I looked up. "You want me to sit with you?"

My lips tipped up. "Thanks, but no. I'll think about it. I want to talk to my mom again. Now will you tell me?" I crossed my legs at the knee and bounced one foot.

"I kind of like this knowing something you don't know thing." He grinned, popping the last bite of sandwich in his mouth.

I offered my sternest glare.

He swallowed, leaning his elbows on the table. "We are off the record?"

I rolled my eyes. "The house isn't bugged."

"Just have to ask."

"Of course," I said, my fingers working a thick lock of my hair into a knot. "So?"

"We've been tracking a weapons ring through twelve states for two years."

"Guns." I stuffed my mouth full of sandwich to keep from saying anything else. Of course Joey knew what was going on. Damn damn damn. "What does the church have to do with a weapons ring?"

"My buddy is pretty sure you're right about money being laundered through Way of Life. And maybe more than that. He said a few of the other guys have the place on watch lists, but he didn't want to let me in on someone else's case without permission."

All that money. It was the perfect cover for anyone looking to clean up massive amounts of cash. And not a casino or a garage, which are typically associated with the criminal underworld. Who would think to look behind Golightly's perfect hair and rows of Stepford Bible students?

Kyle's friend, evidently. "But knowing it and proving it are two different things," I said.

"Indeed. Especially with someone so well-connected. They've got quite a legal firewall over there."

"You're sure it's him?"

"We're not sure of anything. Reasonably convinced it's someone in his outfit? Absolutely. But can I tell you who, or if the good reverend knows anything about it? It's a big place. A lot of employees. And we can't get close enough to find out."

"I don't exactly need a warrant." I half-smiled.

"What you need is a gun of your own." Kyle's voice dropped and he leaned across the table and grabbed my hand. "Listen to me, Nicey. These are not people you want to fuck with. The mob is in this up to their necks."

I squeezed Kyle's hand and fixed him with my most capable stare. "I can't walk away." And I couldn't even tell him the whole reason why.

"I suppose I knew that when I came over."

"Then why talk to me?"

He shook his head. "The phrase 'too damned smart for your own good' mean anything to you? You would have gotten it anyway." He balled up his napkin and drained his soda glass. "I didn't want you stumbling into the middle of this without knowing what you were getting into. You want to make a conscious choice to dig around? I might not approve, but I can't stop you. I couldn't live with the idea that you might happen in and get hurt, when I knew how dangerous it was the whole time. So here I sit."

"That which doesn't kill us makes us superstars, right?"

"I think you took some poetic license." He smiled, folding his arms across his chest and not-so-subtly flexing a bicep.

I met his eyes to find the blue lasers half-lidded, underlined by a grin that made my palms break out in a sweat. Oh, boy. "Thank you." It came out a touch too bright as I scrambled to my feet and moved toward the door. "Really. It looks like I have more research to do."

He shook his head almost imperceptibly and stood, smoothing the creases out of his khakis. "I'm around if you need me," he said as he stepped out the door.

I kissed his stubbly cheek and promised to do my best to avoid getting dead. Leaning against my side of the door after I shut it on the deep indigo gloaming outside, I considered the five million nine hundred ninety eight thousand ninety four questions clamoring for my attention. Following the money was a good strategy. As long as there was a trail.

Large glass of Moscato in hand, I snapped up my laptop and padded to the living room, propping myself on the couch.

I didn't know a huge lot about money laundering or the illegal weapons trade, but if that's what the ATF thought Golightly was into, I'd learn.

The sketches of Jasmine flashed up on my screen when I opened my web browser. We'd run them every day for a week, and they'd spread through the wires to TV stations and newspapers all over the east coast. Still nothing. Why?

Elise's voice floated through my thoughts. "All Jesus, all the time."

Of course. If no one at Way of Life was allowed to watch TV or see the paper, how could anyone ID her? One more tick in the "Way of Life is shady" column. Which was getting longer by the day—and the PD hadn't released anything beyond basics about the second victim yet. I made a note to call Aaron about that first thing and flipped my thoughts back to Golightly, money, and guns.

Joey's face flashed on the backs of my eyelids and my stomach tightened.

Illegal arms trafficking puts weapons in the hands of murderers every day. How many people had died already? How many more would before Kyle could get a warrant?

Whoever was behind this—Golightly, Wolterhall, Jenny of the disdainful glare, the whole damned lot of them—was going down.

No matter who they were in cahoots with.

Or how good he might be in bed.

I clicked into the Google bar on my screen.

Information is a reporter's best friend.

17

Aaron's blue eyes sported weekend-getaway sized bags when he stepped onto the dock where his boat was tethered at five-forty-five on Wednesday.

"Trouble sleeping, detective?" I asked from my perch on a bench in the corner.

I'd spent two days mired in a mess of court cases, phone calls, and copy-writing. And being avoided by the only cops I really wanted to talk to. Which I did not appreciate.

I filed my fourth story of the day at a quarter to five and headed out into a perfect June afternoon, too frustrated with the lack of time to dig around my biggest story to enjoy seeing the sun. Larry was still working on Wolter-hall's photo, and the Internet hadn't coughed up anything new on Way of Life—though it was helpful in explaining the finer points of how to launder money.

As far as I knew, both murder victims were still unidentified.

Add all that to Aaron's sudden scarcity, and my tolerance well was tapped out.

As such, I'd lost my ability to care if I annoyed my generally-favorite police officer. Turnabout's fair play.

Halfway home, I turned for the freeway and drove south to the marina where Aaron kept his boat on the Appomattox River. I knew he liked to fish when wrestling a tough case, and the evening was perfect for it. Clear, warm, and not a hint of a breeze.

He didn't even look surprised to see me.

"You want a Coke?" he asked. "I don't feel much like beer today."

"You want to tell me why?"

"No." He waved me aboard the Alyssa Lynne, named for his daughters.

"You're not playing fair, Aaron," I said.

"I really am sorry." He disappeared into the belly of the boat and returned with two cans.

I opened mine and sat on the bench opposite the captain's chair. Aaron started the engine.

"This whole thing stinks, Nichelle."

His words, his haggard appearance, and Girl Friday's Monday post clicked puzzle pieces into place.

"Who are they arresting, Aaron?"

"Her friend." He sounded somewhere between beaten and disgusted.

"The boyfriend? Or the jealous chick?" Crap. Maybe I was farther off than I thought. Someone who knew her—but the obvious choice, not the crazy mystery one? I wondered if Charlie had anything yet.

"The one who called it in."

No. My eyes fell shut. "But he didn't do it." I didn't bother with a question.

Aaron just shook his head, his eyes on the open river.

"What the hell is going on here?" I asked.

"There was something in the autopsy report we didn't tell you," he said. "We didn't tell anyone."

"You going to tell me now?"

"She'd been pregnant, but she'd never delivered a baby," he said. "The coroner found significant injury to her uterus."

"A miscarriage?"

"Nope. Poorly executed abortion."

Holy crap.

"Like, coat hanger poorly executed, or backwoods doctor poorly executed?"

"Who knows? I don't even know if there's a way to tell. Just another piece of this freaky puzzle."

"When?"

"A year or so ago, based on scarring."

So right before she turned up on the streets of Richmond. Which meant it wasn't Flyboy's kid. "Anything else?"

"The damage was easy to spot, seeing as how the killer removed the organ for us."

I flinched. It didn't take a leap to get that Golightly's congregation probably wasn't the most pro-choice bunch of folks. Her family might not be, either—that could explain why she'd been on the streets.

Picasso's voice pinged around my thoughts, followed by Kyle's. Family. Church family.

Maybe my gut hadn't failed me.

Aaron eased the throttle forward, and I shifted mental gears. "I went back three times and looked for her friends this week," I said. True: I wanted to return the journals. I kept photocopies of several pages, but didn't want to break my promise. "You won't find him."

"We already did," he said. "Landers picked him up at the scene an hour ago. He was drawing it. In horrifying detail, considering it's been cleaned up."

"There's no way he did this, Aaron. I'd stake my shoe closet on it."

He nodded. "I know that. You know that. But the public doesn't know that. And with this blog drawing attention to the gorier aspects of the case, the brass wants you to splash an arrest across the front page. Settle people down. Stop every wacko in the city from calling in confessing. They say it'll give the guy a place to sleep."

"In jail? They're not seriously convincing themselves they're doing him a favor."

"They're sending him to psych. For as long as a court order will keep him there."

Deep breath. "If they want me to 'splash it across the front page,' why have you been giving me the brush-off for two days?"

"They wanted him in custody before we announced an arrest." He sighed. "I may not agree with their method. But they're doing it anyway, and I like my job. So there it is. You showing up here saved me a phone call."

Whatever, I guess. "On the subject of things you're keeping to yourself, do you have an official ID yet?"

He shook his head. "It's the weirdest damned thing I've ever seen. Every media outlet in three states is running the sketches on a loop. We get a dozen nutjobs a day, but nothing we can work with."

I nodded, spearing a chunk of something that looked like one of Darcy's treats onto my hook and casting it. My feet itched to run the fifty miles to Way of Life and broadcast the sketches on their in-house TV.

Time to come clean. I sighed.

"Aaron, I have a hunch." I sucked in a deep breath and spilled my guts for a good fifteen minutes. Journals, doodles, Golightly, money, weird cultish Bible school.

"She was out there," I finished. "I'm sure of it. I just haven't found her real name, or why she ended up here," I finished. "I think I'll take the sketches with me and see what they turn up."

"A TV preacher, huh?"

"They have lawyers coming out their ears," I said.

He nodded. "The simplest thing would be to grab Landers, ride out to have a talk with the local law enforcement, and go question a few folks. But say you are onto something. If we go flashing badges, how fast do you figure any evidence of the victim will disappear? Especially if someone there had something to do with her death?"

He turned the crank on the fishing rod and pulled his line back a little, his face lost in a storm of thought as he stared over the water. "And if they're as lawyer-happy as you say, interrogations won't get me anywhere."

"You could drive out and pop into the service on Sunday." I grinned. "I might've done that last weekend."

He nodded. "I'll talk to Landers and see if he wants to ride along."

"Blend in," I said. "They don't seem to like outsiders much."

"Noted."

I paused. "Anything on the other murder?"

"Waiting for the dental. Forensics is paranoid after the clusterfuck with the first one, and the state police have them elbow-deep in some cemetery relocation business this week."

"Naturally. Keep me posted?"

"Of course."

We fell into easy silence, each lost in our own thoughts.

The room was set up like an altar.

They cut out her freaking uterus.

I grew surer by the cicada chirp that Way of Life was tangled up in Jasmine's murder.

"Where was the cow's blood?" I asked.

"Excuse me?" Aaron furrowed his brow.

"The cow's blood y'all found at the murder scene. Where did the scrapings come from? The walls? The corners?"

He sighed. "The altar. And the floor all around it."

Huh. I pondered as Aaron guided the boat back to the dock.

I told him goodnight and continued the debate the entire way home.

Darcy pawed at my foot, and Emily's comment about a group being in on the murder together surfaced as I bent to pick up the dog.

"I'm lobbying Bob for hazard pay," I told Darcy, grabbing the phone and hoping my brilliant psychologist friend wasn't busy.

* * *

Two glasses of wine later, Em and I had rehashed everything I thought I might know about Jasmine, Golightly, and lots of things in between.

She listened as I described every rabbit trail in this crazy forest, her earring clicking against the receiver when she nodded occasionally.

I took a breath after I described my chat with Aaron. "So. That's where I am."

"Girl. You have had a week. Do I need to come up there?"

I laughed. "I think I'm dealing. Mostly, I want to figure this out. If you want to help play detective, hop a plane. But otherwise, you can stay there and keep your phone on."

"There's a lot here, Nicey." Papers rustled. "You say no way the autistic guy is your killer. You're sure about that?"

"So are the detectives. They're going along with it because the brass wants a show."

"And you're okay with that?"

I gnawed my lower lip. No. But what else could I do?

"I'm pissed. But also in a corner."

"Sure." She didn't sound even a little convinced.

"Okay, I'm going to talk to my boss," I said. "I can't tell which way is forward anymore. But you said last time we talked if it was a sacrificial thing there was probably more than one person. I blew that off because the cops started off so focused on a serial. But the abortion, the murder scene, the freaky amateur hysterectomy—the church fits it better. "

"It's logically sound. Not that most murderers are horribly logical folks," Emily said. "I think you still have two distinct possibilities here. One is you do have a serial. It's not like they kill someone every day. The second victim makes that more likely. It sounds like your cops are still leaning that way, but without knowing what else they're keeping from you, I can't say it's more likely than your theory. Two is this poor woman did run away from the religious outfit. Or maybe even some other one. But you really need a rock-solid connection before anyone is going to take you seriously."

"These people are into some bad stuff, Em," I said. I'd glossed over the nitty-gritty because I was paranoid about Girl Friday's seeming psychic powers. "Really bad. Stuff Kyle's guys have a hand in."

"And Kyle is helping you with this, but Kyle's not the one you slept with." It wasn't a question. She clicked her tongue. "I might hop a plane. At the very least, grab a charger for your phone and the rest of that bottle. We're going to be a while getting you straight."

"I'm not crazy, am I?"

"Nah. But you sure are tangled up right now," she said. "Talk to me."

I did. I told her as much as I dared about Joey, and how much I wished I wanted Kyle as much as he seemed to want me. My mom. My grandparents. The dog, my bloodtype, Shelby, the blogger, my bra size. Words streamed out for an hour.

"It's a good thing you get paid for listening to people ramble," I finished. "You're good at it."

"Everyone needs a good ear now and again."

"So, how do I fix it?"

"What do you think you need to do?"

"Aw, come on, Em," I said. "I want advice, not head shrinkage."

"What I would do for myself in that situation might be entirely different from what you need to do to be happy."

"Right now, I really want to talk to my mom."

"I think that's a wise start," she spaced the words out.

"I know. You think Kyle's right and I should call my grandparents."

"It's not like I haven't made my opinion about that abandonment issue known for years," she said.

"I can't."

"You can. You don't want to. You're afraid of rejection. Which is perfectly understandable. You're also holding a grudge. Again, understandable. But not healthy. And kind of childish. I love you, but it's true. And this is starting to affect other aspects of your life."

A dull ache took up residence in the back of my throat, matching the heaviness in the pit of my stomach.

"I don't want to hurt Kyle," I said finally. "I love Kyle. I think part of me always will. It's complicated."

"I think it's simpler than you want to admit." She wasn't arguing, exactly, but her voice was firm. "You keep telling me there are all these obstacles to being with Mr. Mystery."

"But he's—" I paused. "You don't understand, Em. We just click so well. He fits."

"Uh-huh." She paused. "What's his last name, Nicey?"

"Not fair," I said. "You don't know everything, and you're turning me into a country song."

"Look, sweetie, I'm not saying this is your fault. Commitment phobia as a result of paternal abandonment issues is so common I can't go a week without a new case walking in. You want to conquer it? Call your mother. Call your grandmother. Then let me know why you want the guy it can't work with more than the one it could."

"Emily—" I stopped, my stomach twisting into a boy-scout-worthy knot. Damn.

"I'm here if you need a sounding board, doll," she said. "But I can't tell you what to do."

"Can you tell me where to look for this murderer? That'd be awesome all by itself."

"I'd stay with the church," she said. "I think you're onto something. The reverend might be in the thick of it, or he might not know anything about it. What you need is a friend on the inside."

I nodded agreement. If only that were as easy to come by as question marks this week.

"Thanks, Em. Love you."

"Back at you, girl. Holler if you need me."

I clicked off the call, putting the phone down and picking the dog up.

Staring at the bright reds and blues in the abstract of a mother and child Jenna had painted, I wanted nothing more than to curl up in my mom's lap, tell her all my worries, and have them fixed with a lollipop and a kiss. Maybe I wasn't such a grownup, after all.

I turned Emily's last words over in my thoughts, sifting my fingers though Darcy's fur. A friend on the inside. Elise and Ben were the only people who hadn't been rude, and she'd seemed less drink-the-kool-aid than him. I set Darcy down and went to pick through my wardrobe for pants that covered my ankles, a tunic, and some flats. I'd found two of the three when my doorbell rang.

Nine-thirty. I checked my hair and lip gloss in case it was Joey and rushed to my teensy foyer.

A glance out the windows along the top of the door put my heart in my throat. I fumbled with the locks and threw the door wide.

"Mom?" I swooped her into a fierce hug. "What the hell are you doing here?"

18

My mom is a walking ball of energy—five-seven in flats, she only looks short next to me. She's the picture of grace and confidence. In my almost-thirty years, I'd seen very few things rattle her.

Certainly nothing enough to make her fly halfway across the country unannounced. In June. She's a wedding planner—that's like a CPA taking off on a lark in early April. My stomach clenched, and I squeezed her tighter.

She stretched on tiptoe and clung to my shoulders like she might never hug me again. I knew the feeling, a thousand memories of her frail, chemo-weakened frame barely filling my arms making me thank God for the seventy billionth time I still had her to hug.

I held on tight for a bit too long before I stepped back and took in the makeup-free face half-hidden behind her sunglasses. In the dark.

"It's always good to see you," I said. "But, um..."

She put a hand on my face, not removing the shades.

"We need to talk," she said.

Indeed we did.

I grabbed her stuffed-to-the-seams overnight bag and ushered her inside, Darcy sniffing her ankles.

She bent and fluffed the dog's fur, then followed me to the living room, smiling at the half-empty wine bottle. "I think we need another glass, love."

I settled mom on the sofa and scurried to the kitchen to fetch one, stopping short when I stepped back into the living room. Her beautiful blue eyes were barely visible through puffy, scarlet-rimmed slits in her face.

I poured wine into both glasses and handed her one, a thickness in the air between us.

She opened her mouth, then shook her head and closed it again, dropping her eyes to the floor.

Puzzle pieces rained into place.

Of course.

How could I be so stupid?

"I got it." I put a hand on her shoulder.

Amazing, the things we can miss if we don't want to see them.

"No, I have to tell you something, sweetie." She pulled in a hitching breath. "I came here to talk to you, and I'm not chickening out this time."

"It's about my father, right?"

Tears sprang up and spilled over in the same instant. She nodded. "God, I hoped I was wrong."

"Back up. Wrong?"

"About you finding him."

"Finding—I didn't find him."

"Then how did you know that's why I was here?"

I raised one hand to my temple. "Why do I feel like an Abbot and Costello routine? Can we start at the beginning?"

She shook her head and squeezed my hand. "There's not enough wine in Virginia for that, baby."

I laughed. "I don't want to hear the details of my conception, thanks. But I just clicked a few puzzle pieces here. I always assumed I'd never met him because he was a deadbeat, or maybe because he was young and had grown up and had another family."

The tears about the ATF raid in Waco. The absolute freak-out that led to the hot mess in front of me.

"I was wrong, huh?" I asked.

"He wanted to get married." She drew another shaky breath. "He was older than me, and so sure the money would never dry up. Parts would never run out."

I furrowed my brow. "I thought you met him at school?"

"I lied." She hid her face in her hands. "Please don't be mad. You were always so curious about everything. I didn't want you to go looking. Protecting you has been my first priority since the first time I saw you."

"Questions about everything except him." I shook my head. "How'd you miss that?"

"I suppose I took it as a gift from God and went on with my life," she said. "Always, with seven million questions every day, from the time you could talk. I could have picked your career path when you were in kindergarten. Reporter or therapist. But now that you mention it, why didn't you ask?"

I threw my hands up. "We never even got a Christmas card. Why should I give a second thought to anyone who could treat us that way? We didn't need him, right?"

I worried, growing up, that it hurt my mom. My father not being around. My grandparents disappearing. She never let it show, never said a word—but that didn't mean she didn't feel it. I decided if I loved her enough, they wouldn't matter. We took care of us. We didn't need anybody but each other.

She smiled, tears still dripping down her blotchy cheeks. "Right."

"He was an actor?" Among the few things I knew about my grandparents was that my mom's dad was a film producer. They lived in Malibu. They told my mother, who wanted to have a baby on her own at seventeen, that it was a mistake and I was an "embarrassment." That was it. Oh, and my grandmother had nice handwriting.

If I knew little about them, I knew nothing about my father. Donor? I'd always thought that a more relevant term. Em offered "sire" once when I spilled my guts to her, but that sounded too much like I should be training for the Kentucky Derby.

An actor. Of course. My height, my crazy striking eye color.

"So, he asked you to marry him." I spaced the words out, just as unsure I wanted to know as she seemed to be about wanting to tell me. I snatched my glass off the table and gulped a few swigs of Moscato. "But you didn't want to?"

"I didn't know much about anything except I didn't want an abortion, and I wasn't old enough to get married," she said. "He went nuts. Totally off the deep end. His parents were very conservative. Ultra religious. I didn't know until you came along, but that's why he was with me. Didn't like the starlets because they were 'impure.'"

"When you say 'nuts'...?" I swallowed more wine, my throat suddenly rivaling the Sahara in lack of humidity.

Her face fell, her eyelids following. "He screamed. Called me...awful names. Words I don't say. Threw things. My father asked him to leave. It was the last nice thing daddy did for me."

Her shoulders shook with soft sobs, and I pulled her close, my cheeks heating with indignant anger. What an asshat. We were far better off without him.

"And he disappeared into religion?" I guessed when she sat up and swiped at her eyes.

She nodded. "I don't know where. I don't keep in touch with anyone who knows him. When you were born, I got a postcard from Colorado. It said Jesus knew what was best for us both."

"So when the Waco thing was big news..." I trailed off.

"I was a basket case, wondering how I might explain it to you, hoping he wasn't there."

"He wasn't?"

"No. I tracked down a woman who used to be a secretary at the studio, who talked to his mother and called me back. They wouldn't tell me where he was—fine—but they said it wasn't there. I've watched TV church productions for him for the past several years. He's handsome. Charismatic. Photogenic. It seems like a perfect fit for him. But if that's what he's doing, he's behind the scenes. I have yet to run across him on a program."

The last piece.

"So when Mrs. Miller called and told you Kyle and I went to Golightly's church, you flipped."

"Oh, Nicey." She took my hand in both of hers and squeezed. "You look so much like him. I was terrified you'd walk into him. I called and bawled at you like a nut myself. Forbid you to go back out there. Forbid you!" She dropped her head back and laughed. "I raised you. I bet you've been back since I talked to you. If you went with Kyle, you're chasing a story, as much as I'd like to hope it was a social thing."

"So you came to see me." I felt the corners of my lips turn up in a soft smile.

"I had to warn you. And I couldn't do it over the phone. I've owed you this conversation for many years, baby girl." She downed the rest of her wine and tipped the glass toward me.

I poured. "I appreciate the heads up. And I love any excuse to see you. I've missed you something awful lately. But can we talk about something else now?"

"Please." She glanced around. "Your house is still the same." Her eyes fell on the shelf in the hallway. "You have your beach glass."

"Always." I put an arm around her and leaned my cheek on her head.

"Want to tell me about your gentleman friend?"

"Pardon?" I sat up and raised an eyebrow at her.

"The one who was here Sunday afternoon when I called. Who's not Kyle." She patted my knee.

"How did you—" I began, then waved one hand. "Never mind. You know all."

"This is J of the extravagant Christmas gift, yes?" she asked.

I sighed. First Emily, now my mother.

Dear Universe, I get it. You can stop now. Love, Nichelle.

Standing, I turned for the kitchen and smiled over one shoulder. "We need another bottle."

* * *

I slipped out the next morning with my gym bag slung over one shoulder, leaving a coffee mug and a note on the counter for my mom. She was staying until tomorrow. If I could knock my copy out early, I'd have time to run to Way of Life to look for Elise and still be back in time to take mom to dinner.

Two hours later I'd ap-chagi'ed off all of last night's wine, showered, and bounced my foot through the news budget meeting. Staring at the blinking cursor on my blank computer screen, I waged a silent battle with myself. Emily was right. I'd never knowingly printed anything untrue, and my skin felt a size too small at the thought of the story the PD's command staff wanted me to write.

But Girl Friday had hinted at it since Monday, so surely she'd be all over the arrest. Aaron had warned me it would go to all the TV stations first thing this morning. Charlie, who was desperate to have something I didn't about this case, would blast it from here to Timbuktu. The right thing, or the easy thing? I didn't want Andrews bitching at Bob because it looked like I'd fallen down on the job. Enough tension already stretched between the two of them for an acrobat to do cartwheels across.

I huffed out a sigh and grumbled a few of my favorite swearwords.

Laying my fingers on the keys, I stuck strictly to the facts.

Richmond police continue to search for leads to the identity of a young woman found brutally murdered in an abandoned building at Belle Isle Historical Park last week.

Detectives made an arrest in the case Wednesday, holding the young man who originally called in the body discovery as a person of interest in the investigation. RPD Public Information Officer Aaron White didn't release the man's name, but in an exclusive interview with the Richmond Telegraph *last week, the suspect said the victim was his friend.*

The coroner's report lists massive blood loss due to stab wounds as the cause of death.

I quoted Aaron about the unusual difficulty IDing the victim, especially in the age of computers and online records, added statistics for violent crime perpetrated against homeless people, and sent it to Bob for immediate posting online just in time to dash for the courthouse and snag the last seat for day one of DonnaJo's juvenile murder trial.

I wolfed down a sandwich at my desk as I wrote up the trial, then stuck my head into Bob's office.

"You have email," I said. "And I have some stuff in the works I'm going to go check out."

He turned from his screen to the door, leaning back in his big leather chair. "Anything interesting?"

"Could be." I shrugged. "Not sure yet."

"Larry said he's working on a bear of a photo restore for you."

"I'm anxious to see what he can do with it."

"As anxious as I am for you to let me in on your new lead?"

"Let me see what I can find."

He turned back to his computer. "Don't get shot."

"Not on purpose." I grinned and turned for the elevator.

Shelby rounded the corner from the break room as I punched the down button.

"Hey, Nichelle," she called brightly.

I fought the natural urge to bolt and turned a smile on her.

"Hey there," I said. "How are you?"

"Frustrated with this blogger. I'm following every footprint she has online, but they're all carefully cloaked. I don't know how anyone's going to find out who she is."

"I haven't had time to look at anything not strictly related to my copy for today. Is she getting more followers? Or pissing Aaron off more?"

"Her followers aren't exploding, but I've found several forums in my searches where people are linking to the blog and saying she's not beholden to the PD." She made air quotes around the last words and rolled her eyes. "She's up to two hundred fourteen subscribers."

"From eighty-five a week ago?" I didn't like the sound of that. "That's more than double."

"But still a relatively small group. And a niche, if you read the comments on her site. Conspiracy nuts, mostly. She had a piece this afternoon questioning the validity of the arrest that she herself reported on for the past two days. Got a ton of comments about the cops being corrupt. One guy wrote a thesis about patsys. Compared this homeless dude they picked up to Lee Harvey Oswald."

I swore under my breath. Who was this person?

Shelby arched a brow. "I kinda thought that was funny."

"She's right, Shelby." I sagged back against the wall, barely noticing that the elevator came and went without me. "The whole thing stinks to high Heaven. I interviewed that guy. Twice. He's not a murderer."

"So how does she know that?"

"She has an in at the PD. The question is who? And why hasn't Aaron figured it out yet?" I knew the answer to the last one was simple—he had more pressing matters that needed his attention.

If I was honest with myself, I was most annoyed that Friday had likely written the piece I would have if I didn't care so much about keeping my good relationship with my cops. Politics and playing by the rules sucks sometimes.

"I'll keep trying," she said.

"I have work to do."

I told myself Friday didn't know about Golightly.

Myself said she just didn't know yet.

I'd blabbed to Aaron. Who knew who he might mention it to or where Friday was getting her information? I stifled a growl and punched the elevator button hard enough to jam my finger. Shaking my hand, I turned back to Shelby. "Keep me posted?"

"Yup." She turned to go back to her cube.

"Hey, Shelby," I called. "Thanks."

Her spiky black hair bobbed acknowledgement as she walked away.

I stepped onto the elevator and leaned my head against the wall, my universe seriously askew. My mom in Richmond. To talk about my father, the faithful actor. Shelby Taylor being pleasant. Helpful. Roses from Joey. Kyle treating me almost like an equal on a case.

Rod Serling had to be lurking behind a pillar in the *Telegraph* garage, but I didn't have time to look.

I texted mom I'd be home by seven, pointed the car toward the interstate, and turned up the radio.

19

Twenty or so oxford-clad, fresh-faced young people sat knee-to-knee in a circle on the wide emerald lawn between the main building and the houses that looked like dorms, hands clasped and heads bowed.

I glanced down at my outfit—loose linen pants that grazed the tops of my feet, Tory Burch ballet flats, and an Indian-print cotton tunic. With three-quarter sleeves. Surely, no one could find that objectionable.

Climbing out of the car, I surveyed the grounds. Where to begin? I hadn't met enough people here for the confused visitor routine to fail me— yet, anyway. I set off toward the dorms with my best vacant expression in place.

Nobody paid me any mind, only a couple of people even glancing my way as I strolled around Way of Life's grounds in the June sunshine for half an hour.

No Elise.

I stopped behind the second dorm, perching on a bench and gathering my thoughts. I needed to find someone who'd talk to me, and she was my best bet. The staff didn't like me, and a lot of the rest of these folks looked too invested in all this to be helpful.

My eyes skipped across the grounds, lighting up when I caught sight of the teacher I'd talked to Monday. Before I could get to my feet, a petite blonde woman strolled from the back door of the classroom building to join him. He stopped and bent his head to hers, their serious faces telling me to stay away.

I glanced at my watch. Just after two.

Elise had been cleaning the coffee shop at about the same time Monday.

Worth a shot.

I walked to the far end of the main building and pulled the door open.

The long hallway was nothing short of opulent, the walls lined with heavy red material that looked an awful lot like silk. Wood wainscoting, thick green carpet, and pressed ceiling tiles dripping with crystal chandeliers completed the picture.

Money, money, and more money.

I strolled to the foyer, pausing in front of the six-foot portrait of Golightly in the center of the wall opposite the door. He wore a serious expression, and about half the lines I'd seen in his face on the jumbotron Sunday. I studied the painting, my mom's words echoing in my head. He was handsome. Had charisma by the bucketful. But it wasn't him, because mom said she'd never seen him on TV. I glanced around, my skin prickly with apprehension at the possibility—however remote—my father was in this building. Not a fan of the tight feeling that brought to my chest, I returned my attention to the reverend. Flanked by two table-sized candle sconces, the oil painting was undeniably the focal point of the church's entryway.

"Who are we worshipping here, folks?" I murmured.

Money. Power. Sex. All great motives for murder. Golightly was deep into at least two of them. I could guess about the third.

I spun for the hallway that led to Way of Life's mini-mall, contemplating the scene as I strolled toward the coffee shop. There were more people around. As long as Jenny of the disdainful glare didn't come out of the office, I blended.

I peeked into the narrow space, tables lining one wall and the counter stretching along the other. A three-by-four logo cross dominated the back wall, the razor points on the rays glittering in the soft overhead light. Two of the three tables were occupied by academy students.

Elise bustled around behind the bar, her eyes cast down and away from the man at the counter. I stepped up behind him, catching a whiff of expensive cologne that matched the Bespoke suit covering his broad shoulders. He was tall, his chestnut hair precision-cut across the nape of his neck.

Elise handed over his coffee and he spun for the door, no evidence of payment in sight.

Catching a glimpse of his profile, I froze.

Simon Golightly.

He didn't appear to notice anyone else. Didn't thank her for making his latte, either.

Nice.

I waited 'til he left and turned to the counter, trying to cover my surprise with a grin.

"You again." She smiled, giving me a once over. "Better. At least for fitting in around here."

She kept her voice so low I had to lean halfway across the counter to hear her.

"Thanks," I said. "For the advice the other day, I mean. I haven't gotten nearly as many dirty looks today."

She nodded.

I glanced toward the door. "That was him, right?"

Another nod, this one joined by a downturn in her rose-colored lips. "The prophet must have his coffee," she muttered, almost too low for me to catch it.

The prophet?

No.

Seriously?

"Can I get you something?" she asked.

"Can you make a nonfat white mocha?"

"Sure." She moved to the giant coffee grinder/espresso machine, pulling levers and waiting as it hummed and hissed.

I sipped and smiled when she handed it to me. "You're good," I said, reaching into my bag for cash. "How much?"

She waved a hand. "On the house. Consider it an apology for the way the office staff treated you."

"Thanks." I leaned a hip on the counter, glancing behind me. Not another customer in sight, and everyone loitering at the tables looked absorbed in something else. I turned back.

"Why didn't you?" I asked, keeping my voice carefully low and even.

Her eyebrows drew together. "Pardon?"

"You were nice to me," I said. "Nicer than you had to be. Why?"

"You look nice," she said simply. "It's the Christian thing to do."

"Can I—can we talk? When you're through here? Is there a place we could have some privacy?" I put a hand in my pocket, touching my cell phone. Three years she'd been here, and Jasmine had only been in Richmond one. If I was close to anything, showing her the sketch would prove it, but I wanted away from the eyeballs in this building.

She smiled. "I'm done here at four. At the far end of the property, past all the buildings, there's a pasture. Behind the barn on the other side, there's a feed shed. Meet me there at four-fifteen. And don't walk straight there. Meander a little."

My stomach flipped, and I nodded.

"Go with God, washed in the blood," she said brightly, louder.

I had to find out what that was about.

"You, too?" I couldn't help the question inflection. She winked. I picked up my latte and turned for the door.

My foot froze in midair when Pink Jenny walked in, talking animatedly to a younger woman in a long lavender dress.

I spun for the wall, bending my knees to hide my height and ducking behind the curtain of my hair. Crap hell.

She didn't falter in her monologue, which had something to do with the example set by Biblical women, except to bark out an order for a caramel latte.

More hissing and burbling from the espresso machine.

Another voice, softer, I guessed from the woman in lavender. "Thank you. How are you today?"

"Doing well, thank yo—" A sharp intake of breath followed Elise's stammer.

"Oh?" That was the same disdainful tone Pink Jenny had used on me

Monday. It physically hurt to not turn and stare, but I kept my back to them and my head down.

"Doing well? You know," Pause. "Elise." Reading the name tag. "You can have what you say. I will set my faith in agreement with your 'doing well' if that's what you want."

Chairs scraped back, books snapped shut, and sneakered footsteps beat a hasty retreat. I couldn't blame them. I didn't chance breathing too loudly.

"No, ma'am," Elise's voice was so low I had to strain to hear it. "Forgive me. I rebuke that statement and cover it in blood. What I meant is that I am blessed and highly favored of the Lord this afternoon. And you, ma'am?"

"Blessed and highly favored of the Lord. Go with God, washed in the blood."

My gold-tipped flats grew roots into the marble floor, the resolve that shoved Joey out my front door Sunday night keeping me still.

"And you as well," Elise said.

Two sets of footsteps receded. I stayed still.

"All clear," Elise said.

I turned slowly, finding her slumped against the counter. She rolled her eyes. "I can't believe I did that. Another nasty letter for my file."

"You still want to chat?"

"Do I ever," she said. "I've been written up for 'being oppressed by a spirit of rebellion' more times than anyone else here. What else can they do to me?"

Jasmine's lifeless face flashed on the backs of my lids. I shook it off and smiled. "See you in a bit."

"Sure." Her bright eyes were kind and smart. They held a curious gleam I'd seen a few too many times in the mirror. She wanted to know what I was doing there every bit as much as I wanted to know what was going on.

We could help each other out, she and I. I just had to avoid trouble for forty minutes.

* * *

I meandered to the best of my ability and still made it to the feed shed behind the big red barn with fifteen minutes to spare. They crawled slower than the last moments before a bid on twenty-dollar Louboutins could be finalized on eBay.

Couch-sized bags of organic food supplements for the cattle lined the walls, stacked neatly in alternating columns. I brushed a finger absently over the burlap, checking my watch for the thirtieth time in a minute and a half. My insides looped into tighter knots as I considered what I knew about Way of Life.

By itself, was any of it particularly damning? No. But all together, it set off every alarm bell I could muster.

A soft squeak from the double doors pulled my attention to the sunlight spilling through them.

"Hey." I smiled as Elise scooted through the door. "Thanks for coming to talk to me."

"What did you want to ask me?" She dropped a navy backpack on the straw-covered floor.

"Well, I..." I snapped my mouth shut, turning my gaze to the bags of feed on the opposite wall. And babbling. "I'm curious. By nature. I've never been to a church like this one. Never met people like most of the ones here. The more I see, the more I wonder." Every word true.

She slid down the wall and sat by her bag, and I took a spot beside her. Pulling the cell phone out of my pocket, I called up the sketch and flipped the screen around.

"Do you know this woman?" I asked.

Her eyes popped wide, then narrowed into a squint as she reached for my phone.

"Jasmine?" The whisper was so soft I was sure I'd imagined it. That couldn't be her real name. Could it?

She raised shining eyes to mine, tracing a finger along the screen.

It could.

"How—where did you get this? Her hair is longer, and she looks thinner, but," Elise pulled in a hitching breath, a tear falling, "I'm pretty sure this is my friend. Where is she? She left, and they all just acted like she was never here. Never talked about her, never prayed for her. It was crazy."

I knew it.

I closed my eyes, throwing a silent thank you to the Heavens and keeping myself from sprinting for Aaron only by the grace of God.

"Leigh? Where is she?" Elise repeated, a frantic edge making her voice too high.

I bit my lip. Crap. I'd interviewed plenty of grieving friends and family members, but I'd never had to be the bearer of news this bad.

"She—" the rest of the sentence stuck in my throat. I cleared it and tried again. "She passed away, sweetie. I'm so sorry."

She nodded, her eyes falling shut, tears spattering the blue cotton of her uniform pants. I patted her shoulder and let her cry.

It seemed a small eternity passed before she handed me the phone back and raised her head. Her happy blue eyes were red-rimmed and puffy with sorrow. "How?" she choked.

Oh, good Heavens.

"She. Um. Well." I stammered, searching for the right words. "The police suspect foul play," I said.

"But you're not the police?" she asked, only half-questioning.

I returned her unblinking stare. If Joey had a friend out here who knew who I was—and knew Kyle on sight—then what the hell?

"I'm a reporter at the *Richmond Telegraph*," I said. "I'd like for that to stay between us. I'm following the story about her, and the trail I picked up led here."

"I don't understand," she said.

"Maybe you don't need to understand everything," I said. God knew she'd sleep better if she didn't.

"Why? Where was she?"

"Living in an abandoned building in Richmond," I said. "She had friends. They were talking about moving away."

She nodded, sobs taking over again.

"Elise, I'd like to ask you some more questions," I said. "But I don't want to upset you more. I'm so sorry for your loss."

Another nod. "I appreciate that," she said, looking up and dragging the back of one hand across her face. "But I get the feeling you're trying to find out exactly what happened to her."

"I'd like to know who she was, too," I said.

"She was one of the happiest people I ever met, though goodness knows she had no reason to be. She chose it."

"How long was she here?"

"Two years." She sniffled. "Just under."

"Why was she here?"

"Her parents sent her. Thought it would reform the sin out of her. She had sex with her boyfriend. She cried a lot the first month. Said her momma called her an 'abomination.' She changed her name. Said her parents didn't want her, so they didn't have any say-so in her identity. She ignored her given name for two solid months, and everyone finally started calling her Jasmine. For the vines on the porch. She liked the swing."

I pulled out a notebook and scribbled all that.

"Why isn't she here anymore?"

Elise shrugged, hurt creeping into her voice. "She didn't even tell me she was going. She was sick for a couple of weeks, didn't get out of bed. When they moved her out of our room, I thought she was going to die. But she got better. Came back to the dorms for a day. Then she disappeared." A tear slipped down her round cheek. "I would've gone with her if she'd just said where she was going."

Not the best idea ever.

"How about you?" I asked, looking up. "Why are you here?"

"A long story that amounts to a rough year." She picked up a piece of straw and twirled it between her fingers. "My folks got divorced. My grandparents died. My choices were pretty much get Jesus or get meth."

Jesus worked for me. Normal Jesus, anyway. Golightly's Jesus, I wasn't sure about.

She must've read it in my eyes. Her lips tipped up the barest inch. "I love the Lord. There are other people here who do, too. Pastor Brady. Mr. Mathers —you can hear it in every word they say. But I see things that don't make sense. And asking questions isn't popular. I don't have anyone to talk to anymore."

I opened my mouth to reply and the sound of an approaching engine snapped it shut.

"What's that?" I breathed.

"I don't know, but you'd better hide," she hissed, jumping to her feet and scooping up her bag. "Get under the workbench, and don't make any noise."

I crawled to the table and folded myself into the tight space between the wall and a rolling tool chest.

Elise stood, looked around, then sat again, dragging a thick Bible from her bag and opening it across her lap.

The engine idled a few feet away, doors opening and closing and low voices floating through the thin walls of the shed. No words, just tones.

Men. The roughest bass I'd ever heard, with an accent I couldn't make out enough to place. The other lighter, higher-pitched.

I held my breath, and it looked like Elise was doing the same. No idea how long we sat that way, her staring blankly at the Good Book and me praying silently that we weren't about to get caught—more for her sake than mine.

The car door finally opened and shut again, and the engine receded. I blew out a long breath.

Raising my head, I met Elise's blue eyes. "I guess He does answer prayers when they're repeated urgently enough," I said.

She nodded. "They have maintenance trucks that go all over the property. Probably someone spraying Roundup. The Lord can cure us of everything but weeds, if you watch the gardeners."

I smiled. The more I talked to her, the more I liked her. "Elise, will you help me?"

"Help you what?"

"My gut says Jasmine's ties to this place have something to do with her death. I need to know about her." Picasso's deadpan 'they killed her,' floated up. "And her family. Who's who and how things work here."

She kept her eyes on the floor. "What is it you want to know? You can't put my name in the paper. They...wouldn't be happy about that."

"No worries," I said, pulling a notebook and pen from my bag. "Top secret source. For starters, what was Jasmine's given name? The police want to contact her next of kin."

"Ruth," Elise said softly. "Ruth Galloway."

I jotted it down, a sigh of relief escaping my chest. Nearly two weeks of searching, and there it was. "Do you know her parents' names? Or where they live?"

"Her mother's name is Wanda. She was from a little town in South Carolina called Wallingford. In the mountains."

"Is that why she'd never been to a dentist?"

Elise shook her head. "She used to complain about her back teeth hurting. She never ate anything sweet—that's part of the reason she was so thin. But her folks have plenty of money. Her mom's dad owned some kind of mine. Copper, I think. But they were really into Golightly's schtick. Watched every sermon. Even traveled here a few times a year to come to service. Donated tons of money. But she didn't go to the dentist or the doctor. Like, ever."

"Why couldn't she go to the doctor?"

"Doctors are for the weak of spirit." Bitterness dripped from the words. "If you are faithful enough, the Lord will take your ailments from you."

"Because God didn't give us doctors?" It popped out before I could stop it.

"Exactly." She grinned. "That's exactly what I said the first time I heard that."

"Wow."

Elise touched the picture on my screen again. "I'm pretty sure she had endometriosis," she said. "She said she'd had a bad attack right before she left. She was still bleeding pretty badly when she came back to our room."

I scribbled so fast my fingers ached from gripping the pen, not missing a word. I put a star by that because of what Aaron said about an abortion, a thousand questions firing in my brain. Was she "sick" because of an early pregnancy? And had someone here ended it? Because that seemed...hypocritical was too light a term.

I looked up. "You said Jasmine had a boyfriend before she came here. Was she seeing someone here, too?" I asked.

She sighed. "I don't know." Her mouth twisted to one side.

"You don't know, or you don't want to tell me?" I softened my voice. "It could be really important."

"She didn't say. She was acting funny, and I asked her a few times what was up, but she wouldn't tell me. Said she was protecting me. She spent a lot of time looking moody and scribbling in her journal."

Of course she did. Please God. One more favor today.

"A journal? I don't suppose she left it here?"

She tipped her head to one side. "Maybe. There's a box of her things under the floor in the closet. I kept thinking she'd come back for it, or she'd get in touch and I could return it."

"Any chance I could see it?"

She glanced around, then checked her watch. "We have to hurry. And you have to be quiet."

* * *

The hallways were tastefully decorated, but not in the opulent overabundance of the main church building and offices. The dry air held the faintly floral antiseptic smell of college dorms and old folks' homes everywhere. They must buy that cleaning solution in bulk from a secret supplier.

"It felt wrong to look through her things," Elise whispered as she climbed the stairs. "But I found stuff moved around every day for three weeks after she disappeared. Someone wanted this. Maybe it will help you."

In her room with the door closed, Elise moved a chair from one desk and hooked the ladder back of it under the doorknob. "We don't have locks," she said. "The Lord sees all, so the ministry does, too."

For real?

"I've been here three times and I'm skeptical of their motives, too, Elise," I said, shaking my head as I perched on the bare mattress on the far side of the room. "Your instincts are good."

"Sometimes I wish they weren't," she said. "I wanted to fit in. To lose myself and my worries in the glory of God. I guess part of me still does or I'd go somewhere else. I could get a job in any Starbucks in America, thanks to the reverend's fondness for lattes."

"I hear they have great benefits." I grinned.

She turned for the closet, then paused with her back to me. "Do you really think it could have been someone from here? Who killed her?"

"The more I learn, the more I think that's likely."

She nodded, opening the door and dropping to her knees. I caught a glimpse of a cross on the back wall of the closet before she stood and turned back to me with a pink lockbox in her hands. She set it on the desk and took a step back. I crossed the room and knelt in front of the desk. The box wasn't much bigger than your average Stephen King hardcover, a scratched-up pink metal rectangle with a dented corner and a bitsy silver lock on the front.

"You don't have the key, do you?" I raised an eyebrow at Elise.

"I do not."

I waved one hand. "S'ok. I have a friend who's pretty good with picking locks. How about a paperclip?"

She rifled through the desk and came up with one. I poked one end of it at the lock.

No dice. The lock was too small.

"Do you have a smaller one?" I asked.

She shook her head, and I racked my brain, lifting the box. It was heavy, but I couldn't tell if that was the container itself or the contents.

I asked for a staple. She didn't have a stapler. "Ball point pen?"

She handed me a retractable one and I took it apart and straightened the spring I pulled from the pen barrel. Folding it in half, I tried it in the end of the keyhole. It slid in. I jiggled it and it slid further. Blowing out a slow breath, I tried to leverage it to turn the lock.

It broke.

"Dammit!" I clapped a hand over my mouth, glancing toward the ceiling. "Sorry. Habit. That was loud, too."

Elise smiled. "I think if your worst sin is the occasional curse, you're in decent shape. No matter what the secretarial staff has to say about your shoes."

Not sure swearing even made my top five worst sins, I focused on the box. For all I knew it held the key to the whole mess, and someone hunting it after the victim left the academy smacked of motive. Jasmine wasn't coming back for it, so who'd get upset about it being broken?

"Do you have a hammer? Or anything we could use as one?" I turned to Elise.

"I don't think so." She bit her lip, looking around.

I stood. A lamp on the night table with a heavy silver base caught my eye. "What about that?" I pointed.

"What are you going to do with it?"

"Break the lock."

She grinned and pulled the lamp's plug from the wall. "I knew I liked you."

It took three swings, only because I didn't want to draw too much attention. I pulled back for number four, and Elise put a finger on the lid and opened the box.

Papers. At least two journals, plus a stack of rubber-banded index cards. And photos.

I caught my breath. "You said you're doing work-study. Does everyone?"

She nodded. "Idle hands are the devil's playground, and all that," she said.

"And free labor is better than paid." I didn't say it out loud, but from the look she shot me, I might as well have.

"What did Jasmine do?"

"She worked in the executive offices." Elise tried to cover a smirk. "All the talking they do about lust being the biggest obstacle to faith, but you should see who works up there."

Of course. I blew out a sigh and grabbed the photos.

Jasmine smiled up at me. She posed with four other girls, arms slung around shoulders, in cap and gown. A magnolia arched over their heads, graceful blooms dotting the branches. I flipped it around. "High school graduation?"

Elise shrugged and nodded. I laid it on the desk.

Photos of Jasmine with several combinations of the girls from the other photo lay beneath it.

"They were her friends. Her mom didn't approve, and she was never allowed to talk to them after she came here."

"How old was she?" I asked, squinting at the tassel in the graduation picture. "Twenty-three? Twenty-four?"

"Twenty-three when she left. So twenty-four," Elise said.

Same range as the dead girl in the car trunk. Hmm. I shoved that aside. This whole thing was too intricately webbed for Jasmine's murder to be random, but I understood Landers's mission. I just didn't agree with his theory.

"So her folks made her come here." I put the photos down and turned. "But she was a grown woman. I was almost finished with college at twenty-one. How does that work? Why did she do it? I mean, leaving home, couldn't she have gotten a job and an apartment? Or moved in with the boyfriend?"

"She'd never really worked." Elise shook her head. "She came from a lot of money. She didn't even know how to make a bed when she came here. They threatened to cut her off. She used to tell me this was better than living on the street. Said she had nightmares about not having a place to sleep or food to eat. I guess when you think about it, that would be pretty motivating in her shoes."

Indeed. And it would take serious motivation to face that nightmare. I picked up one of the journals, but the dates in it were four years old. Maybe this was just a memory box.

I flipped through the index cards. Schedules, names, abbreviations. I passed them to Elise. "Do you recognize any of this?"

She shook her head.

A second journal had entries from the year before she was sent to Way of Life. I turned pages slowly, skimming the months leading up to her arrival. She wrote pages about how much she loved her boyfriend—his name was Jared—and how they were going to be together forever. Pressed flowers slid down every other page as I turned it, and her descriptions of their dates got more graphic and heated as the summer went on.

I kept scanning, the story sucking me in better than the last romance I'd read. Jared was a mechanic. A black mechanic, from the nasty names Jasmine said her father called him. The pages crinkled and blurred with tear stains. I kept turning.

Three pages later, the detective Jasmine's mother hired got photos of the young couple in compromising positions. Oh, boy.

Four pages after that, she met Elise at Way of Life.

The entries stopped after she started classes. I closed the book, drumming my fingers on the cover and glancing around.

"I wonder if he knows," I murmured, looking back at the empty box.

"Who knows what?" Elise asked.

"Jared. That was her boyfriend. He wasn't exactly what her folks called marriage material, according to this, but she writes about him with such passion. She loved him. If he loved her, he should know what happened to her."

"She said at first he was waiting for her," Elise said. "Then she stopped answering his letters."

"Letters?" My eyes flew back to the box.

"She kept them in her night table."

I turned for the drawer, but Elise shook her head. "They disappeared after she left."

I furrowed my brow, "I thought you guys weren't allowed contact with people outside the church."

"Letter privileges have to be earned," she said. "But if you're devout enough, you can be favored by the Lord with mail. They read it all, of course."

"Of course."

"They had a code. So he would write things to her like about the beauty of the grass, and it was supposed to mean her eyes. Or something."

I nodded. "How does one earn letter privileges?"

"Being faithful. Toeing the line. Getting praise from the ministers. You know—God telling them you could get letters."

"I'm not sure I see God concerning himself with my method of correspondence."

"Their God concerns himself with everything. Especially how much money you have. Some people who work here drive fifty miles each way in the most awful cars. No air conditioning, and it's getting hot. No heat in the winter. They sincerely believe if they're faithful enough and believe enough, God will bless them with a better car."

I scribbled that down, then reached into my pocket and tried to find the voice recorder on my cell phone from memory. Pretty sure I took a picture of the inside of my pants.

"How does this pass for logic?" I blurted, biting down on the tip of my tongue as the words slid out anyway. "If they really believe God cares about such small details, then why wouldn't a benevolent diety want people to be comfortable?"

"Couldn't tell you," Elise said. "They don't like when I ask questions. That's how I got moved from the offices to the coffee bar."

"You used to work in the offices?" I asked.

"Just as an assistant. Answering phones, filing papers."

Watching people?

Thirty minutes of careful questions all but confirmed my suspicions about Wolterhall. He was from California. He liked women, but of course no one acknowledged that. The younger and prettier, the better, according to Elise. Yes, he was married. He handled all the ministry's financial affairs. And they overlooked his extramarital ones in return. Holy cow.

"How many women are we talking about?" I asked.

"I was only there for about two months, but I saw seven," Elise said.

Seven. That was playing the field, all right. It was damned near a whole softball team.

"And his wife?"

"The wives don't stay with the ministers the night before a service," her tone was beyond sincere and straight into matter of fact. Her face said she believed what she was saying, no matter how kooky I thought it sounded, so I held mine carefully neutral. No judgment. Only facts. "They have to be alone to receive God's anointing. You can speak to them if they talk to you first, but not unless."

"But the women he was with?"

"Needed saving. I asked about it, and Miss Jenny strongly suggested I never speak of it again. The next day I learned how to make the reverend's favorite latte."

I nodded slowly. Needed saving from him, maybe. "Young women from the congregation?"

"Newer ones. Never the same one twice. Usually the ones who came in wearing heels. I told you about the lustful thoughts and the shoes. My guess is Mrs. Wolterhall got them banned from the whole church. None of us were allowed to wear them already, but they started with the flip flop welcome and the insurance thing about a year ago."

"Does Wolterhall have an assistant?"

"Matthew. He's the only boy who works in the offices."

Damn. I paused. Jasmine was pregnant before she left.

"And Jasmine? Who did she work with?"

"Pastor Brady. He's the reverend's right hand."

Pastor Brady. Mister B? I'd have to check him out.

"He like pretty girls, too?"

She shook her head. "His wife is a knockout. They seem really in love."

Strike one.

"How well do you know Matthew?"

"We're friends. Kind of," she said.

"Was he seeing Jasmine?"

She started to shake her head, then paused. "Dating is a distraction," she said. "From the work of the Lord. I think she had a boyfriend, but I don't know who. Nobody talks about it."

"Can you find out? Without getting in trouble?"

"I can try." She nodded, an idea forming behind her blue eyes. "You want to talk to people, right?" she asked.

I nodded.

"Can you come back on Saturday? We don't have classes, and the offices are closed. Just the shops and stuff are open."

"What do you have in mind?" I asked.

She leaned closer, her face lit up like a mischievous child's, and outlined a plan.

I listened, my thoughts racing ahead. Just as she stopped talking and smiled, the floor vibrated and her eyes popped wide. "I have to get you out of here. We can't have anyone in the dorm but another student."

I grabbed a photo off the stack. "Can I borrow this?"

She nodded and peeked out into the hallway. I followed when she waved the all-clear.

Too much spinning through my head. My fingers ached for a pen. Or a keyboard.

I finally had names—not just Ruth's, either. The back-home boyfriend and the parents hung just below Wolterhall and Violet on my suspect list.

And those were only the people I knew about. What if Jasmine had a dorm romance? I wanted to talk to the ministers more than I wanted Eunice's white chocolate banana bread.

I climbed into the car and started the engine.

Saturday.

20

Way of Life vanished in the rearview, the adrenaline rush that went with being right making my head a little hazy as I dialed Aaron's cell.

"You psychic or something?" he said by way of hello.

"Nope." I stopped at the intersection with the main road, wondering which way to town. I tried right first. "But I have good instincts. Why?"

He chuckled. "I just picked up the phone to call you. Can you come by here?"

"Not for a while," I said. "I'm in Fauquier."

"Landers has a lead he wants to talk to you about. In person. We're getting slightly paranoid, thanks to your blogger friend. When are you free?"

"First thing in the morning?" I asked. "I have dinner plans I can't break."

"Sure," he said. "So, what did you find out there?"

I took a deep breath. We were both on cell phones. If Girl Friday had figured out how to listen in, I had bigger problems than a blog with two hundred followers. "Between you and me, right?" I dropped my voice, anyway. "Until I say otherwise?"

"Of course."

"Ruth Galloway. Her name is Ruth Galloway."

"Who her?"

"Jasmine."

A sharp intake of breath followed by silence put a goofy grin on my face.

Home. Run.

"Holy shit, Nichelle. Where did you get that?"

"Magic."

"I'm serious."

"So am I, kind of. Maybe I am a little psychic. Following my gut has rarely failed me."

"This time it led you to the TV preacher. Is that where you found her name?"

"I talked to a girl who goes to the Bible college he runs. Turns out, our Ruth was this girl's BFF. Both of them not quite drinking the Kool-Aid. She actually changed her name to Jasmine while she was there—something about the vines that grow on their porches and hating her uber-controlling parents. Disappeared suddenly after a strange illness a little over a year ago."

I knew the silence on the other end of the line meant he was taking down every word. "Hometown: Wallingford, South Carolina. The folks are big fans of Golightly."

"Got it," he said. "I'll find them."

"Have you checked specifically with the Fauquier sheriff's office for missing persons?"

"Fauquier has a sheriff?"

I laughed. "I'm headed there now. I'll let you know what I find."

"Nichelle." He paused. "This is—thanks for calling."

"I keep my word, Aaron. I still have faith you'll do the same."

"Not that I've earned that this week, but I appreciate it."

I clicked off the call and pulled over to the shoulder, searching for an address for the local sheriff. GPS said I was halfway there. I followed robot-woman's directions to a squat, cinderblock building on a sparse main street. A feed store and a bank were the station's only company.

Parking the car, I climbed out and went inside.

Two uniformed deputies played cards across a single desk. Their heads swiveled to the door in unison when the little brass bell over my head tinkled as I stepped through.

Their faces betrayed shock for a few seconds, both of them scanning me from head to toe—twice—before they scrambled to stand and spoke in unison. "Can we help you, ma'am?"

I smiled. "I hope so. I'm looking for information on a missing person's case."

The taller one shouldered past his buddy to get to the counter first. "We'd love to be of assistance, but I'm afraid we don't get too many of those around here. Missing horses or hunting dogs are more regular for us."

"It should be easy to find, then," I said. "Ruth Galloway, age twenty-four. Tall, dark hair. Pretty."

The shorter one tipped his broad-brimmed hat backward. "Don't ring a bell."

"It would have been more than a year ago. Perhaps the sheriff would remember?"

"Don ain't in today," the shorter one said. "I can try him on the CB. He's out taking care of some county business this afternoon." He paused. "I'm Buck, and this is Malcom."

"Nice to meet you," I said. "I'm Nichelle." I stopped there. Police reports are a matter of public record, and I wasn't ready to tell them why I wanted this information.

"Where'd she live?" Buck asked, moving to a file cabinet in the far corner.

"She was a student at Way of Life's Bible academy," I said.

A quick look passed between them.

"I see," Malcom said, leaning on the counter. "The thing is, ma'am—"

"Malcom," Buck's tone held an unmistakable warning. Malcom turned a questioning gaze on his cards partner, who had yet to open a file drawer.

Buck shook his head slightly. Almost like he thought I wouldn't notice.

"The thing is what?" I pasted on my best confused smile.

Buck stepped away from the file cabinet. "I'm afraid we can't help you. We don't ever have no trouble out of the reverend and his folks."

"You didn't even look for the report," I said, keeping my voice even.

"No need. I know we didn't take one from the church. We'd remember something like that."

Sure. I glanced between the two of them, Buck's face frozen in a much less welcoming smile, and Malcom suddenly preoccupied with his shiny black shoes.

"I see," I said. "And if I wanted to ask the sheriff about that, when might he be available?"

"I'm not sure of his schedule for the rest of the week, ma'am." Buck kept the smile in place as he talked. Creepy.

"Could you try his radio?" I asked.

"I don't want to interrupt his business just now." Still with the smile.

But you were going to before I said the reverend's name. I didn't bother to say it. One more crazy piece for this puzzle, though it was at least pretty easy to see where this one fit. Golightly had money and wanted to be left alone. These guys were happy to oblige in exchange for the occasional under-the-table envelope stuffed with cash. Fantastic.

I smiled and nodded, turning back for the door. Buck hustled around the counter and opened it for me. His attempt at nonchalant as his eyes lingered on my plate failed. Especially since his lips moved while he read.

Shit.

I peeled out of the lot and dialed Kyle's cell.

"Hey you." His voice was warm.

"I was right about the girl," I said. "Ruth Galloway, twenty-four, of some little mountain mining town in South Carolina. Student at the Bible academy. I just pissed off the local sheriff's deputy, who I'm pretty sure is on Golightly's off-the-books payroll. And he got my plate number on my way out."

Kyle was quiet.

"You still there?" I asked after thirty seconds of dead air.

He huffed out a short sigh. "Keeping you out of trouble is a full-time job. Where are you now?"

"Speeding back toward Richmond. My mom is here. We have dinner plans."

"Don't speed." The edge in his voice could have sliced through steel. "You're handing those yahoos an excuse to arrest you. Stay five under until you get clear of the county by twenty miles, and call me when you get back to Richmond."

"Want to come to dinner? I know mom would love to see you."

"Can I meet you at your house when I get out of here?" he asked.

"Sure. I'll be there in a couple hours. Have to run by the office."

I clicked off the call and tossed the phone in the cupholder, my brain racing way faster than the posted speed limit. It wasn't proof. But it was more than I'd had that morning by a hundredfold. And it had Charlie beat by a country mile. All things Bob would be pleased with. I kept a paranoid eye on the rearview all the way into downtown, piecing a story together in my head. Swinging into the *Telegraph's* garage, I hurried upstairs and flipped my laptop open. Kyle and mom would enjoy catching up if I was a few minutes late.

The Richmond Telegraph has learned the identity of the young woman found brutally murdered on Belle Isle earlier this month. In an exclusive interview, a friend of the victim identified her from sketches as Ruth Galloway, 24, of Wallingford, South Carolina.

Richmond police were cautiously optimistic about the turn in the case Thursday, though department spokesman Aaron White said they'd wait for confirmation from a second source.

The RPD made an arrest in the case this week, holding a young man who was a friend of the victim's for the past year on suspicion of being involved in her death.

I paused, not wanting to tip my hand about Golightly and Way of Life for a number of reasons—and keeping my exclusive wasn't even at the top of the list. Leaving that out made the story thinner, but it was still an Earth-shattering headline with the amount of space and airtime that had been devoted to the mystery woman in the past ten days.

White said the victim's identity could move the investigation along faster.

· · ·

I recapped the investigation, leaving out the part where Landers was still looking for Son of Sam while an innocent young man sat in custody. There'd be time to take the PD to task for that when everything had been set straight. And I had a way slimmer chance of making sure that happened if I pissed off the brass tonight.

I searched for Wanda Galloway on Whitepages and found only one in Wallingford. Bingo.

Punching the number into my desk phone, I held my breath, letting it out in a whoosh when a machine picked up.

Hoping Aaron had talked to them already, I left my cell number and a deliberately vague message. Just in case he hadn't.

I attached the story to an email to Bob and stood, looking toward his door. His light was still on. I ran to his office, tapping on the door before I plowed around the corner and stopped short. Andrews was in my usual chair, an irritated look on his face as he turned to me.

Bob raised his bushy white eyebrows. "You okay, Nichelle?"

"I'm so sorry to interrupt, but I have an exclusive for tomorrow. Is the front already gone?" I glanced at the Virginia Tech clock on the wall. Seven-fifteen. Nothing like playing to the wire.

Bob shook his head. "It's done, but they haven't started the run. What've you got?"

"The murder victim? I got her name. And a photo. Nobody else has it."

"Did you call White?"

"I had to. He promised not to give it to anyone 'til we run it. So if we can get it in the morning edition and wait 'til the racks fill to put it on the web, we'll sell some papers with it."

"I do like the sound of that," Andrews said, standing. "Nice work, Miss Clarke."

"Thank you." I couldn't keep the frost out of my voice. I had a feeling I knew why he was there, and I didn't appreciate it.

Bob turned for his computer monitor. "It sounds like I have some rearranging to do, Rick, if you'll excuse me." He didn't sound apologetic in the least.

Andrews nodded. "Thank you for your time, Bob."

Bob nodded. I shut the door behind Andrews when he left. "What gives?" I asked.

"What do you mean?" Bob asked absently, his attention on my story.

"Bob," I sighed. "What did he want?"

"Same thing he wants every day. To try to talk me into retiring and handing the reins over to Les. He's not going to win. I plan to drop dead right here in this chair."

"Not funny, chief," I said.

"But true." He grinned, turning his focus back to the screen. "Nice. Do I want to know where you got it?"

No. "A source. I have art, too." I pulled the photo from my bag and handed it over.

"Pretty." He shook his head, passing it back. "See how big Larry can make it without losing quality. Tell him to let me know."

"Yes, sir." I stood and turned for the door.

"Nichelle." Bob leaned back in his chair, a smile softening the worried lines in his face when I turned back. "This is good work."

"Thank you." I grinned. "You think we're okay waiting for morning? I mean, with Girl Friday lurking about?" Damned never-ending deadline. I was not a fan.

He drummed his fingers on his mouse. "I'll post it to the web at eleven-oh-one—TV won't have time to get it on air without giving us credit. The rack sales will still get a bump. This search has been a big story."

I nodded. "G'night, chief."

Larry scanned and sharpened the photo and emailed Bob a two-column-by-four-inch image, handing me the original back. I tucked it into my wallet.

I thanked Larry for his help and he swiveled his chair to face me. "I meant to call you earlier today, but it looks like I wouldn't have caught up with you, anyhow. I worked some magic on your other photo. Where's the one you're trying to match it to?"

I leaned over his desk and pulled Wolterhall's picture up on the Way of Life website. Larry studied it for a minute when I stood, then raised one unruly gray eyebrow. "Way of Life Ministries? What are you into now?"

"Don't ask," I said. "Trust me. You don't want to know. How much of a chance this is the same dude from the other photo?"

He opened a program on his laptop and moved it to the giant monitor in front of him, pulling up a much sharper version of the *Register's* photo. I peered over his shoulder and whistled. "Okay, Merlin. That's some magic if I've ever seen it."

"Thanks. The facial recognition software we use to tag images for the website should tell us if this is the same guy. But my photo eye says there's a good chance it is. What did he do?"

"The one in the old news shot was an armed child molester."

"And you think he works for this ministry outfit? Nice." Larry pulled the photo from the Way of Life site over.

"If only that were all there was to it."

A little rainbow-colored wheel spun in the middle of the screen for a few seconds. A dialog box flashed up.

Match.

Holy Manolos.

"Larry, hang onto those images for me, will you?" I asked, backing toward the door. "Thanks so much for your help. I owe you a six pack."

"Sam Adams," he said.

"You got it."

My cell phone binged a text arrival as I stepped into the elevator. Mom: "Starving to death. When did Kyle get giant biceps?"

I snorted and punched the button for the garage. Right?

"On my way," I tapped, unlocking the car. "And I dunno. Nice to look at, though." It sent as I pulled out of the garage.

Bing. "If you like that sort of thing."

Red light. "There are people who don't?"

Bing. "He's such a sweet boy, Nicey."

I let that one go, Emily's words from the night before flitting about and irritating me. I didn't have time to consider them, but ignoring her analysis didn't make it wrong.

21

Déjà vu wasn't a strong enough term to describe dinner. Mom and Kyle fell back into their old, easy banter with remarkable speed, and I laughed more than I had in weeks. Kyle's blue eyes sparkled in the candle light, his grin widening a touch every time he made someone laugh. Twenty-four hours worked a miracle on my mom—relaxed and smiling before she finished her first glass of Sangria, she was positively bubbly after two.

One no-arguments glare hushed Kyle's complaint when I snatched the check from the server before he could. I tucked my MasterCard into the folder and handed it back to her with a smile, and he winked a gracious thank-you.

He walked back to the car with an arm slung around my mom's shoulders, her grinning at him and shooting what-the-hell's-the-matter-with-you glances at me. Oh, boy.

Mom invited Kyle in for a nightcap (subtlety isn't her thing), leading him to the living room while I scurried to the kitchen for wine and glasses. I returned to find her sprawled all over the chaise lounge, Darcy in her lap, and Kyle relaxing on the sofa. He'd taken the opposite of Joey's usual corner, which made me want to giggle for some reason.

Kyle was getting to the good part of a heroic rescue story (mine), mom hanging on every word.

I perched on the edge of the sofa and she shot me a Look. The kind with a capital "L" that mothers everywhere use to mean "behave yourself, young lady."

I rolled my eyes and smiled when Kyle rubbed one hand lightly over my shoulder. "She can take pretty good care of herself, Lila. You'd be proud."

"I always am," Mom said, her eyes softening when she looked at me. Dammit. I couldn't be annoyed with her cupid attempts when she looked at me like that. Making her proud was sort of my singular goal in life for as long as I could remember.

"Can we discuss something else?" I asked. "Not my favorite day in the life of Nichelle."

Kyle's light touch morphed into a massage. I dropped my chin to my chest and let his magic fingers work. "You still carry all your stress in your shoulders," he said.

I sighed. "And you still know how to make it ebb away."

Hand to God, I heard applause from the direction of the chaise. Immediately followed by an over-dramatized yawn. "Kids, I've had such a lovely evening," Mom said, standing and meeting my warning glare with a sweet smile. Kyle's fingers kept up slow, rhythmic circles over the muscles in my neck.

"I'm afraid it's been a long couple of days, and I have an early flight. I'm going to bed." She ruffled Darcy's fur and set her in the floor. "With earplugs."

My eyes popped wide. She did not just say that. Kyle stifled a snort behind me.

"Coffee in the morning?" Mom asked, turning for the door.

"Of course," I chirped. "I wouldn't miss seeing you off. Sleep well. Love you."

"Back at you, baby." She disappeared.

Kyle dropped his head to my shoulder, laughter shaking him hard enough to shake me, too. "She's something else," he said when he sat up. "I've missed her."

I leaned back against his chest.

"I have to tell you, I admire your restraint," he said, resting his chin on the crown of my head.

"You do not quit, do you?" I laughed in spite of myself. "You know, if I didn't know you well enough to see through the bravado, this whole I'm-God's-Gift thing would be a huge turnoff."

"Not me, Goober," he said. "I waited all through dinner for an I told you so, but you didn't say it. Lord knows you'd be justified in it. Please tell me you let White have it today. And don't spare the details."

Oh. That. I grinned. "Maybe a little. But he tripped all over himself thanking me, and I have the exclusive. I can be gracious about being right."

"And your boss?"

"I didn't tell him a damned thing," I said. "I wanted my attagirl, not an ass chewing. I'm not ready to put Golightly and company in the story, so Bob's still on the no need to know list."

"Won't the TV stations pounce on it with her name out there?"

"Only if her parents return their calls," I said. "They didn't return mine yet. I'm curious to see if they'll even talk to Aaron."

"Oh, yeah?" He launched into a story about tracking down a dead drug dealer's family and getting the cold shoulder. His breathing was deep and even. Soothing. I closed my eyes and listened to his voice, trying to conjure up the tingly feeling I got with Joey. Swing and a miss.

I sat up. "But this woman wasn't a criminal." I recounted Elise's version of how her friend ended up at Way of Life.

"Sounds like she might as well have been, according to them," Kyle said.

"Aaron told me something else, too. She had an abortion before she left Way of Life. And the killer cut out her uterus."

He gaped. "Jesus. No pun intended. Yeah, I'd say the parents are worth looking at. And so far you've been right about more here than the PD has."

I smiled. "Hey, thanks."

His fingers tickled my face as he tucked a stray lock of hair behind my ear with a grin. "You're smart. You know how sexy that is?" His eyelids dropped halfway, the heat in the gaze flushing my skin.

My heart took off at a gallop. I leaned my cheek into his palm. "As sexy as your eyes when you do that with them?"

He leaned forward half a millimeter, then stopped, holding my gaze.

Waiting.

Daring.

From the corner of my eye, I caught a flash of something bright through the picture window behind the sofa.

Just before it exploded.

22

Glass.

Screams.

Barking.

Kyle vaulted us to the floor, covering my body with his and groping for his ankle. A second later he pushed himself up with one arm, a small black pistol in his other hand, and scanned my face with worried eyes. Rocking back onto his knees, he wiped my forehead with a gentle thumb and swore under his breath. "What the hell have you gotten yourself into?" he asked.

I shook my head, words failing me as my eyes locked on the gun. Whoever was outside had one, too.

More explosions, followed by a roar.

"Stay. Here." Kyle dropped a kiss on my head and turned, still crouching behind the sofa.

I couldn't breathe. Darcy nosed at my hand and I pulled her to my chest, petting and shushing her as she struggled against my grip. Kyle moved to the end of the couch, then darted to the doorway. From the foyer, he peeked back around the corner, both hands around the butt of the snub-nose semi-automatic, his right index finger on the trigger.

Darcy growled. I squeezed her tighter, stroking her head. "Be still. I don't want you to get hurt," I whispered.

Kyle edged down the wall until I couldn't even see his shoes anymore, moving methodically toward the gaping maw that used to be my favorite window.

His boots crackled across shattered glass, the sound all I could hear over the blood pounding in my ears. Darcy nipped at my hand, and I flinched and let her go. She scooted under the coffee table and shot me a glare.

"Kyle?" It came out as barely a whisper. I cleared my throat and tried again.

He appeared at the end of the couch. "I think whoever it was is long gone, but I'd like to look around outside, and I have to call the RPD."

Tears pricked at the backs of my eyes, and I blinked, annoyed. Focusing on how scared I felt, I tried to channel some of that into anger. Kyle grabbed my hand and pulled me to my feet. Something warm and wet trickled over my cheek when I stood. I flicked at it with my hand, blinking at the red streak when I pulled it away from my face. Blood, not tears. Fabulous.

Kyle already had his phone to his ear, but he stepped toward me and smoothed my hair gently away from my forehead. "There are three or four places it hit you," he said, thumbing thin trickles of blood off my forehead and cheek. "I don't think any of them need stitches, but some Neosporin and Band-Aids would be nice."

I nodded, turning for the bathroom. Behind me, Kyle listed his credentials for the nine-one-one operator. "Shots fired, probable drive-by. Requesting assistance." He reeled off my address as I stepped into my nineteen-twenties pink-tiled bathroom, flipping on the light and the water. I stared into the mirror. The longest cut was at the crest of my cheekbone, maybe three centimeters. But Kyle was right—they were all shallow, and my ginger fingers didn't find any shards buried in my skin.

I leaned both hands on the countertop, increasingly furious violet eyes staring out of the mirror. My mom, my dog, Kyle—someone shot out the front window of my house. Someone who could have hurt any one of them. Who the hell did these people think they were?

I grabbed the first aid kit from the white cabinet over the toilet and turned back for the living room. Pausing outside the guest room door, I inched it open.

A sliver of light spilled across the floor. Mom's cell phone lay on the nightstand, white noise blaring from it. The covers moved up and down in regular rhythm, the little orange dot in her ear peeking over the edge of the blankets.

"Sweet dreams, mom," I whispered, pulling the door shut. Just as well. She'd come here to get something off her chest, not give herself a stroke. If I could get her on the plane in the morning without her going into the living room, everyone would be happy.

Kyle stood just inside the front door, and I could already hear sirens on the next block over. He looked between me and the dark front yard for a second, then took the plastic box from my hands and opened an alcohol wipe, gesturing to the chaise. "Let's get you patched up, Lois." He tried for a grin.

"I don't believe there will be any lightening of my mood tonight, but thanks." I sat, tipping my face up to his. His long fingers were gentle as they worked, cleaning and dressing the cuts. I pulled in a sharp hiss of breath at the sting of the alcohol and he winced. "Sorry."

"Eh." I waved a hand. "Thanks for...being you."

His lips tipped up. "After a moment of thought, I believe I'll take that as a compliment."

"It is."

He pressed the last Band-Aid into place as the doorbell rang. I followed Kyle to the foyer and swung the door wide to reveal Chris Landers and Aaron White, along with a couple of uniformed officers.

I tried to raise my eyebrows, but stopped when the cut at the edge of my temple protested. "What are you two doing here?"

"We need to talk," Landers said. Aaron nodded.

I opened my mouth and then snapped it shut again, stepping out of the way and waving them inside. Kyle stepped forward and introduced himself.

The way Aaron bit down on a smile as he shook Kyle's hand made me groan to myself. I'd never hear the end of this.

I led them to the kitchen. Aaron rattled off a list of instructions for the patrol officers behind us and they moved into the living room.

I opened the fridge and offered all three stoic-faced cops a drink, then busied myself getting glasses and ice, my chest tightening again for some reason.

Kyle, Landers, and Aaron tossed around lots of big official-sounding words, almost like they'd forgotten I'd covered cops for eight years. Work mode—it was easier to keep my hands from shaking if I treated it like a story. That wasn't about me.

I set the drinks on the table and took one of the chairs. Aaron sat across from me. Kyle and Landers paced.

"At the risk of redundancy," I said, "what are you two doing here?"

"I heard the call," Aaron said. "I know your address."

"Um. Why?"

He rolled his eyes. "I know Charlie's, too. And every other cops reporter in town. You people can get the wrong folks pissed off at you sometimes. Though no one does it quite like you do."

"Everybody has to be good at something, right?" I tried to smile.

"Pick another thing," Kyle growled, leaning against the edge of the yellow-tiled countertop.

Landers chuckled. "I assume the ATF doesn't respond to drive-by calls these days, so you were here for social reasons, Special Agent Miller?"

Heat rose into my cheeks and Aaron reached across the table and patted my hand. "I'm not sure that's pertinent, Chris."

"I'm getting the lay of the land," Landers said. "And in point, it could be. What if the shooter wasn't aiming for Miss Clarke at all? You got a collar who made parole lately, Miller?"

I turned to Kyle. It hadn't occurred to me whoever blasted out my front window might not be after me. From the look on Kyle's face, it hadn't occurred to him, either.

"I—" His hand moved to his face, his fingers sliding absently over the bristles around his mouth. "I don't know."

I turned back to Landers. "You didn't answer my question, detective."

"I was coming here to talk to you about my case," he said. "Aaron found me on the sidewalk outside and filled me in." He turned to Kyle. "You said it was a drive by?"

"I think so." Kyle shook his head as though trying to clear it. "I've never been on this end of one, and everything happened so fast."

Aaron excused himself, returning a minute later to say he'd sent an officer outside to set up lights and comb the yard for casings. "If it was a drive-by, they're in the car," he said. "But we're looking. How many shots?"

"Three?" I said just as Kyle said, "Five." He sounded way surer than I did.

"Which?" Landers pulled out a notebook and pen.

"Five." Kyle repeated, his tone certain.

"I'll defer to Kyle on grounds of experience with firearms."

"The window exploded with the first one," Kyle said. "It was a large-caliber that hit just right, or a shotgun. At least two people in the car. One to drive and one to shoot."

Watching them think it through was akin to having my own *Law and Order* episode in my kitchen.

"Why aren't the neighbors outside?" Landers moved to the kitchen door and stepped out onto the little side porch.

I followed. "I don't understand the question."

"Your neighbors. It's not like there's gunfire in this part of town every night. Why aren't they out here being nosy?"

"They work?" I asked.

He gestured to the house next door. "No one sleeps that soundly."

"That one's empty," I said. "Creepy, really. I looked it up right after I moved here. The woman who owned it passed away and it's tied up in probate court. Has been for ten years. It's like a mini museum if you peek in the windows. Everything's still right where she left it. The neighborhood kids think it's haunted." I didn't add that I kind of did, too. I shrugged. "People probably assumed it was firecrackers. The Fourth is coming up."

He shook his head, muttering about desensitization to violence and turning back for the house.

I looked around, suddenly chilled in the balmy June air, and jogged up the steps, locking the door behind me.

Aaron drained his glass and put it back on the table. "Okay, Nichelle. If we go on the assumption our shooter was after you, give me your best guess."

I exchanged a look with Kyle and he nodded.

"A cop," I said.

Landers jerked his head up. "Do I want to know?"

"I'm not sure I do," Aaron said, his lips disappearing into a grim line.

"Not a Richmond cop," I said, offering the short version of my visit to the Fauquier sheriff's office.

"Subtlety wasn't this guy's strong suit," I finished. "He got my plate number before I left there. And that was just this afternoon."

Aaron leaned back, raising the front two feet of the chair off the floor, and laced his fingers behind his head. "It's certainly plausible," he said. "And the timing fits."

"What if it wasn't the deputies themselves, but whoever they're protecting?" Landers asked.

I turned to look at him. He raked a hand through his curls, everything about his lanky frame agitated as he paced a five-step pattern across my tiny kitchen. "What do you mean?"

"They got your plates, they looked you up, and they called whoever the head honcho is at the church and handed you over. Maybe even for a price. A reporter from Richmond nosing around an outfit like that—especially if they did have something to do with this murder...that's worth something."

Shit. I slumped in the chair. Could be. Not that we had any way to know for sure.

I raised my head and caught a look passing between all three of them.

"Time to wake up the neighbors?" Kyle asked.

Aaron pulled out his cell phone. "I'll have a perimeter set up. Six blocks? Where's the closest gas station?"

"Three blocks down and one to the north," I said. Security video from the outdoor cameras and a bit of luck could turn up a plate number if they could get a description of the car.

Aaron stepped into the hall, his phone to his ear.

"We're assuming they left when Agent Miller heard the engine rev," Landers said. "But someone could come back to make sure they did the job right. We'll keep an eye out. And interview everyone we can find. Maybe someone saw something."

Kyle moved to stand behind my chair, laying a hand on my shoulder.

Aaron returned, nodding. "They're on their way." He turned to me and his face softened. "I'm sorry, Nichelle."

I tried to smile. "My life is never boring, at least."

"You should go somewhere else tonight," he raised a questioning eyebrow at Kyle.

Kyle's fingers sank into my shoulder. "My loft is safer," he said, his voice uncertain.

"My mom is here," I reminded him. "Once she's on her plane in the morning, we'll discuss it. But I'm not waking her up and telling her this. She'll stay. Or drag me home by my ear."

"There's someone else in the house?" Aaron and Landers both stood up straight, though I couldn't swear to which one spoke.

"She went to bed before everything broke loose. With earplugs. And it's my mother. She's not plotting to murder me." I moved to the kitchen door. They weren't waking her up, either. "I'm serious, guys. I just need to get her on her way home."

"You never did tell me why she came up here," Kyle said.

I shot him a shut-the-hell-up look. "We can talk about it later. Personal stuff, is all." Every word true.

Aaron and Landers shared a sigh.

"I suppose the stubborn streak that can make you such a pain in my ass is working against me here, too," Aaron said.

"You love me anyway." I managed a flash of a grin.

"She didn't see anything?" Landers asked.

I shook my head. "She didn't hear anything, either, or she'd already have me on a plane back to Dallas. The miracle of Ambien and ear plugs."

Aaron patted my arm. "I'm going to supervise outside."

"Thanks, Aaron."

"I'm going to see if they've found slugs. Or pellets." Landers turned for the living room.

I sagged back against Kyle. His lips brushed the top of my head, and he led me to my bedroom, flipping on the light. "Go to bed. I'm going to help. And tomorrow, I'm getting myself assigned to your preacher. If this had anything to do with that guy, his days are numbered."

23

I stared at the ceiling fan until the last of the cops left just after three. Landers and Kyle had a debriefing outside my door, wherein Kyle promised to have me call Landers the next morning. It didn't occur to me until then I hadn't asked Landers why he'd been on his way to my house at eleven o'clock. At least I had a good excuse for the lapse.

I heard the door whisper across the floor and turned my head. "I'm not asleep."

Kyle crossed the room in four long strides, laying a hand on my arm. "It'll be okay. They found a couple of guys a few blocks up who were drinking on the front porch. Saw them speeding off. Got a good description of the vehicle. We'll find them."

"What about what Landers said?" My voice thickened. "What if they come back? I'm scared, Kyle."

He pulled me up into a hug, his arms offering a harbor I needed more than air.

I buried my face in his chest and sobbed. He stroked my hair until I was through, then crooked a finger under my chin and tipped my face up to his. "You really think I'm going to let anything happen to you? Sleep. One of us should. I'm on sentry duty. White has a patrol car across the street until sunrise. Let's get Lila on her way home, and then we'll figure this out."

I squeezed him again. "Thank you."

He shook his head in dismissal, stepping toward the door. "Of course."

I fell back onto the pillows, Darcy sighing from her bed.

Another half hour of staring at the fan and the clock later, my eyes fell shut.

I was so tired I didn't even dream.

* * *

My mom's grin when she saw Kyle the next morning would've cracked anyone else's face. He just smiled and nodded, positioning himself in the hallway to block her view of the living room as she got ready for her flight. I followed her back and forth from the bedroom to the bathroom, chattering about nothing with an energy I must've borrowed from someone who got more than three hours' sleep.

Mom hummed through putting her makeup on, stealing I-told-you-so glances at me. Pretty sure she mistook my jitters for some kind of afterglow.

A big cup of coffee in one hand, she loaded her bags into the rental car and turned to hug me. "I love you, baby. I'm so sorry about all this. I just want you to be happy."

I tightened my arms around her. "I know that feeling," I said. "Be safe. Call me when you get home." I pulled my head back. "And hey—any excuse to see you is a good one. I miss you."

She kissed my cheek and slid into the car. "I have to go now, or I'm going to cry. Love you best, baby girl."

"No, I love you best," I said, pushing the door closed and waving.

She turned right out of the drive at my direction, never seeing the boarded-up window or the police tape littering the front porch.

"Nice work," Kyle said.

"Thanks."

"Get a bag and grab the dog. You're coming home with me."

I opened my mouth to protest, turning to face him.

He raised one hand, a stubborn set to his jaw. "I won't take no for an answer, Nicey. These people are dangerous. I'm not leaving you here alone with a six-pound dog for protection."

I sighed. "I appreciate that, but I have so much going on the next few days. I'm sure it will be fine. You said Aaron had a good lead on them."

Kyle folded his arms across his chest, his biceps visible through the cotton of his wrinkled shirt. "You have what stuff going on?"

I bit my lip. The kind of stuff he wouldn't like, but an edict from Jesus himself wouldn't stop me from going to Way of Life Saturday.

"No." Kyle shook his head, his eyes narrowing. "No way, Nichelle. You're not going back out there. Are you kidding me?"

"I have to." My eyes flicked to where my mom had disappeared to a few seconds before. I wanted to know what happened to Jasmine. I also wanted a face-to-face with the who's who of the ministry, and Elise's plan might actually work. I set my own jaw and snapped my eyes at him. "Last time I checked, I wasn't under investigation by the ATF. You don't get to tell me what to do."

"You are determined to get yourself killed," he said through his teeth. "Why? Give White what you've got and let them go after this guy. If they killed that girl, Landers will turn it up. I watched him last night. He's a good cop."

"The legal fortress around that place could put the Alamo to shame," I said. "It'll be so much easier for me to get the truth and hand it to Landers."

"Not if you die before you can tell him what you know. These people obviously have no qualms about shutting you up. And if they shot up your house last night, they're not exactly going to sit for an interview."

"I'm not going in with a pen and pad asking them questions," I huffed, looping a thick strand of hair into a knot. "Give me a little credit."

He stepped forward and put his hands on my shoulders. "I'm giving you a lot of credit. But you're no match for these guys."

I bit the inside of my cheek. "You know why my mother was here?"

"I'm guessing because she was worried, after what you told me the other night. She's a smart lady."

"My father."

Kyle's eyes widened. "No shit? What about him?"

"He got Jesus in a big way when she wouldn't marry him. Turns out he was an actor from the studio, not a friend from school."

"It's not this Golightly guy?" He didn't manage to keep his jaw hinged at that.

"No, he's too old, and she said she's never seen him on TV. But she thinks he's involved with a televangelism outfit somewhere, somehow. That's why she flipped when she heard we went out there."

"Do you want to find him?" he moved his hands to my back, pulling me close to him.

"No." I rested my head on his shoulder, slowly shaking it. "Can I tell you something I haven't even had the guts to admit to myself yet?" I mumbled into his shirt.

"What's that, honey?"

"I want to make sure he didn't murder this girl."

Kyle pulled in a deep breath, his arms tightening around me. "Damn."

The thought had whispered in the corners of my brain since about five minutes after my mom finished talking Wednesday night, and shored up the more I thought about the things I knew, precious and few that they were.

He went batshit when my mom didn't want to get married. Jasmine worked in the offices. She was pretty. Not unlike my mom—willowy, with long, thick hair. Men often fixate on a type of woman from an early age. And the men at Way of Life tried a little too hard to keep themselves from being attracted to the opposite sex, evidenced by their insane unwritten dress code.

Sex and money: in my years at the crime desk, only a handful of murders had motive outside those two.

What if Ruth Galloway had been sleeping with my father? Crazy as it sounded, I couldn't say it was impossible.

"What did your mom tell you?" Kyle asked finally.

"He was always religious, but he went really deep in when she refused to marry him," I said. "She said he called her horrible names. Threw things at her. In her parents' house, with them there."

Kyle nodded. "Violent temper."

"I don't know for sure he's ever heard of Golightly. But Jasmine worked in the executive offices. Elise has a plan to get me in tomorrow morning, and I will find a way to talk to them. I have to."

"I can't let you go alone," Kyle said.

"I don't see where you have a choice."

"I have twenty-four hours to come up with something."

I pushed back and smiled. "I'll make you a deal. I'll come to your place with Darcy if you'll back off with the overprotective routine."

"Somehow I think I'm getting shafted. You get to not stay here and be a sitting duck, and I get to keep my mouth shut about you strolling into the wolf's den. How is that a good deal for me?"

I smiled. "It's the only one I'm offering?"

He rolled his eyes. "Deal."

I turned back for the door. "Coffee?" I asked over my shoulder.

"As thick as you can get it." Kyle stepped into the kitchen and pinched the bridge of his nose. His eyes were test-cramming bloodshot.

"You really stayed up all night." I didn't bother with the question mark, laying a hand on his bristly cheek.

"Of course I did," he smiled. My chest tightened. Swallowing an onslaught of tears, I reached up and kissed him, just a gentle thank-you.

He smiled when I pulled away. "Get your stuff. It sounds like I have more work to do than I have day left. We'll come by here this evening to grab the dog."

I made him a triple-strength cup of coffee and handed him a package of Pop-Tarts. "Ten minutes."

24

Overnight bag stowed in the back of my little red SUV, I parked in the garage at the *Telegraph* office at seven-fifteen. Resting my head on the steering wheel for a second, I tried to collect my thoughts.

There were too many to corral, let alone compartmentalize. I shoved the personal stuff into a drawer in the back of my brain and focused on the murders. Two young women in a week's time was odd for anywhere smaller than New York. It was too early to call Landers, but I planned to ring his phone at eight sharp.

I closed my eyes, memory of the crime scene tape leftover from Landers's midnight visit to my house breaking my concentration for a second.

A tap at the window nearly sent me through the roof of the car.

Rubbing the back of my head where I'd whacked it, I turned to the window, my hand flying to the key that was still in the ignition.

"Jesus, Parker." Closing my eyes, I pulled the key out and opened the door. "You scared the hell out of me."

"Sorry." He took my bag and threw it over his shoulder. "Here, I'll make it up to you. I just wanted to say thanks for whatever the heck you told Mel. She said you talked some sense into her the other night, and things are...way better."

I punched the elevator button and smiled. "I'm glad I helped. And excessively in need of good news this week. Yay for you two."

He frowned, stepping into the elevator. "Why so jumpy?"

I leaned against the wall and smiled. "The cops digging bullets out of my living room walls kept me up half the night."

He flashed the grin that made women in five counties call for smelling salts—and read our sports section. It faded when his emerald eyes met my serious gaze. "You're not kidding?"

I shook my head. "Oh, how I wish I was."

He laid a hand on my arm. "You playing Nancy Drew again?"

I chuckled. "How ever did you guess?" I batted my lashes.

He shook his head. "Not funny. What did the cops say?"

"They have a good lead," I said, waving one hand in a show of bravado I would've given my shoe closet to actually feel. "It'll be fine."

"Someone shot at you. I see no scenario in which that's 'fine.'" His voice carried as he stepped off the elevator and an intern spun to stare at us. I smiled and nodded at the kid and he continued in the direction of the break room.

Turning to Parker, I shushed him. "I'd prefer to keep this to us for as long as I can," I said. "In particular, I don't want Bob knowing about it."

"You know this is a newsroom, right?" He shook his head. "Good luck with that."

I sighed because he was right. "Just, shhh. Please?"

"The cops really have a good lead?"

"And I'm staying with Kyle for at least the weekend. My landlord will be thrilled about having the window replaced, I'm sure."

"That's what insurance is for," Parker said. "Kyle is the federal agent ex?"

I nodded, and he patted my shoulder. "That makes me feel at least a little better. Let me know if you need anything. Budget season. I'm doing a lot of sitting around watching TV while Mel listens to the council argue over which programs get what money they have."

"Thanks, Parker."

"Watch yourself."

"I don't fancy getting shot again."

"Then stop pissing off criminals."

"It appears to be an occupational hazard."

He rolled his eyes. "Maybe you need an new occupation. Do I know anyone at the *Post*? Maybe Tony does."

I smiled. Parker's friend Tony Okerson was a retired Redskins quarterback, and my dreams of covering the White House for the *Washington Post* were common knowledge. "I wouldn't turn down a good word or two from him."

"I'll see what I can do." He turned toward his office, then stopped and grinned at me again. "No, I won't. We'd miss you. But do me a favor and dodge the bullets, okay!"

"Doing my best."

I continued to the break room and flipped on the coffee maker, my thoughts racing as the thing burbled. Thirty thousand items on my to-do list. Better start checking them off.

I plopped into my chair, my coffee mug already half-empty and the newsroom still fairly quiet. Opening my laptop, I stared at Google. How could I find Ruth's back-home flame if her folks wouldn't talk to me? Jared. A first name was all I had to go on.

I tried searching for her name.

And found a Facebook profile. Clicking the link, I held my breath.

Last update: about a month before she arrived at Way of Life. I scrolled through her photos. She liked selfies—especially ones of her kissing a tall, gorgeous guy with dark skin and a dazzling smile.

"Damn," I mumbled. Jared the mechanic looked like a Calvin Klein ad. I clicked the tags. His last name was Abernathy. Whitepages got me an address, but no phone number. Probably only had a cell. Crap.

I clicked back to Facebook, finding his profile. And the name of the shop where he worked.

They had a phone.

I dialed, sending a silent prayer up.

"Motors and More, this's Mel," a voice said.

"May I speak to Jared, please?" I drew loops and squiggles with my pen.

"Hang on." The phone clattered to a desk, and Mel bellowed.

"Jared. Can I help you?" His voice was deep and rough.

I hauled in a deep breath. Could I tell anything about him from a phone call? Maybe. Especially if he didn't know she was dead.

I introduced myself.

"What can I do for you?" he sounded more curious than guarded.

"I'm working on a story about a murder case, Jared. I'm so sorry, but I think you knew the victim."

A rush of air issued from his chest through the phone.

"It's her isn't it? She's gone," his voice was soft.

I froze. How did he know? No way Aaron had called him.

"Who?" I asked.

"My Ruthie." A sob cut off his sentence. He cleared his throat. "I saw a drawing in the paper. It said the cops in Richmond were looking for information on a murder victim they couldn't identify. But she'd never been to Richmond. Her hair was longer, I thought. And she was so thin."

"A friend has identified the victim as Ruth Galloway," I said. "You two were involved?"

"We were engaged," he choked out. "In love. Her folks hated it. Hated me. Bigoted control freaks. But I've been saving up to open my own shop, and I'm almost there. She was coming home."

I scribbled. News to me.

"When did you last talk to her?"

"Last spring," he said. "My letters started coming back in the summer. But she'd have found me. She loved me."

Engaged? But she had a boyfriend at Way of Life, and another in Richmond.

I stared at the photo of Jared on my screen, my thoughts roaming back to the murder scene. So much blood. I bet there were cows in Wallingford. Someone she trusted enough to let into the loft. Someone who knew the altar set up might point to her folks or the church?

Hot damn.

"Have you ever been to Richmond, Jared?" I asked.

"No. Why was Ruthie in Richmond?"

"She was living on the streets," I said. "Ran away from Way of Life."

He gasped, then fell silent. "Lady, you have the wrong guy," he said finally, relief flooding through the speaker. "She would never." I could hear the smile in his voice.

"I'm afraid she would. Did," I said.

"But why would anyone stab Ruthie?" he asked. "She was such a happy person. Always found the bright side."

Now that jived with her rainbows and unicorns journal of life on the street.

Wait. My pen froze mid-word.

I didn't say anything about a knife.

"Thanks so much for your time, Jared," I said, scribbling the rest of his comments. "I'm so sorry for your loss."

Not a speck of red tape near this guy. A phone call from any of the cops I'd entertained at midnight would have him in his local sheriff's lockup before lunch. "I appreciate your help."

He hung up.

I texted Kyle and Aaron his name and place of employment, plus a rundown of the conversation.

Kyle pinged right back. "You solved it! Now you can stay home tomorrow."

"Nice try." I tapped. "See you at six."

Aaron shot back a thank you ten minutes later.

I saved screenshots of both Facebook profiles, re-reading my notes. Maybe he saw the M.O. in the paper—he did say he read the story.

But he still thought she planned to marry him when she'd carried someone else's child for at least a few weeks. Definite motive. And he looked plenty strong enough.

I highlighted his comments about her folks, too—if they got wind of an engagement, they'd have motive.

Staring at my notes until the letters swam didn't get me anything else.

Next up: email. Seventy-eight new messages. I deleted the morning round of "lose weight without trying!" and "bigger breasts TODAY!" spam, stopping at a message from Shelby. Three-fourteen in the morning. I should make an extra pot of coffee.

Hey Nichelle,

I think I found something. Will you be around in the morning?

ST

I looked toward the cluster of cubes that made up our copy corral. Still silent. I clicked reply.

I'm here for at least a while. May have to run to police HQ after the meeting. Can't wait to hear.

Another ten spam messages and I found one from Landers.

Call me.

That was it. I checked the clock and rifled through my bag for the card he'd scribbled his cell number on. No way he was still asleep with so much going on, anyway. Dialing, I glanced around the newsroom, pondering Shelby's cryptic email and wondering for the first time if Bob had a point about the blogger. What if Girl Friday worked at the *Telegraph*?

Landers picked up before I had time to get very far with that. "How are you this morning?" he asked in place of hello.

"About done being scared," I said. "Getting pissed. Kyle said you had a good lead."

"We'll find them. May take a few days, but we will." His tone left no room for doubt.

"Thank you." I picked up a pen. "So, in all the excitement, I never asked you what you wanted to talk to me about last night."

"And I never mentioned it. You have time to come by here this morning?"

"Are you already at the office?"

"I haven't been home in two days. I got an ID on the second vic late yesterday. Haven't released it yet."

Definitely front page. Probably lead story, unless Congress was up to anything interesting.

"I'll be there in fifteen minutes," I said. "Thanks."

"People are shooting at you. It's the least I can do."

"But you were going to tell me before you knew about that. I appreciate it."

"See you in a few."

I shot Bob an email telling him to save me space on the front for the second victim and scribbled an apology for missing the news budget meeting on a Post-it. I stuck it to his closed door on my way to the elevator.

Two birds, one stone: I could avoid Bob for the morning and get a great scoop. We might even get it on the website before Charlie could get it on the air at noon if I hurried.

My cell phone binged a text when I started the car. I glanced at the screen. Kyle again. "Got myself a new assignment. The good reverend should watch who he shoots at."

"That was quick. It's not even 8:00," I tapped back.

Bing. "I'm charming. Everyone sees it but you."

Red light. I smiled. "And modest, too." I hit send as the light turned green.

I slid the car into a tight space on Grace Street a few minutes later, checking in with the desk sergeant and dropping my bag on the belt for the x-ray machine. I stepped through the metal detector, smiling at the patrolman watching the monitor.

Landers picked up my bag. "Good morning."

"To you, too, detective," I said, turning the smile on him. He was serious about the two days at the office, his jaw shaded with a half-inch of scruff and the same rumpled blue button-down and khakis I'd seen at one a.m. still hanging on his spindly frame. I checked his left hand. Married. I bet his wife was super excited about this case.

He punched the button for the elevator and leaned against the wall. "Cecilia Erickson, age twenty-four."

"The same age as Ruth Galloway," I said, my brain whirling. Crap. What if it was a serial? "How did you get the ID?"

"Dental."

Well, that was more normal, anyway.

I dug a pad and pen out of my bag and scribbled as I followed him into the elevator. He didn't speak again until he shut the door to his office.

"She was a paralegal," he said. "Working on a law degree."

"The law school isn't far from the Bottom," I said, glancing up from my notes.

"It's not. But the school isn't what caught my eye."

I held his gaze until he dropped his eyes to the papers on his desk. I was almost afraid to ask.

"Where did she work?"

"Jessup and Poole."

I only managed to hold onto my pen because I'd felt it coming. The firm was an old one. Powerful, with tentacles in political lobbying. And ties to the Mafia.

"That's the second employee they've had turn up murdered in a year." I scribbled as I talked, mentally sorting puzzle pieces.

"She didn't work for the murdered lawyer," Landers said. "But she did work for one of the senior partners. Aaron tells me you might have seen him last Sunday morning. If you sat close enough to the front."

My pen clattered to the floor.

"These people are so far in the middle of this they can't see their way out," I said, more to myself than to Landers as I picked it up.

"It certainly appears that's more of a possibility than I thought," he said. "What are they hiding that's worth killing two young women in the space of a week?"

I kept my face neutral, which wasn't easy under his scrutiny. Things I had found on my own—like Ruth's name and hometown—I was happy to share. But the ATF information Kyle had given me was off the record. Landers would have to find that himself.

"Could that be why Agent Miller was at your house last night?" Landers drummed his fingers on the desktop.

"You'd have to ask him," I said.

He slammed his hands down on the desk. "Two people are dead and someone's trying to kill you," he got louder with every word. "Isn't that more important than your story?"

"You wouldn't trust me if I passed on information someone else gave me in confidence. My reputation is much more important to me than the story. Kyle likes you. He got himself assigned to a new investigation this morning. Call him." I jotted Kyle's cell down and passed it across the desk.

He leaned back in his chair, eyes flashing. "I don't have time for games."

"I'm not playing one." I kept a handle on my temper—not simple, with so much frustration and so little sleep in the way. Landers wasn't a bad guy. He just wanted to figure this out. I could sympathize.

"You have any suspects?" he asked.

"A few. I wouldn't rule out Ruth's parents, though I'm not sure how they'd fit with the second victim."

"Me, either. The mother hung up on me. Right after she told me she hadn't had a daughter in three years and gave me an alibi. They were hosting a tent revival. Three thousand people watched their every move all week long."

I closed my eyes, giving my head a little shake. "Could they have paid someone to do it?"

He tipped his head to one side. "The M.O. doesn't really fit with a professional hit."

"But they seem a little crazy, don't they? Not surprisingly, they didn't return my call."

Landers nodded. "You're better off. It was like talking to a Stephen King character." He jotted a note. "I'll have a chat with the local law enforcement in South Carolina."

"Ask them about her old boyfriend. I talked to him this morning. Big time torch for her. If he knew she was seeing other guys, he'd have motive. Aaron and Kyle are trying to get him picked up."

"Thanks." He scribbled Jared's name when I offered it.

"I'm not ruling out a serial. Like you said, the law school is near the Bottom." He leaned forward, resting his elbows on the desk. "But I'm getting more interested in your theory about this ministry outfit. Or maybe there's another connection between the victims and the killer. I'm not going to give away your headline, Miss Clarke. I just want to catch this bastard."

I tapped my pen on my notebook, scanning his walls. The case had taken over his office, marked-up maps and horrifying photos dotting the drab-gray interior matte. "I've become very interested in a CPA who works for Golightly," I said slowly. "Edwin Wolterhall. Has a violent sex offender history and a penchant for young brunettes. And she might have been trying to blackmail him. Her friends here said she talked about getting money for them to move."

He picked up his pen. "Spell his name for me?"

I obliged. "Kyle seems to think getting a warrant through all the lawyers Way of Life has on staff will be difficult."

Landers nodded. "It will. But nothing's impossible if you keep at it long enough. Thanks for coming by."

I asked for and jotted down contact information for Cecilia's next of kin before I tucked the pen and paper back into my bag. "Thanks for coming to the rescue last night."

"We'll get to the bottom of it." He stood, waving me toward the door. "I'll keep you posted."

I settled back into the driver's seat of my car, the second victim, the law firm, and Wolterhall spinning through my thoughts. There had to be a link. Maybe more coffee and another round with Google could help me find it.

25

Richmond detectives have identified the remains of a young woman found in a car trunk in Church Hill last week as Cecilia Erickson, 24, of Richmond. Erickson was a paralegal and a student at Richmond American University Law School, where she was in her second year.

"We're pursuing every angle in this case," RPD Det. Chris Landers, who's leading the investigation, said.

Erickson was the same age as Ruth Galloway, the young woman found brutally murdered on Belle Isle earlier this month. Landers said that while an arrest has been made in that case, he can't dismiss the similarities between the women without further investigation.

I sat back in my chair. That was as close as I could get to saying "possible serial killer" and still sleep at night.

Finishing the story with background from my earlier reports, I sent it to Bob with a note to pop it on the web as soon as he read it through. Lord, I missed the days when Charlie was my biggest worry. At least Charlie had a schedule. A week of constant deadline mode was wearing on my nerves.

More caffeine.

Fresh coffee in hand, I clicked into my web browser ten minutes later, checking Channel Four's site to see if Charlie had anything.

Coffee sloshed all over my desk when I thumped the cup down, and I snatched the computer out of harm's way, my eyes locked on the headline: "Police search Bottom for possible serial killer."

I muttered every swearword I knew—including a few my mother didn't know I knew—as I scrolled through the story. Which led off "Cecilia Erickson, a twenty-four-year-old Richmond paralegal…"

Damn, damn, damn.

I wasn't sure where my anger was directed yet, but I was good and pissed at someone. Surely Landers hadn't blabbed to her. But then who did?

I tapped one finger on the edge of my laptop as the four-one-one blog loaded.

A grinning photo lifted from Cecilia's Facebook wall smiled at me, two different "unnamed police sources" quoted about the search for Richmond's very own John Wayne Gacy.

Heat rose in my cheeks as I read, each line sending my blood pressure closer to the danger zone. By the time I clicked it off, I was surprised my head was still intact.

"Dammit!" I dropped my head back and shouted at the ceiling. It shouldn't have taken Charlie this long to find the blog, honestly. But having to race both of them to this story wasn't what I needed.

"Everything okay, Nicey?" Bob's voice came from behind me, and I tipped the chair back and studied his upside-down furrowed brow.

"No. Things are so not okay for me this morning, I can't even see okay in the rearview." And the people who shot up my house less than twelve hours ago weren't even the biggest reason why. Not that I was telling Bob that. "You can take your time with the exclusive I just sent you. Charlie has it already. She got it from Girl Friday." I sat up and spun the chair around.

"Damn."

"I don't get it, Bob," I said. "Landers was so careful. Hell, he came by my house last night to tell me about this."

His brow furrowed. "Why didn't you write it up then?"

"Because—" my lips froze. Shit. That wasn't smart. "Because we were discussing other things and we didn't make it around to this. That's why I missed the meeting to go see him this morning."

Bob was a good reporter, too. Of all the rotten luck. "What were you discussing with him that was so important you missed being first to a huge story?"

I bit the inside of my cheek. "Personal stuff?"

He groaned. "Jesus, Nichelle, were those roses from a cop? I can't even begin to tell you what kind of headache that's going to create for the both of us."

I blinked, giving that a second to sink in. In the balance, it hurt him less to think I was seeing a detective outside work than it would to know why Landers had been at my house at midnight—or who the flowers were really from. Two problems, one unintentional fib. Win.

Shrugging, I changed the subject. "Shelby thinks she has a lead," I said. "I'm ready to level my playing field. What did you need?"

"You weren't in the meeting. Just wanted to see what other copy you had for today. I wasn't looking for the ulcer you just gave me, that's for damned sure."

"Sorry." No, I wasn't. Ulcer beats heart palpitations. "I'm headed to the courthouse this morning, and I'll have the murder trial day two. Not sure what else. I haven't gotten through all the police reports. Not that they're doing much but waiting for another dead woman to pop up."

"Your friend think this really is a serial?" Bob's bushy eyebrows met his hairline.

"He doesn't know. He can't rule it out, because if it is..." I didn't finish the sentence.

Bob nodded. "Right. And what about your preacher? You turn up anything but the girl's name out there?"

I laughed and shook my head. "No comment?"

"I'm not stupid, Nichelle. Telling you to stay off a lead like that is like tossing a ribeye in front of a dog and telling him to sit. Just don't get us sued. And if you're playing Nancy Drew, let's have the story first, huh?"

"I'm trying."

"If Girl Friday is getting her information from the PD, perhaps we should run it before you take it to them."

"I—" I stopped.

He was right. I promised to have my copy ready by deadline (for all the good it would do me) and clicked the blog back up on my screen, scrolling to previous entries.

She hadn't had Ruth's identity until six hours after we put it on the web.

But Cecilia, she had first.

Why?

I jumped to my feet and snatched up my bag, hoping Shelby was a decent detective.

* * *

Shelby grinned so genuinely when I tapped her shoulder I had to force myself not to flinch. She's always been pretty, and a true smile directed my way was almost enough to make me like her.

"I got her," she said, grin still in place.

"Her who? You're sure?" I bounced on the balls of my feet.

"Ninety-nine-point-nine percent," Shelby said.

Two solid weeks of competing with a ghost had me ready to punch someone. But I might settle for yelling. "Where can we find her?"

"Your cops should be able to tell you that," she said, clicking her computer screen to life. "She works at RPD headquarters."

"A cop?" Damned if Aaron wasn't right. "Why on Earth would a cop run a blog like that? Dragging information out of the PD is harder than pulling teeth out of a lion. For most people, anyway."

Shelby clicked a window up, full of bitsy type I couldn't read from where I stood. "She's not a cop. She's a dispatcher." She waved toward the screen. "Alexa Reading—she graduated from RAU with a bachelor's in journalism last month, but—"

"She couldn't find a job," I breathed, my thoughts straying to Violet and her useless econ degree as I squinted at the screen.

"Not the one she wanted. But she has good communications skills and a college degree. So the PD snapped her up," Shelby said, scooting her chair to one side so I could see better.

The screen was split, showing a side-by-side of snippets from the blog next to articles from the RAU Eagle.

"It's a writing style analyzer," Shelby said. "It's as close to certain as you could be that the same person wrote this stuff."

"How did you find her?" I asked, scanning the highlights in the excerpts. Phrasing—especially odd ones—matched. It had to be her. And it all fit. Working in dispatch, she had 24/7 access to every radio in the department. Her "unnamed sources" didn't even know they were talking to her.

"I read every post on her blog three hundred times, and some stuff started to pop out at me. She has a good grasp of writing and structuring a news story. But she's green. So I started looking at the college papers," Shelby said. "I pulled samples from several issues throughout the year and ran them through the analyzer."

"That had to be hours of work." I smiled. "And it's brilliant. Thanks, Shelby."

"I hit this about three this morning, and then I couldn't sleep, I was so excited," she said. "I guess that's how you feel when you're working on one of your Nancy Drew stories."

"Just about. You're not a bad Nancy yourself."

"I'm more of a Bess," she said. "But I'm good with that. This was fun, Nichelle. Thanks for letting me help."

I wasn't sure I'd "let" her do anything. But since she seemed to want to think that, I just nodded.

"Let's go find a dispatcher, shall we?" I asked, another puzzle piece falling in as the times on the blog flitted through my head. "She works the early shift–that's why she doesn't post between seven and three."

Shelby was quiet on the short ride to police headquarters. I was glad of it, too many things whirling through my fried brain to make small talk.

We checked in at the desk and the sergeant smiled. "You here to see White or Landers?" he asked.

"Neither." Yet. "We're actually looking for a dispatcher this morning, Sam." I glanced at Shelby, waiting for the name.

"Alexa," she said brightly. "Alexa Reading."

"You aren't supposed to interview anyone without Detective White's say-so." Sam frowned.

"I'm not really looking for an interview." I smiled. "And I promise, Aaron would approve of my intentions."

He stared at me for half a second and smiled. "I've never known you to be a liar, Nichelle. Don't prove me wrong today, huh?"

I nodded.

"She's a quiet one." He stood, turning for the door that led to dispatch. "Be right back."

"I just bet she is," I mumbled to Shelby, mentally rehearsing what to say to Girl Friday.

"What are we going to do?" Shelby asked.

"Try to explain that she's being irresponsible," I said as Sam appeared in the doorway, a slight young woman with a soft brown bob on his heels.

"Can I help you?" She stopped in the doorway. "I have important work to do."

"I was hoping we could take a walk," I said, skipping an introduction because the look on her face said she knew good and well who I was. "I understand how important being near your desk is to four-one-one, but I'd like to talk to you for a few minutes."

Her eyes widened a touch, then flew to Sam, who didn't appear to be paying us any mind.

"I can't be away from nine-one-one long." She stressed the numbers. "But okay."

Shelby and I led her outside and a half-block down before we turned on her.

"How's it going, Girl Friday?" I asked.

"I don't know what you're talking about, Nichelle." She pursed her lips, folding her arms over her chest.

"But you know who I am," I said, my eyebrows going up.

"You work at the newspaper."

"It's not like my photo runs with my byline," I told her. "And Shelby here has pretty good proof that you're behind River City Four-one-one, so give it a rest. I'm not here to argue with you. I'm here to offer a few words of friendly advice."

"Let me guess," she said, her mouth twisting into a sneer. "You want me to go easy on the cops. They have an innocent man in jail and you couldn't care less. You don't deserve to have a byline."

Shelby took a step forward and opened her mouth. Since I wasn't sure I wanted to hear her opinion on that topic, I raised one hand and turned back to Alexa.

"You don't have the first damned clue what I do or don't care about," I said. "So if I were you, I'd watch the accusatory tone. I care very much about that guy and about this story. And you seem dead-set on wrecking everything anyone is trying to do here. That's not journalism, it's muckraking. It's irresponsible. Do you even understand the headlines you're running could incite a panic if your following gets any bigger?"

"The people deserve the truth," she said, eyes flashing.

I rolled mine. "Not at the expense of public safety."

"There's a serial killer running around the city, and you think not warning people is in the interest of public safety?" She shook her head. "Unbelievable. How did you end up with a job when I didn't?"

I blinked.

"First, I worked my ass off to get a job, and I work my ass off every day to keep it," I said. "Second, nobody is sure this is a serial killer, except maybe the people you've managed to convince with your sensational reports."

"You're just pissed because I beat you to the punch on the victim's identity this morning." She smirked, and my fingers itched to smack the look off her face. I folded them behind my back.

"I'd be lying if I said I wasn't annoyed, but I got my information honestly, and you didn't," I said.

"And Nichelle's story was better," Shelby piped up.

"I—" I glanced around. No Rod Serling. "Thanks, Shelby." I turned back to Alexa. "Look, you're stealing confidential police department information and broadcasting it online. And you're spinning it in a way that could cause big trouble. I get being young and passionate about the First Amendment, but you're going about this all wrong."

"And I suppose your way—letting the cops get away with whatever the hell they want—that's better?"

I closed my eyes as Shelby snorted. "I think someone missed a homework assignment," she said.

I grinned, meeting Alexa's angry stare. "Look, I don't know you, and to be honest, I don't really give a damn why you're so mad. I came to talk to you instead of turning your name over to Aaron, because he will fire you, and I don't fancy being responsible for anyone being out of work. I saw you were a recent j-school grad and I thought I could give you some advice. Maybe even help you out. Clearly, my mistake."

She blinked. "You can't get me fired."

"I have no authority over PD human resources, but if you think they won't can you when they find out it's you who's caused so many headaches this week, you are not as smart as I thought you were."

"You thought I was smart?" Something that looked like a smile touched her lips for half a blink.

"Anyone who can keep up with me and Charlie on a story this big isn't stupid," I said. "But you have an awful lot to learn about ethics."

"Get me fired." She lifted her head, glaring at me. "I'm not going away. Blogging is the next evolution of journalism. Newspapers will continue their slow death, and someone has to fill that void."

"And you're going to make a living at this...how?"

"Ad sales," she said, glancing at her watch. "My break is over. Are you finished lecturing me now?"

Twelve years and a hundred thousand subscribers in, the *Telegraph's* website only made a paltry amount from ads.

I glanced at Shelby. "We're done here," I said, flashing a smile at Alexa. "Good luck with your ad sales, Friday. You'll need it."

We walked further down Grace toward the car as she turned back to the PD.

"You're not going to see your detective friend?" Shelby asked.

I unlocked the car. "I'm going to think about it," I said. "She is causing trouble, but I want to make sure I'm ratting her out for the right reason— not because I'm tired of her constantly hanging over my head."

Shelby nodded. "You're a decent person, Nichelle."

I started the engine. "You're not so bad yourself, Shelby."

"When I'm not trying to get you killed," she muttered.

"I wasn't going to say it."

"It's okay," she said. "I deserve it."

I spent the drive back to the office wondering if my epic war with Shelby Taylor had reached a peace accord.

* * *

I let Shelby out and sped to the courthouse, standing through the morning arguments thanks to the packed gallery in DonnaJo's courtroom. I wrote the first half of the day two when we broke for lunch, emailing Bob a request for fifteen inches in Metro for the trial. I ran back early to snag a seat, then opened a text to Kyle.

"Wondering if you've had a chance to read background on your new assignment."

I tapped one finger on the edge of the screen, hoping he'd reply.

"Working on that now. Anything I should look for?"

"Edwin Wolterhall might have an interesting file," I said. "If you can lay your hands on a court transcript from his trial in California, I'll kiss you."

"Tempting. FOI?"

"Case is years old. Records sealed bc it involved a minor."

"Won't be easy. Let me work on it."

I grinned as the gallery started to refill, and DonnaJo winked at me from her seat at the Commonwealth's table. "Anything good?" she mouthed.

"Could be," I replied.

She nodded and turned as the judge called the court back to order.

I spent the next three hours trying to focus, but mostly taking notes on autopilot.

Speeding back to the office, I guessed it would take less than an hour to finish and file my story, which meant I could call Aaron about Girl Friday before I was supposed to meet Kyle. If I wanted to. Which I still hadn't decided.

Until I got to my desk and found a box sitting on top of the pile of press releases and messages in the center.

A camera. One of those little flat HD video ones. With a note from Andrews on *Telegraph* letterhead.

. . .

Our editor isn't interested in moving the paper forward, but perhaps his favorite reporter might be. Just try it. For Bob's sake.

I plopped into my chair, wadding up the note and tossing it in the recycle before I snatched the camera from the box and plugged it in, cursing Alexa Reading and her video.

Damn Rick Andrews. He wasn't getting rid of Bob if I could help it.

I texted Aaron. "Girl Friday works in dispatch on your first floor. Day shift. Alexa Reading."

Three seconds went by. "Are you sure?"

"Yeah. I talked to her," I tapped. "I feel a little stoogey, but thought you deserved to know."

"She signed a confidentiality agreement. Not your fault she violated it."

"Thanks." I added a smiley face.

Aaron did, too. "You just made my day."

I flipped open my laptop and banged out the rest of the trial day two, which included a lot of expert testimony on bullet trajectories and ballistics reports. This kid would spend the best years of his life behind bars before DonnaJo was through with him.

I sent the story to Bob as my cell phone started tinkling Disney classics. Unknown number. I frowned.

"Clarke," I said.

"Miss Clarke," the man whispered, and I covered my free ear and strained to hear him. "My name is Richard Galloway. I just wanted to—" His breath hitched in. "I don't know. You called about my little girl, and I had to call back. Thank you for caring about her."

My tongue was super-glued to the roof of my mouth. Landers said the mom was a nutcase.

"Hello?" he whisper-shouted.

"I'm here," I managed. "I'm surprised to hear from you. The detective I saw this morning said your wife was..." I trailed off, no clue how to finish inoffensively.

"She is." His hushed tone took on a hard edge. "I'm not. She holds her money over everyone like a noose. But I will see my baby have a Christian burial."

"I can let the police know that," I said. "Would you like to tell me a little about your daughter?"

I got only a muffled sob in response. "I loved her," he said. "I'm sorry I wasn't stronger."

A clatter in the background was followed by a shout and the line went dead.

I dropped the phone and grabbed a pen, scribbling.

He certainly sounded sincere. And didn't seem fond of his wife. But Landers was sure a man had killed Ruth and Cecilia both, and I was inclined to agree. Unless Wanda Galloway was unusually buff, she'd have had a hard time inflicting that kind of damage. I typed the Galloways into Google and found photos from the local paper in Wallingford. Wanda's flat scowl could wilt a whole garden, but neither of them looked like they'd been inside a gym in at least a decade. As I stared at the woman, my cell phone binged again.

Kyle: "I earned that kiss today. Check your email. And meet me at your place to get the dog in an hour."

I grabbed my bag and went to fill Bob in on Girl Friday before I headed out. Between Wolterhall's court transcript and Elise's plan to get me into Way of Life the next morning, my weekend was looking good.

26

I saw the car first.

It took half a second for cold to spread from my free-falling stomach to my fingers and toes. No. *Nonononono.*

Joey.

Who was invited for the weekend.

Joey.

Who I'd forgotten was coming.

He paced the length of my front porch with long, agitated strides, his shoulders coiled under his tailored navy jacket.

I slowed the car, still out of his sight line, my brain racing for what I could tell him. Certainly not that I was spending the weekend at Kyle's—even if I did intend (really) to sleep on the couch. Hello there, disaster waiting to happen.

Joey raised his phone to his ear, and my cell phone commenced buzzing in my bag.

I kept my foot on the brake, any semblance of a plan failing me.

The phone went silent and he pulled out a key and opened my front door, disappearing inside. To where the bullet holes were. I sped into the driveway.

Bolting for the porch and through the open door, I stopped short when he stepped into the foyer, Darcy snuggled under his left arm. "Nice shotgun scatter patterns someone left on your wall," his tone sounded almost conversational, but I caught the undercurrent of fury.

"It was an interesting Thursday." I leaned against the wall and tried for nonchalance, folding my arms across my chest.

"Dammit, Nichelle!" Beach glass trembled on the shelf behind me, and I flinched. I'd never heard Joey yell. He reached for me and froze, pulling in a deep breath before he set the dog deliberately on the floor and stood, his voice under tight rein, muscles standing out all around his collar. "You can't keep dismissing this like it's a game. When the other team has guns and knows where you live, you stop playing."

"I'm not playing at anything," I snapped. "And I'm more than a little offended at the insinuation. This is important."

"Why? Why is it so important you figure it out? No headline is worth this." Again with the yelling. Darcy scooted behind the coat rack. I kept flashing eyes on Joey, annoyed because I was excited to see him even with him treating me like I was five.

"I have several reasons, none of which I'm inclined to describe in detail for you right now," I said. "But the top of my list is that scatter pattern on the wall. I'm not backing off the story because they shot at me. If you don't already know that, you don't know me at all." I blinked, the telltale pricking in the backs of my eyes that went with tears just making me madder. Damn PMS.

He stepped toward me, his voice softening, and ran his index finger lightly over the bandages Kyle had put on my face. "Let the cops do their job." He tried to smile, catching me by the shoulders and pulling me to his chest.

I held my whole torso stiff.

"Why must you be so stubborn?" His arms tightened around me, his face buried in my hair. "I just want you to be safe."

I sighed, tension leaking from my body as I let the solid wall of his shoulders take the weight I'd been carrying all day. My arms looped around his waist. "My mother was here," I said into the butter-soft fabric of his jacket.

"What?" His chin thumped into the top of my head.

"She was here. She came to talk to me about," I paused, his happy family story from Sunday rolling around my thoughts. "Something. And she just left this morning."

"After this happened? She didn't take you with her because why?"

"She was sleeping. Pills and earplugs block out drive-bys, it appears."

"Drive-by. That's what the cops think?"

"That's what it was. I was on the couch. The window exploded, there were a few more shots, and a car sped off. RPD found a couple of guys a few blocks down who gave them a good description of the vehicle."

"You know anything else?" His voice sharpened again. I raised my head and pulled back. Guns, money, and the Mafia danced on the edges of my thoughts.

"I think the sheriff out in Fauquier is in Golightly's pocket."

"You're not wrong." The safe circle of his arms dropped, and he resumed prowling my little wood-floored foyer like a caged panther, one hand raking through his hair on repeat.

"I went by there when I got the ID on the victim yesterday, looking for a missing person's report. They were pretty uncooperative. I didn't flash my press credentials or anything, but the deputy followed me out and looked a little too long at my plates. This happened a few hours later."

He paused midstep, closing his eyes and resting his forehead on a clenched fist.

"Dammit, dammit, dammit." The last one carried rock-concert decibels. He straightened and slammed his fist into the wall. A hairline crack ran up the plaster from just above his hand to the ceiling.

I took a deep breath, trying to keep my adrenaline levels down. Joey never lost his cool. Twice in five minutes was enough to rattle me.

"This would all be a lot easier if you'd just tell me who killed—" The rest of the sentence stuck in my throat when Darcy darted out onto the porch, bouncing and yipping.

At Kyle.

He grinned and bent to scratch her ears. "You ladies ready to go?"

"Go where?" Joey threw me a questioning glance, and Kyle's grin vanished quicker than Eunice's armadillo eggs at the sports desk, his blue eyes settling on the scene before him.

I watched them both step closer to me, questions flashing in neon across their faces.

Damn. Damn. Damn.

* * *

Everything moved through Jell-O.

Kyle's eyes hit on the leather overnight case at Joey's feet before they flew to mine. "I see."

Crap. I'd been perfectly honest about wanting to be friends, but that didn't stop the hurt in his blue eyes from stabbing me in the gut. "Kyle, it's...complicated."

"Looks pretty self-explanatory to me." He set his jaw, one foot edging back toward the door.

"But... I don't think...it's not..." I fumbled for words and found none, so I laid one hand on his arm. "Please don't go away mad."

Joey stayed in the doorway to the living room, keeping his mouth shut. Thank God.

I tossed him a please-don't-leave glance and ushered Kyle out onto the porch.

"The last thing in the world I want is for you to be hurt, Kyle."

"That's the same guy. The one who was here wanting to go for a walk last Fall." The ice in his voice could've frozen the ninth ring of Hell. Which was currently located on my front porch. "He's the reason you're not 'feeling it' with me?"

"No!" It came out too fast, with too much force. He shook his head and I threw up my hands. "Not entirely. I'm at least sure of that. I came to pick up Darcy and you weren't here yet, but he was. The window and the shotgun holes freaked him out. We had plans I forgot about in all the trigger-happy bumpkin insanity."

Kyle slumped against the wall under the coach light and hauled in a deep breath, his jaw clenching and unclenching. The air whooshed back out and he turned serious blue eyes on me. "So, are you coming with me?"

Time stopped.

I didn't know.

But I couldn't tell him that. I turned back for the door, my brain racing for a solution that wouldn't leave someone with hurt feelings.

Total blank.

Joey's wingtips echoed across the floor inside, and he pulled the door open.

"I take it you knew about this?" He gestured to the boarded-up window, his eyes on Kyle.

Kyle stood up straight, the two of them practically nose-to-nose. "I was here when it happened."

Joey tipped his head to one side, his dark eyes flicking to me. "I see." The words were crisp. "At least you didn't let her get killed."

"She tries way too hard."

Lord save me. Where was a good plague of locusts or lightning strike when I needed one?

Kyle moved away from the wall, hands in his pockets affecting a casual pose. Joey stepped onto the porch, folding his arms across his chest. They moved in orbit around me, sizing each other up, both of them watching me like I might grow another head. If the physics had worked out in my favor, I would've. Anything to stop this testosterone fest.

"Miller, right?" Joey asked. My eyebrows shot to the top of my head.

Kyle nodded. "Special Agent," he hit that hard, "Miller. ATF. I'd like Nicey to stay at my place this weekend. I can keep her safe there."

He reached a hand toward me, then pulled it back when I glared at him. The words were sweet, but his motive had less to do with protecting me than it did beating Joey. And I wasn't too stupid to realize that.

Joey nodded, pretending to think that over for an endless minute. He turned his dark eyes on me. "If you'd be more comfortable at home, I'm happy to stay here with you," he said, the corners of his mouth edging up in that sardonic grin that usually turned my knees to gelato. "That was the plan anyway, right?"

I shot Joey the same watch-yourself glare I'd just thrown at Kyle. He wasn't lying. But he was being unnecessarily cruel, and that struck me as beneath him.

Kyle stiffened. "I'm a trained sharpshooter," was all he said. Crap.

"I'm pretty handy with a gun myself," Joey replied, his voice dropping ominously. I knew that tone. Double crap.

"And why would that be?" Kyle asked, his eyes going to Joey's midsection in search of a gun bulge under his jacket. There wasn't one. "It seems you know quite a bit more about me than I do about you."

"I do my homework," Joey said.

"I wasn't aware there was an assignment." Kyle's eyes flashed.

"I don't think that's my fault," Joey's voice kept the dangerous weight. "Or my problem. Agent Miller."

My eyes dropped to Kyle's calf, where I'd never known he carried a gun until last night. Not that I thought he would start shooting at people. But the tension in the air would've withstood a chainsaw.

"Why don't we rectify that?" Kyle's words had a hard edge. Commanding. I'd only ever heard it once before. My thoughts flashed back to a gasoline-soaked warehouse and a very different standoff. "Starting with your name."

"I don't think that's any of your business. I'm sure Nichelle will tell you anything about me she thinks you need to know." Joey's fingers curled into a fist at his side, his eyes cutting to me as he stepped toward Kyle.

"I'm sorry, did it sound like a question?" Kyle put one foot forward, his nostrils flaring. "It wasn't."

Joey's arm twitched.

My eyes ping-ponged between them for half a heartbeat. No matter who swung first, Joey would wind up in handcuffs for decking a federal agent, and Kyle would waste no time with fingerprints and a background check that would produce everything including Grandma's lasagna recipe.

And that was only the first reason I didn't want them in a brawl on my porch.

Profiles tense and fists balled, they each took another step.

I jumped into the middle.

"That's enough," I said, wriggling around so I had one hand on each chest. Their heart rates would've convinced any doctor they'd just run a marathon.

"Go in the house, Nichelle," the words slid through someone's teeth, so low I couldn't swear who said them. So I lost my temper with them both.

"Did I stutter? That's enough!" I stomped one Manolo and shoved with both arms. They each staggered back half a step, tight jaws going slack. "While I think you both have honorable intentions—or you did when you got here, at least—I feel a bit too much like that baby in King Solomon's court. So I'll thank you to take your hormone overdose elsewhere."

Kyle looked like I'd slapped him. "Nichelle—" he began.

I kept my hand up. "Not right now."

"You're not safe here," he said.

"I assure you, she's perfectly safe with me," Joey said.

I whirled on one heel, my head verging on explosion. "Stop. It." I bit out.

"You can't stay here alone." Kyle stepped to the door, laying a hand on the knob. "If you don't want to come with me," his Adam's apple bobbed with a hard swallow, "at least let your friend here stay."

"The one who offers to give up the baby keeps her in that parable, yes?" Joey murmured, glancing between me and Kyle. He arranged his face into the stoically unreadable drive-Nichelle-batshit-crazy look, his armor of composure settling back around him.

"This isn't about winning," Kyle said, his eyes on me. "It's about keeping you from getting killed."

"If that's the objective, I suggest we consider the possibility our friends with the shotgun could be the least of our worries," Joey said, pulling a folded newspaper from inside his jacket.

Kyle and I both turned questioning eyes on him. He opened the paper to my story on Jasmine (Ruth. Whatever.)'s identity, and folded it back, holding up the photo Larry had sharpened and enlarged.

"Say the cops are right and this is a serial," Joey said, his gaze flicking between me and Kyle.

I opened my mouth to object, and he raised one hand. "I'm not agreeing with them. Just asking you to consider it. Maybe a serial with ties to your televangelist, even."

"I'm listening," I said.

"You don't see it?" That was directed at Kyle, whose sharp intake of breath told me I was out of the loop.

"She's pretty," I said, snatching the paper and studying the picture. "She looks happy. Friendly."

"She looks..." Joey exchanged a glance with Kyle, who turned horrified eyes on me.

"Like you." Kyle finished, barely above a whisper. "She looks like you. Nichelle, please come home with me."

Joey leaned against the porch railing. "Your call, sweetheart."

My brain reeled, my eyes flashing from one of them to the other and back to the photograph in my hands. She had long dark hair. A straight nose. Nicely-almond-shaped green eyes. With their words rolling around my head, she didn't look unlike me. Cecilia Erickson's Facebook photo skated through my thoughts, and my stomach plummeted to my knees.

"Your involvement with the story would put you on a serial's radar," Kyle said. "Nichelle—" he stopped, his gaze screaming a plea.

Mine jumped back and forth across the porch.

"I can't." The words strangled around the lump in my throat.

Joey reached for my hand, but I pulled away, brushing past Kyle and grabbing the dog and her bag before I turned for my car.

"You're right. Both of you. It'd be stupid to stay here alone before someone figures out what's going on. But I can't choose. So I choose me. I'm sorry if I've done anything to hurt either of you—please, please know it wasn't intentional." My breath hitched, and I put my free hand to my throat.

"Nichelle," Joey's pitch rose with alarm.

"We'll be fine."

I ran for the car before the tears could spill over. Backing out of the driveway, I caught a watery glimpse of something I never thought I'd see— Kyle and Joey standing together, gesturing and talking like they were planning a golf weekend—or maybe about to pick up where I'd interrupted their fistfight.

I didn't stick around to see which.

27

Driving northwest out of Richmond, I didn't spare the horses until Culpepper. I found a four-room inn nestled on a corner in the historic district. Where better to hide from the world than a charming Victorian with wraparound porches and plenty of rockers?

And an owner who might take a check. With no idea who was looking for me, I didn't want to use a credit card or visit an ATM anytime soon.

I parked in a gravel lot out back with only one other car and tucked Darcy under one arm.

A brass bell over the front door announced my arrival and a woman who looked much more like Mrs. Claus than anyone I'd ever actually met closed the ledger on her antique cherry desk and looked up. "Can I help you, doll?" She flashed two rows of denture-perfect teeth.

She could. And did. I took a key ten minutes later and climbed the sweeping staircase to the Jefferson room.

It was just as period and lovely as the rest of the house, dominated by a giant claw-footed tub and a stone fireplace. I set up Darcy's bed, food, and water in the opposite corner from the tub and kicked my heels off, crossing the plush rug to the canopy bed. Flinging myself across it, I let my thoughts wander.

A dead woman who looked like me. Enough to scare both of the men I refused to think about.

It wasn't a serial—and if it was, I was in the best place I could be. But my gut said Landers was lifting rocks to no avail. Twelve hours ago, he'd seemed on the verge of admitting as much.

I knew why he had to focus there. Public safety was his first priority.

The truth was mine.

So what did I know?

Aaron and Landers had the wrong person in jail. I'd eat my Manolos if I was wrong about that. And I knew they knew it, too. Politics in policework irritates me on a good day, but this nonsense had me plain old pissed off. The sooner they knew who really did it, the sooner Picasso would be free. A little voice in the back of my head said I'd be freeing him to go back to peddling portraits for pennies.

Wait. What if it didn't have to be that way?

I sat up, snatching up the phone.

Jenna sounded out of breath when she picked up, but her tone brightened when she heard my voice. "What's going on with you?"

"Enough for a half-dozen margaritas," I said. "But until we have time for that, I have a question for you: do you still know anyone in the RAU art department?"

"My favorite prof is the department chair there," she said. "We had lunch just last month. Why? Did an artist kill those women?"

"The cops have one in custody, but I don't think he did," I said. "He's homeless. Young. I think he's mildly autistic. Nice guy, and he's really talented, Jen. I've only seen pencil sketches, but—"

"Did he do the sketches I saw in the paper?" She pulled in a sharp breath. "I knew those didn't come from the PD. The lines, the subtle shadows—that was great work."

"He did. I'd like for him to not return to being homeless when they have to let him go. You think you can help?" It was a big favor.

I needed desperately to do something good for someone.

"Worth a shot. There's always room for that kind of talent on a faculty," she said. "You think he could teach?"

"I think so." I sighed, a smile flitting across my face. "Thank you, doll."

"Anytime. You okay?"

"Eh," I said. "I'll be better when this story is filed and we can catch up."

I hung up and flipped my laptop open, clicking into the sealed court transcript Kyle sent me.

Three hours later, I looked up from my screen when Darcy yipped and scratched at the foot of the bed.

If it wasn't Jealous Jared, it was Wolterhall.

It had to be. The testimony was horrifying. Violent. And his weapon of choice? A knife.

Somebody bought a juror to cause that dismissal.

I stood and clipped Darcy's leash to her collar. "Two seconds, girl," I said, looping the leash over my wrist and unzipping my bag. I pulled out navy cotton slacks and a white oxford with a button-down collar, laying them carefully over the armchair and smoothing out wrinkles before I clicked my tongue at Darcy and turned for the door.

Elise said the ministers at Way of Life worked Saturdays.

Hopefully Mr. Wolterhall did, too.

* * *

My alarm buzzed before the stars faded from the inky sky, and Darcy growled from her bed when I turned the lamp on.

"This is not my idea of fun, either," I said as I pulled on the academy uniform and brushed my hair. She tucked her face under a paw.

No makeup, per Elise's instructions, meant a little moisturizer and a quick look in the mirror, and I was ready to go. I slid Andrews's infernal camera into my pocket, just in case I could get Bob a few brownie points with it. Laying a potty pad next to the tub for Darcy, I ruffled her fur on my way out the door.

I started the car, pausing to open the text messages on my cell phone before I started the half-hour drive to Way of Life.

Swallowing hard, I clicked Joey's number. "Have some snooping to do today. Know you're mad, but you love D. She's at the Rose House Inn in Culpepper. Just in case. Wish this weekend had gone as planned. Really." I hit send before I could chicken out.

My cell phone binged ten minutes into my drive. I didn't look. The heaviness in my stomach said I couldn't deal with Joey's goodbye and still focus on work. Psycho first. Tears later.

I cranked up Janis Joplin, questions from the list I'd made during the world's longest soak in that fabulous tub the night before flitting around my head. If I could manage a chat with Wolterhall and find the minister Jasmine worked with, I'd call the day a win. And maybe help Aaron get the warrant he was after, too.

I parked alongside a narrow dirt drive behind the barn, the first cantaloupe-colored rays of day peeking over the horizon. Thankful for my sneakers, I turned toward the shed, probably a quarter-mile across the pasture.

Easing the door open, I peeked through the crack. Empty. I slipped inside and leaned on the edge of the workbench stretching the length of the back wall. Deep breaths. As long as I wasn't obvious, I was safe.

Elise said the ministerial staff didn't keep track of the students closely, no matter how well their assistants helped them fake it. That was the crucial thing about Saturday: no assistants. I was fuzzy on the why, but it had something to do with preparing for service in solitude to receive God's anointing. And saving people's souls from the fires of eternal Hell. The day off was a bonus for the secretaries.

My gaze roamed over the feed bags, still in their perfectly symmetrical stacks. Four days since I'd been there last, and there wasn't a single bag missing. Surely they didn't order those one at a time?

Before I could consider that fully, voices—male ones—took over ninety percent of my attention. The other ten whirled desperately for an escape route.

Early morning. When they feed the livestock.

Shit, shit, double shit.

I shoved the toolbox aside and dove under the bench, pulling the case back in front of me and trying not to yelp when I lost a nail to the corner. Putting the end of my smarting finger in my mouth, I tasted blood and blinked back tears, but dropped my head to my knees and stayed quiet.

The door crashed open half a minute later, the guys divvying up work. "Let's get done and go back to bed" was the general theme of their conversation. Sending a thank you heavenward, I hugged my knees and tried to be as small and invisible as possible.

"Why do we have to do this on Saturday, anyway?" One guy said. "They have miles of grass out there. They won't starve."

"A glad heart and many hands make light work," another replied. "Your outlook is selfish. We're saving the eternal souls of every person here by keeping our food sources pure. Like the reverend says, pure food makes a pure soul and brings us closer to God."

The road to Hell was paved with Pop-Tarts? My eyes popped wide, but I kept quiet.

The other voice grouched quieter. Plastic met plastic—bins opening and closing, maybe. Mr. Pure began singing a hymn under his breath, which sounded so close I was too petrified to look up.

A rattling that signified buckets being picked up followed, then retreating footsteps. The doors opening and closing. Three heartbeats. Five. I raised my head and blinked. Easing the toolbox aside, I peeked out from under the workbench. Alone again. I wanted out of the shed before they came back, and I had no frame of reference for when that might be. But if I ran, I might miss Elise. I also might be spotted by the cow feeder guys. Damn.

I bit my lip and pulled the ragged fingernail the rest of the way off, flinging a drop of blood to the floor and trying not to get any on my clothes.

Just as I rocked onto all fours to crawl out of my hidey hole, the door opened. "Leigh?" Elise hissed.

"Present," I whispered.

She scurried through the door and pulled me to my feet. "I saw those guys and almost had a stroke," she said. "They're early. And it's Saturday, too."

"They said something about going back to bed." I dusted off my pants.

"I'm sorry," she said. "They didn't see you?"

"No."

"Let's get out of here before they come back," she said.

"Where are we going at this hour?"

"To open the coffee shop. You're new. I'm training you." She winked and waved me outside. "No one has a way to confirm anything until Monday, not that they'll ask." She gave me a once-over. "Nice work. You'll blend perfectly."

I followed her out into the thick summer air, curiosity burning a hole in my frontal lobe. "Why do you stay if you don't believe?" I asked.

"Oh, I believe." She smiled. "In normal circles, I'd be considered a zealot. But I believe in Jesus and Heaven and the Bible. And I'm not sure the reverend believes in the same ones. I've just never been able to decide if I'm right. What if it's Satan planting seeds of doubt about the mission? Jasmine..." she trailed off, her voice breaking.

I laid a hand on her arm. "There are too many people looking at this for it to go unanswered, Elise. We'll figure it out."

"She deserved better," she said.

I nodded. I'd never seen a murder wrapped in quite so much intrigue, but every dead end made me more determined to dig up an answer. The boyfriend and Wolterhall jostled for top of my suspect list.

"So, where do we start?" I asked, following her into the main building.

"You know how to make a latte? Two of the ministers are always up early on Saturdays. Even without your makeup, I have a feeling they'll want to talk to you."

I grinned and quickened my steps. I would leave Way of Life with some answers today. I could feel it.

28

Few things are creepier than a big, empty building. Except maybe a big, empty building full of ginormous, razor-edged gold crosses.

I followed Elise to the coffee bar. She made me a white mocha while I followed her prompts to punch it into the touch screen register. "Three-twenty-six?" I asked.

"You're hired." She grinned.

I sipped my coffee and studied her. "I gather you haven't always been so suspicious of the reverend?"

"Oh, no. The first year I was here saved my life. I found purpose." She made herself a coffee and took a sip, pulling a worn Bible from her bag under the counter and laying it on the bar. "I found faith. We never went to church when I was growing up. Funny, they say kids who grow up with religion rebel by leaving the church. Like Jazz. I guess the grass is always greener."

"What changed for you?"

"I still didn't fit in," she said. "Everyone is always nice, because it's unchristian to be mean. But I'm the odd duck. Jasmine was my first real friend. Some of the things she said, put together with things I saw when I worked in the office and things I see here every day—I'm just not sure the reverend is as invested in everyone's spiritual well-being as he professes to be."

"Why?"

She sighed. "The revival started it. Once, during a summer revival, they asked for extra volunteers to pray over the donations. People came from all over that week, and the reverend touched so many of them with God's grace. It was amazing. People walked for the first time in years after he laid hands on them. Miracles left and right for three straight days."

"Wow."

"We're supposed to pray for those who made donations at the end of every service. I mean, we do it at the academy, but to be in the room while the reverend blesses the donations and prays for the people who gave, that's a big deal. I wanted it so badly. I prayed all week. And I was chosen." Her tone took a left into darkness, her fingers moving to rifle the edges of her Bible's pages.

"What happened?"

"There was a thirty-second plea for God to bless the generous souls, and then we sat at tables and counted while his assistant reported the totals to him every few minutes. There was so much money. Too much money. I counted thirty thousand dollars in small bills, and there were twenty other people in the room doing the same thing." She looked up, her eyes screaming questions I had no answers for. "If you read this book, Jesus didn't have much. He was a simple man. He talked about the poor and meek being blessed. The people with the money were the ones who killed him, right? How can it be Godly to take in that much money?"

Oh, boy. "I suppose it depends on what you do with it," I said.

"They don't use the majority of it to help those less fortunate than themselves, that's for sure," she said. "Which is something else Jesus said. But when I started asking questions about it, at first they told me God wanted to bless them for their hard work and faith. Then they just asked me to leave them alone. Questions aren't favored around here, I warn you."

Of course not.

People who have something to hide never like questions.

Before I could consider that further, the door to the office across the hall opened and the young minister who'd introduced Golightly on Sunday stepped to the counter. He flashed a Colgate-commercial grin and asked Elise for a caramel latte.

She whipped it together and passed it to me, blessing him and poking me, her you're-on look barely registering.

Nothing registered, really—because for the first time in my life, I was staring into eyes that looked just like mine.

I scanned his face, running mentally through my bio file. Brady. The guy's last name was Brady. And he was the only minister on the staff who was younger than me.

Tall, well-built, amazing hair.

And the eyes. Holy freaking mirror image, Batman.

Elise poked me again, and I shook my head. Maybe he wore contacts.

And maybe Richmond had a serial killer. Eight years at the crime desk had taught me true coincidences are few and far between.

Brady smiled. "Good morning. How are you on this beautiful day the Lord has blessed us with?"

I jabbed at the register screen. Focus. They were just contacts. Right? What had Elise said to that wretched woman the other day?

"Blessed and favored of the Lord," she chirped. "Oh, I'm sorry, sir. Leigh, I think he was talking to you."

"Blessed and favored of the Lord." And confused as hell. "Three-twenty-six, sir."

He handed me a five and told Elise to keep the change.

"You're blowing it," she muttered out of the corner of her mouth.

What? I looked up as he turned for the offices, searching the facts I had.

Brady was the one Jasmine worked for. Double hell.

"Pastor," I blurted. All this work to get in spitting distance of these guys. I couldn't let him leave when he was right there.

He paused, the jumbotron smile turning back to face me. "Yes?"

"I was wondering, if you, um, could maybe pray with me about something?" The words flowed out as fast as I could think them.

His smile widened. "Of course. I'm never too busy to pray with a young sister in the Lord."

I glanced at Elise, and his brow furrowed. "Would you be more comfortable speaking in confidence?"

I nodded, and he motioned for me to follow him.

Point Nichelle.

Now, what did I need prayers for that wasn't catching the killer? Lying to a minister felt—well, like I'd go to Hell, no matter how honorable my intentions. Southern Baptist Sunday school lessons whispered through my thoughts as I followed Brady to his office.

Which was...damn. I had to bite my cheek to keep from whistling. The Oval Office had nothing on Way of Life in terms of opulence. Polished floors, Persian rugs, a stone fireplace, and dark, heavy furniture filled the space. Pentagonal beams outlined a star in the ceiling, a crystal and bronze chandelier dangling from the center.

Brady shut the door and gestured to the sofa in front of the fireplace. "Please. I hope you're well."

"I'm just worried," I said.

"Phillippians chapter four: Don't worry about anything, instead pray about everything." He smiled, sitting in a chair opposite me. "Tell God your needs and don't forget to thank Him for His answers. If you do this you will experience God's peace."

"Maybe worried is the wrong word. I guess I'm feeling a little lost."

"How?" He leaned forward, resting his elbows on his knees, his eyes laser-focused on me. He was charming. And all in this conversation. Could he have killed someone?

I returned the stare. My creep radar said no. I groped for an honest reply. "I just...how can we find our true path with certainty?" I actually wanted the answer to that more than I'd thought when I walked in there.

"Ah." He nodded. "I hear this from many students every year. I was lucky, I guess, because I never questioned the path. I was always headed for the ministry, and I'm right where I want to be."

"But how did you know?" I pressed.

"I was raised for it," he said. "My parents—they were deeply religious people. My father was very involved in several ministries in California where I grew up. He and the reverend developed a friendship, and I came here to the Academy when my mom and dad went home to Jesus."

I flinched. His father was dead? And from California? "I'm—I'm so sorry."

"I'm not. Death is the last obstacle to eternal peace. I really believe that, but I know not everyone has my faith."

"I think that's lovely," I said, perfectly sincere. The idea of losing my mother terrified me to my bones. I admired Brady's ability to have peace with his loss.

His loss. Not mine. Even if the universe had a seriously skewed sense of humor here, I'd never met my father, and never had any desire to.

He nodded, opening a book on the coffee table to reveal a hollow interior filled with chocolates. He plucked one from the pile and nodded to me. "One of my weaknesses. But they make me happy." He winked.

I took one and returned his smile. "Thank you." I paused, drumming my fingers on my knee. I wanted to ask him about Jasmine, but wasn't sure how far to push. On one hand, Elise said they didn't like questions. On the other, I was here. What did I have to lose?

"That is comforting," I said. "Especially when we lose friends young. Like Jasmine. She and Elise were close, but thinking of her being with the Lord makes it easier."

His face fell, but he recovered the smile before most people would have noticed. It didn't reach his eyes.

"I wasn't aware anyone was still in touch with Jasmine." He blinked hard, clearing his throat. "She was a good assistant and a sweet young woman. Heaven has gained another angel if she's no longer with us."

I left it. Either he'd inherited some acting skills from my mom's old flame, or he really didn't know she was dead. Elise said they told the Academy students TV and newspaper would cloud their faith. Maybe Brady practiced what he preached?

I switched gears before my brain could get too mired in the possibility of this guy being my half-brother. Remote? I couldn't say for sure. The evidence certainly appeared stacked in favor of it. Not that I knew how to start that conversation, even if I'd wanted to.

"You're very sure about God's purpose for you." I leaned forward, clasping my hands in front of me. "But you look so young. How old are you? Can I ask?"

"I'm twenty-seven," he said. Two years younger than me. My stomach did a slow somersault as he went on. "I was raised for this. Chosen. Age has no bearing on destiny. By the time Jesus was my age, he had performed many miracles."

"When you put it that way, I feel like a slacker." I smiled

"Everyone who seeks faith will find their way to it," he said. "That's something the reverend says often, and I believe it."

In my experience, the truth works the same way.

He smiled and bowed his head. "Shall we pray?"

I closed my eyes and listened to his strong baritone, asking silently for some insight into Jasmine's murder.

"Amen," I said in unison with Brady.

"Go with God, washed in the blood," he said as I turned to leave.

I stumbled at the words. Washing in blood was a thing with these folks. Could that have something to do with the horror scene—and cow's blood —in the switch house?

29

I pulled Brady's door shut behind me, so deep in trying to finagle a connection I didn't hear the other door open.

"Good morning." A smooth baritone pulled my attention back to the present, and I tossed my hair back as I looked up.

At a grinning, gray-at-the-temples Edwin Wolterhall.

My eyes flitted toward the ceiling. That was quick.

"Good morning," I said. "What a beautiful day the Lord has graced us with today." I followed the words with a smile. The greetings they offered each other were nice, as long as they were sincere. The scripted vibe was the creepy part. It smacked of overlord-type control. I glanced at Golightly's closed door.

"It is indeed." Wolterhall paused outside his door. "Can we help you with something?"

"Pastor Brady was praying with me," I said.

His brows flew up, his eyes skimming over me before they went to the clock. "I see."

Somehow I thought he saw wrong, but I wasn't sure how to correct that. Elise said Wolterhall was no stranger to mistresses, though his taste seemed to run ten or more years my junior.

He put one hand on his doorknob.

"We prayed for Jasmine," I blabbed, my only thought to stop him from walking away. "For the people here who knew her. For her soul. She was murdered."

His whole face sagged, the polished mahogany door catching his body when it followed suit. "She what? She...No. She left. She wasn't happy here. Didn't want to be here in the first place."

Afraid to even breathe as I watched him talk through it, I felt a little more wind leave my sails.

I'd walked through the door almost sure Wolterhall—or maybe Wolterhall and someone else—had killed Jasmine. And in less than ten minutes, these guys had both convinced me of their innocence. They didn't even seem to know she was dead.

I reconsidered my suspect list: someone from the streets? Maybe someone who knew enough about her past to set the scene in an effort to point here?

Jealous Violet.

But she was so tiny, I couldn't see that unless she had help.

Back home boyfriend Jared.

He should be in custody by now, so if it was him, I'd know soon enough.

I twisted my fingers together, wishing this were a less convoluted mess.

"Did anyone know when she left or where she went?"

He shook his head. "I didn't. I don't know about anyone else. It was God's will. Better for everyone."

"How was it God's will for her to leave the path you provide here?" The question popped out before I could stop it, hanging in the air like a storm cloud.

Wolterhall's brow furrowed, his eyes searching my face. I kept it as neutral and naive as I could.

"The Lord blesses us for our faith." His face said the words were chosen with care. "In many ways. Jasmine was not one of our flock."

Then why would God send her there in the first place? I wanted to ask, but I also didn't want to make him any more skeptical of my presence. Either he was a damned good actor, or he wasn't my killer. But he was still a shady dude.

And I was stuck for who killed Jasmine. And/or Cecilia, whose death may or may not be related. This story had more blanks than a Mad Libs.

Wolterhall opened his office door just as my brain produced an idea.

The mother.

"Her family must be devastated," I said.

"I'm sure they'll find solace in their faith," he said. "Her parents are longtime members of the church. Staunch believers."

"Do they come for Sunday service?" I'd need a whopping disguise to come back the next day without them noticing something was off, but assuming I could slip under the shoe police's radar, I could look for her folks. And Cecilia's boss, too.

"Her mother is housebound," he said. "For physical reasons."

Well, crap.

The abortion stuck out as motive. So did the possible blackmail.

Had Elise found out who the Way of Life boyfriend was?

Too many questions. I needed more coffee. And a notebook.

A notebook.

Jasmine's journals.

Someone who'd kept them so compulsively for so many years didn't take a two-year hiatus. Elise said so—"she was always writing in them." But they weren't in the box.

Except what if they were?

What if her box worked like Brady's hollow book?

Because she'd written something worth hiding?

I smiled at Wolterhall, who was lost in his own thoughts.

"I will pray for her. And her loved ones." Who may or may not claim her body. Those people needed some prayers, if you asked me.

"We will, as well." He turned and disappeared into his office without the customary blood-farewell thingy. I'd rattled him, but why?

Halfway back to the coffee shop, I froze. What if Elise was asking the wrong people about who Jasmine was seeing?

What if Jasmine had been seeing Wolterhall?

Running the last few steps to the coffee bar, I spotted the teacher, Mathers, at the back of the line and dropped my hair over my profile before he could stare long enough to figure out why I didn't belong. I tapped two fingers on the counter in time to *Suspicious Minds* as Elise made coffee for two hundred and thirty nine people. (Or five. Who took forever.)

When Mathers took his latte and turned for the doors that led out to a gorgeous summer day, I leaned across the counter.

"I need that box. The one Jasmine kept her things in." I fought to restrain my voice. "I have an idea."

* * *

Counting doors in Elise's hallway, I repeated "blessed and favored of the Lord," in my head on a loop, hoping it would pop out of my mouth if someone asked me how I was. Elise couldn't get away from the coffee counter in the middle of the morning, but she winked and told me which door was hers when I asked for a key.

No locks. How could I forget?

I held my breath for the second it took me to open the seventh door on the left and scan the room. I half-expected to find someone inside, searching for the journals. But they'd done that months ago. I hoped I was right about where they might be hidden.

Shutting the door behind me, I scooted the chair in front of it for good measure before I knelt in the floor of the closet. The loose board was right where Elise said it was, the box nestled safely in the space beneath.

I shot a glance at the cross on the wall and hoped I myself was blessed and favored of the Lord right then.

I raised the lid, the broken lock offering no resistance, and emptied the contents carefully into the floor. Scanning it inside and out, I noticed a two-inch difference in the depth of the thing. Clever girl, that Jasmine.

Raising the box to my ear, I shook it.

Muffled clunking.

"Thank you," I whispered, examining the side for a telltale crack.

No luck.

I flipped it upside down.

Nothing.

But there was something in that two inches of space.

If it didn't open from the side, it had to open from the middle.

I ran a fingernail around the edge of the fake bottom plate. And found a crack.

Bingo.

I stood and moved to the dresser, hunting a nail file. Maybe I could pry it loose.

No dice. Searching the bathroom turned up a fat purple emery board. Ugh. I flopped onto the edge of the bed that had been Jasmine's. So. Freaking. Close.

I pulled open the little drawer in the nightstand. Three hair bands, a tube of honey-almond lotion, and a razor case.

A silver one.

I snatched it out of the drawer, my fingers shaking as I popped the tab on the side and watched it flip open.

How on Earth had this woman gone from shaving her legs with something from Tiffany's to living on the streets?

Maybe Tiffany's could help me find out.

Wriggling a replacement blade from the top of the case, I turned back for the closet.

Running the corner of the blade along the teensy crack, I found three catches. I went back to each in turn, working them with the sliver of steel. Two pushes on the third one, and the plate popped out like a jack-in-the-box.

I flipped the razor aside, pulling three fabric-covered journals from the bottom of the box.

Flipping the first open, I checked the dates. It covered Jasmine's first year at Way of Life. The second covered her last.

The first page of the third screamed "VICE" in all capital letters.

I pulled my cell phone from my pocket and checked the time. Quarter to eleven. Elise said she wouldn't be done 'til after five.

I had time to start back in Wallingford, then. I added the older journals from the floor to my stack and settled myself on Jasmine's bed, ready for some reading—and some answers.

30

Ruth Galloway loved Jesus, puppies, and the smell of fresh cut roses.

She also hated and feared her mother enough to keep Emily busy for the rest of her career.

But not her father. She idolized him. Missed him.

And pitied his inability to say boo to her mother.

Tear-stained pages held diatribes about Jesus being benevolent, and the Bible never being intended as a club to beat people into a certain way of thinking.

Others were scarred with angry grooves from harsh pen strokes, labeling Wanda Galloway a "prude" and detailing beatings that would give Satan himself nightmares.

She'd been sent to Way of Life as a pseudo-punishment, like Elise said.

But the hope she'd arrived with poured from the pages.

People were nice.

Jesus was love.

Everything was so beautiful, she changed her name to match the flowers that bloomed near the porch swing where she studied her Bible every night.

I flipped pages as fast as my fingers could manage, so engrossed in the story I didn't notice the hours slipping by.

Halfway through the last journal, Jasmine went to work in the church offices. While a few passages here and there had echoed some of the doubts Elise voiced about the reverend and his mission, Jasmine was mostly happy. Ben Mathers's music class was her favorite, Christian philosophy a close second.

All of page fifty-eight was rimmed in haloed-cross-doodles. She'd been chosen. To work with the ministers. To help save souls.

Her father would be so proud. Maybe her mother, too—those words were between the lines, but came through as clear as any on the page.

On page sixty-three, Wolterhall hit on her for the first time.

More tearstains spattered hurried scribbles that, best I could decipher, detailed Elise's story about Wolterhall's dalliances.

Faith wounded, Jasmine turned him down. Again on page sixty-eight. A third time on seventy-two.

How did she get pregnant? I flipped faster.

On page eighty-four, she asked Brady to join her for coffee after work one day. She trusted him. She wanted to confide that Wolterhall's advances were shaking her belief and ask for help.

Page eighty-eight: *Prayers answered. Pastor Brady is such a wonderful man. He loves having my help and will speak to Mr. Wolterhall.*

Page ninety-three: *Pastor Brady's hand brushed over my breast when he reached past me for a book this afternoon. I didn't know a simple touch could make me feel that way.*

Page ninety-seven: *Pastor Brady offered me a dinner out in Warrenton as a thank you for my help with this week's sermon. We shared a bottle of wine, my first since I arrived here—I guess it went to my head, because I told him how attractive he was. But when I apologized and said no woman except his wife should say such things, he smiled and said feelings aren't a sin. Because if they were, why would God give them to us? Then he said he felt the same way about me. That his marriage has been a sham for years.*

My breath stopped.

Flip.

On page ninety-nine, Jasmine slept with Brady for the first time.

* * *

I skimmed the rest of the journal entries from that year—they read like an erotic Christian romance (if that were a real thing).

They stopped the day her period was officially a month late.

I opened the Vice book. The dates spanned a two-week period between the end of her last journal and the day she left the academy. The second page had only a quote from first John chapter one.

If we confess our sins, he is faithful and just to forgive us our sins, and to cleanse us from all unrighteousness.

Each pastor and employee at Way of Life had a page, except Golightly.

Each page listed different behaviors and labeled the person named at the top with a vice of some sort.

I scanned for names I recognized.

Wolterhall's was lust.

Pink Jenny's was righteousness

Ben Mathers's was envy.

Brady's was power.

I closed the book, looking around and wishing there was an unobtrusive way to get the journals out of the room and into Aaron's hands. Surely the killer's MO and what was in those books was enough for a warrant to turn this joint upside down and shake it good. And if a few gun runners fell out with the riffraff, so much the better.

But my button-down wasn't baggy enough to smuggle six-hundred-plus pages out of the dorm without raising some eyebrows.

Dammit.

I took them back to the closet, tucking them into the lockbox. Picking up a photo of a laughing Jasmine and her friends, I stared into her happy green eyes. Eyes that looked nothing like the glassy ones haunting my nightmares.

"What happened to you?" I whispered.

She only smiled. I felt my own lips turn down, sorrow at the loss of the light in her eyes washing over me. She'd written such beautiful words about dreams and hope, despite the hopelessness of her situation. I would find the truth—she deserved it. Truth, and a proper burial. Reading her journals brought her to life. Made her a friend. No matter whether anybody else cared what happened to her, I did.

I stowed the box back in its hidey-hole. Elise could help me get it to the car when she got through with work.

In the meantime, I wanted to see if I could talk to anyone else without getting in too much trouble.

Power, envy, lust, righteousness—people had killed for less.

I moved the chair from in front of the door and opened it, my eyes taking a minute to adjust to the dim hallway. I turned to check the window, where solidly late-afternoon beams seeped through the sheers.

I reached for my cell phone as I stepped into the hallway, blinking at the numbers on my screen. How in God's name was it five-forty?

Before I had time to ponder that, something round and blunt—and about an inch and a half across—poked into the small of my back, a large hand landing on my shoulder.

"Snooping," an accented, sandpapery bass murmured into my ear, "is the eighth deadly sin. Step into my office, and let's pray for your soul."

* * *

It wasn't Golightly. The voice didn't match the smooth-as-warm-honey tenor that had flowed from the speakers in my car all week.

Marching across the lawn to the church building, I cut my eyes side to side several times, not catching enough of the guy holding the gun in my back to ID him. People milled all around us, but the thought of what might happen to the Bible scholars if I called attention to my predicament was enough to keep me from trying it.

Inside, my invisible friend opened a door almost hidden in a wood-paneled wall and hustled me through a labyrinth of hallways lined with offices. I scanned for names, but the plain brown doors were unmarked.

Opening a corner one, he shoved me inside and closed it behind him. "Please have a seat." The way he waved the gun said it wasn't a request. I did, fixing a neutral expression on my face before I looked up to study his.

"So nice to meet you, Miss Clarke." Silver hair. Olive skin. Straight nose. Strong jaw. Slight belly bulge. Lines around the eyes. Impeccably tailored suit.

Crap hell.

Joey's "friend" paced the floor gracefully, tucking the black semi-automatic back under his jacket and shaking his head at my stoic once-over. "I admit, I rather hoped this wouldn't happen. I have an associate who's going to be sorry to lose you."

The temperature in the room plummeted thirty degrees on the last two words, the needle on my creep radar buried in the far end of "murderer."

Maybe not as sorry as he thought, but he didn't need to know that. Hopefully, I could work Joey to my advantage.

"I don't think I'd want him upset with me." My voice sounded controlled. Amazing, since my emotional state bordered on hysteria.

The chuckle and hand wave told me this guy wasn't impressed. If I thought too hard about what kind of man wasn't afraid of Joey, my toes went numb. So I refused.

"Work around the edges of the law, he said. Use the media." Don Hugo Boss clicked his tongue in disapproval. "I told him it wouldn't work. Told him to stay away from you when he started getting that damned lovesick dog look every time he went anywhere near Richmond. Should've listened."

Gear switch. "Actually, I'm pretty sure he's not speaking to me." If I couldn't save myself, maybe I could save Joey's...whatever appendage they broke for insubordination in the Mafia these days.

"He's not?" One brow rose in a casual I'm-not-interested-but-tell-me-anyway.

"We had a fight."

"Since last Sunday?"

Yikes. "People don't get a lot of privacy around here," I said.

"I suppose in that respect, Simon and I aren't so different."

"I suspect that's not the only similarity," I said.

"Touché," he said. "You're a smart lady, Miss Clarke. And I admire determination. I am sorry it's come to this, but we're dealing with a lot of money. And some very sensitive people. You wandered into the middle of the wrong thing."

One question for all the marbles. "Why kill the girl?"

"Which girl?"

"Jasmine. The one who'd rather live on the streets of Shockoe Bottom than stay here. She's the reason I'm here."

His pacing paused mid-step. He whirled on tiptoe, facing me but not looking at me. "I didn't." The words didn't even sound like they were directed my way. He touched a finger to his chin. "The girl you've been writing about for the past couple of weeks. That's who you're talking about? I could swear I read the police made an arrest."

Nice to know someone still reads the paper. I opened my mouth to reply and gunfire split the air outside.

* * *

Just like that, I was the least of the Don's worries. Gun back in his hand, he disappeared through the door. And left it open.

What kind of church has a firefight on a random Saturday evening?

The kind of church where the Mafia has an office.

I jumped to my feet and scurried out behind him.

"Don't die first. Get the story second. That's what Bob would say," I muttered under my breath, looking around a corner in the maze of hallways. I didn't even have my shoes to use as a weapon—the worst I could do with a sneaker was piss someone off flinging it at them.

I paused halfway to the back door. "Dammit."

The killer was in this building. Every goosebump pricking on my arms was sure of it.

"Because it's Brady." I wasn't sure who I was talking to, but my every instinct screamed that the minister's easy charm had skated under my radar somehow. Maybe I was too busy wondering if we shared a family tree.

The first journals. It seemed like months since I'd read them, but the answer was there—Mister B.

For Brady. Who told her she'd be free if she ran away.

She had an abortion, because he got her pregnant. And then scooted her out the door. Why wait a year to track her down and butcher her? Because she came back looking for money. From him, not Golightly. I nodded to myself. It all fit.

My eyes searched the hallways. It was quiet. Too quiet. I moved toward a red exit sign, eyes darting between the doors all around me, half expecting Brady to pop out like an arcade game and shoot me himself.

I needed to get back to the dorm and get the lockbox. Surely with that, Aaron would have enough to get a warrant.

And I would have the exclusive of a lifetime.

I opened the door and stepped into a warm breeze.

Just in time to see Kyle duck behind a tree, a gun with a long silencer in his hand. His eyes widened as far as mine did when our gazes locked. "Nichelle! Get back inside!" He stepped toward me, his trigger hand crossed over the arm he stretched my way. "Now!"

"What the hell are you doing here?" I stared, my sneakers morphing into cinderblocks.

"I knew you were coming—" the rest of that was lost in a scream—his or mine, I didn't know—as a splash of deep red exploded across his upper arm. Half a second later, his jeans got a matching splotch. I rushed forward, and he shouted something I couldn't hear over the sudden hail of bullets. I didn't care who was shooting. Or why. Kyle was bleeding.

My heart twisted in my chest.

Kyle was bleeding because of me.

He stumbled forward three steps and fell into me. "Get. Down." He breathed, his eyes fluttering shut. I staggered backward, but kept my feet under me. One arm around him, I reached back for the doorknob, half-dragging my friend into the church.

Collapsing, I eased him to the floor. "You're hurt."

"It's just a flesh wound."

I glanced at his arm. Probably. But the leg gushed blood too quickly. There was an artery there somewhere. Shit.

I looked around for a cloth. Nothing, of course. Unbuttoning my oxford, I whipped it off. Kyle tried to smile. "I appreciate the gesture, but I don't think I'm in the mood. For once."

I managed a tight smile. "You keep making jokes, so I know you're not dying," I said, tugging at the sleeves of the shirt. Not cheap, this one. It wouldn't tear. And the whole thing was too big to cinch around his leg. I glanced down.

"Close your eyes," I said.

He obliged, raising his brows. "Why?"

"Not telling." I slipped my bra off, pulling the shirt back on and fastening a few buttons in the front before I wrapped my favorite purple Victoria's Secret around his leg in a messy knot, pulling the ends tight. Kyle winced, opening his eyes. I kept mine on his wound. The bleeding slowed by more than half.

"Thank God," I sighed.

He tried to raise his head, then moved the fingers of his uninjured arm to his thigh, running them over the lace.

"Did you make me a tourniquet out of your bra?" He grinned. "Next time, I won't close my eyes."

"Hardy har. What are you doing here?"

"You said you were coming here. We got a tip something was going down today. A money run with the mob. I couldn't let you get caught in the middle, so I brought a team to serve a search warrant."

"How on Earth did you get a search warrant?"

"I told the judge I suspected a hostage situation."

"What? Why?"

"I needed in."

"You lied to a judge for me?" There was something almost better than chocolate in there somewhere.

"Not technically. If they'd caught you, you'd be a hostage. Or a corpse. I just went with the hopeful scenario." He smiled. "We made it five steps toward the front door before their security guys started shooting."

"They have security guys?" I couldn't recall seeing one.

"Of course they do. We took out the first two and then this old guy in a suit came out and opened fire. I think it was him who got me. Wasn't the preacher, though."

The Don.

A money run.

The feed bags.

I smoothed Kyle's hair back. "I have to get you some help." No way he could make it to my car. It was a half-mile or more across the compound. I stood, hooking my hands under his arms and apologizing with every step as I pulled him into a doorway. By the time I lowered his shoulders back to the floor, every drop of color had drained from his face and his lips were a thin white line.

"Stay here." I tried to look stern.

"I don't think I'm going anywhere." He gestured with his nine-millimeter. "I hope they stay out there. At least until we've secured the building. My guys will find me."

"You've saved me twice now," I stood. "My turn."

I fumbled for my cell phone. Scrambled signal. No bars.

Joey's pre-dawn text waited on my home screen: "They know you're coming. Stay put. I'll tell you everything you need to know. I'll even testify."

I swore a purple streak under my breath, shoving the phone back into my pocket and looking around. I didn't have time to feel stupid. With Kyle losing blood by the minute, I couldn't focus on anything but a way out of Golightly's fortress.

The big doors at the end of the hallway opened, the front office chandelier framed in the empty doorway. I ducked around a corner before anyone came in.

"It's my fault." A man's voice, smooth, but with a tinge of sorrow and a heaping of panic. "Have you seen the newspapers? I might as well have handed her to this monster myself." He swallowed a choked sob. "I loved her. More than I should have."

I stopped breathing. Brady.

"You took her the money she needed," he continued. "And someone killed her for it."

So she did blackmail Brady.

I'd been ready to hang Brady two minutes ago, but that didn't sound like the denial of a murderer. Especially not given the method.

"Now, Pastor." Another voice. Male. Young. Completely calm.

It took everything in me to resist peeking. But I liked breathing.

"No one could possibly blame you for her errant ways. As for what happened in that crumbling old building—you couldn't have known."

My heart stuttered. How did Captain Serenity know the building was crumbling?

Because he was there. He took her the money.

But she never got it.

Because he killed her.

Cow's blood. Their whole "washed in the blood" thing. And the guy sounded so cool: "You need to be with the Savior tonight. Let me take care of this."

"Please," Brady said. A door closed. Then another.

I peeked. Empty hallway.

Sprinting for the door at the end, I prayed for a glimpse of whoever owned the creepy-happy voice. It was familiar, but I couldn't pin down why.

I shoved the door open just in time to see a brown head and white shirt disappear out into the main hall. A guy. Which I already knew. In a uniform? Maybe an overzealous student?

I glanced between the door and the phones on the desks. Kyle needed help. But from where? Not nine-one-one, since it routed to Golightly's personal sheriff.

Lifting the receiver on a desk phone, I hit nine and dialed Aaron's cell number from memory, blurting "hello" before he could.

"It's Saturday night," he said. "Don't you have a life?"

"Shut up, Aaron," I hissed. "I'm at Way of Life and Kyle Miller has been shot. Twice. He's losing a lot of blood. I need an ambulance, and they're still shooting outside."

"Jesus, Nichelle," he said. "Keep your head down. I'm on it."

"I'm thirty-five feet from your murderer. I'll call you back." I hung up, darting to the door.

The guy had disappeared in the direction of the foyer, so I sprinted that way. Empty. The shoe closet room, too.

My shoulders sagged. "So very close."

Outside? I turned.

Not a soul in sight. No evidence of a firefight, either, save the ambulances I heard in the distance and the lack of students dotting the lawn. I shot a glance Heavenward. "I could use a break."

Silence.

And then, music.

A concert-worthy piano rendition of *How Great Thou Art* filled the air around me.

I spun around.

The piano was in the sanctuary.

Easing a door open, I slipped inside. A dark head bobbed over top of the beautiful black grand, which looked roughly the size of a matchbox from where I stood.

I moved closer, stepping carefully and keeping to the shadows.

I found a dark doorway to the left of the stage, goosebumps rising on my arms at the crescendo of the song.

"Hey." Mathers didn't miss a note. "Did you find what you were looking for?"

I nodded, my eyes drifting from his white shirt to the flat gaze behind his wire-rims. Glasses. He was the guy—the one staring at me during the service last Sunday. Did he know who I was all this time?

Aaron's voice floated up. *"In case whoever did this was watching."*

Mathers knew I was a reporter—because he saw me at the murder scene. My gut twisted.

"You play beautifully." I managed to affect a conversational tone.

"Seventeen years of classical piano. My mother said it helped steady a surgeon's hands. But my heart wasn't in medicine. Too much science. No faith. No beauty. So I help out with the music on Sunday when they need me to."

He'd studied medicine.

I swallowed nausea.

"The reverend has quite a devoted following," I said.

"He's a devoted man of God." He nodded, melody still issuing effortlessly from the regal instrument as he tapped the keys. "People flock to that."

I slid my hand behind my back. I couldn't confront him with no weapon and no help. And Kyle was still bleeding in the back hallway.

Get the box.

Get Kyle.

Get out.

Write the story.

Send the cops for this Looney Tune.

I pushed the door and the deadbolt rattled in the frame. Shit.

The music fell silent. "Leaving so soon? I thought I was a better player."

"I'm just anxious to get home."

He heaved a sigh, pushing back from the piano and rising in one motion. "I have to handle everything no one else wants to do around here. Teachers are so underpaid."

I didn't answer, my eyes on the foot-long knife in his right hand.

31

Heart pounding in my throat, I spun for the hulking sets of double doors at the back of the room and took off.

Mathers was faster. Halfway up the aisle, I saw him overtake me and knew I couldn't outrun him. I zagged to the left and sprinted for the doors on the far side of the room.

He watched from halfway back. "Locked," he called when I rattled them.

Deep breath. He had a knife, not a gun. I just had to stay away from him until I could figure out what to do.

Get the truth.

Suddenly thankful for Andrews's asshattery, I reached into my pocket and flipped on the camera as I backed toward the stage.

"Why?" I called, hoping the audio would pick up.

"Why not?" He chuckled. "She was a slut. And a murderer."

Wait.

Mathers hacks up a perfectly healthy young woman, but she's a murderer? Brady cheats on his wife, but Jasmine's the slut? I shook off the urge to launch into a diatribe about that and focused on the fruitcake in front of me. I could write a column on it, but I had to live to see Sunday first.

"She left. Why go find her after a year? Why not just let it be?" I moved back from him and to the side, toward the stage.

"She wanted money." He stepped forward. "She threatened to tell the press the reverend made her have an abortion. Do you know what that would do to our membership?"

"And your donations."

"The reverend does the Lord's work with that money."

"I've seen his tax returns. I'm pretty sure the Bible doesn't say the preacher gets a yacht."

"Blessings come to the faithful. I believe the Lord will bless me for my faith."

"Bless you how?" I asked. "With a yacht of your own, maybe?"

He laughed. "Material things are temporary. Love is forever. Someday, my prayers will be enough to make Chloe see that."

"Chloe?" Bios spun through my head. "Isn't that Pastor Brady's wife?"

"How a man could be married to her and want anything else, I'll never know. But she doesn't love him."

"Because she loves you?" I kept pace toward the stage, my peripheral vision catching a two-by-three gold logo cross with sharp ray-of-light edges on the front of the lectern.

"She came to me at first because she was lonely. But what we have is special." His creepy grin went all dreamy. I paused, staring. Peyton Place with Bibles, this joint.

"When he got the slut pregnant, my Chloe came apart at the seams," Mathers said. "She's tried for a baby with him for nine years. She was terrified Brady would leave her, and I couldn't stand to see her so unhappy. I'm devout. I believe. And the Lord showed me the way. Ruth came to me for advice. She wanted to keep it, of course. That would've killed Chloe. I convinced her it was a mistake. Reminded her how disappointed her father would be."

We danced, him moving toward me, me moving toward the pulpit, as he talked. I kept the corner of my eye on the cross, but it wasn't in reach yet.

He took three easy steps forward. "I took her to the clinic and got rid of it." He grinned. "She screamed. She was sick for days. Plenty of time to convince her to run. I told her the other students would hate her for being a whore, and Brady would hate her for killing his bastard. Away from here, she'd be free."

Mr. B was right. I'm free.

Her journals did have the magical key. I just didn't know which lock it fit.

Until now.

"Ben," I mumbled, stepping backward. "The students call you Ben."

"Actually, most of them call me Mr. B." A step forward.

"Why the cow's blood?" Two steps back.

"Washing in blood cleanses a soul." He shot me an are-you-stupid look. "She deserved to die, but I couldn't send anyone to Hell."

Wow. Just...Wow.

"Why not take her the money, if that's what Brady wanted you to do?"

"What right did she have to it? She wasn't favored of the Lord. Not like my Chloe."

The blonde. "Is Brady having another affair, too?"

"His vice isn't women."

"It's power," I said, the words from Jasmine's journal flitting through my head.

He inched toward me. "Mine is only her."

Envy.

Righteousness.

Jasmine saw them all for what they were.

And this jackass killed her for it.

"But she's married. That's pretty clearly coveting another man's wife." My foot hit the bottom tier of the stage.

"He's going to prison." Three steps forward. "The slut was trying to blackmail him. Perfect motive."

"But he thinks he paid her. He thinks you paid her. He'll tell the cops that." Two steps up.

"And who's going to believe a minister accused of two murders?" Two steps forward, and another grin when my eyes flicked to the knife. "Hers and yours. You're a reporter—the media loves nothing more than to crucify men who have fallen from grace."

"How is it you think that won't destroy the church?" One more step.

He shook his head. "Losing Brady won't hurt us in the long run. The reverend will be appalled. He'll pray for their souls. The faithful will prevail. As long as that's all the story they get." Four steps, and he jogged up the stairs crossing the front of the stage. Shit.

I whirled for the podium and grabbed the cross.

I turned back just as he got within arm's reach, blade glinting in the dim light as he swung it down. Throwing my arm out, I raised the cross. Freaking thing was heavy.

Metal met metal with a deafening ring. I staggered backward. He sprang forward. I swung again.

"There's something poetic in that, but I can't quite put a finger on it," he said, sidestepping it easily.

I slashed the other way. Grazed his arm.

He didn't seem to notice. Two steps forward.

I stepped back.

And fell over the curled foot of Golightly's throne.

My ass hit the carpet.

The cross dropped to the floor.

I scooted back, reaching blindly for it.

Nothing but air.

Mathers planted a foot on my chest and shoved. The crack when my head hit the base of the baptismal turned my stomach, stars exploding behind my eyes.

"Good thing the carpet is dark," Mathers said, almost to himself, straddling my waist and looking down.

I raised one foot and tried to nail his groin, but he brought the knife down and slashed through my polyester pants into my calf. I screamed, grabbing for the wound. Flames raced up my leg, my vision swimming. He raised the blade again, squarely over my heart.

I closed my eyes, hoping the medics had found Kyle.

A roar ripped through the stillness, a soft gurgle punctuating the silence that followed.

A blow forced the wind from my chest, the blade biting into my shoulder. I couldn't scream. I couldn't move.

"Nichelle? Nichelle!"

Joey?

My eyes popped wide. Mathers sprawled across my torso, his knife buried in my shoulder. His lifeless gaze stared through me, blood running from his mouth. My eyes snapped shut again. Shot. He'd been shot.

Footfalls pounded over the ringing in my ears.

"Nichelle?"

Joey flung Mathers aside like a wet rag, dropping to his knees next to me and studying the knife. He didn't try to remove it. I ignored it for fear of fainting.

I grabbed his hand. "You can't be here. There's a guy. He shot Kyle." God, my leg hurt. I winced, whining, when Joey touched it with gentle hands.

Swatting at his shoulder, I tried to prop up on my good elbow. "Listen to me, dammit. That dude was scary. And he knows you. Said he told you to stay away from me."

"He did. I don't follow orders well."

"You have to go. The ATF is here, Kyle is hurt, and that guy—I don't want you on his shit list." I fell back to the carpet, my voice sounding far away. "I like your kneecaps the way they are."

The corners of his lips flashed up. "Miller is okay. They're loading him into an ambulance. The ATF is so shaken by the firefight they weren't expecting, they didn't even notice me. And I'm pretty sure that 'scary dude' you're so worried about was in the body bag I saw before I slipped in the back door." He smoothed my hair off my forehead. "Be still. I'll grab a paramedic."

I caught his hand. "Why did you come?"

"I heard early this morning the wire they had in the dead woman's room had clued Mario in to your plan today."

"Wire?"

"When you showed up here, I had to tell Mario something. He remembered your victim, but he didn't know who killed her. Or why. He thought she knew about his business arrangement with the accountant. He didn't trust them. Wanted to know what her roommate knew, so he bugged the room. He heard you planning this. And they had an important meeting here today."

"The money."

He just nodded."You never answered my text. By lunchtime, I was going nuts waiting."

"I thought you were telling me to go to Hell. I didn't read it until just now."

He shook his head. "You think I'd let you get killed chasing a story because I'm pissed you didn't want to spend the night with me? What kind of guy would that make me?"

I squeezed his hand. "A bad one?"

"Maybe I'm not so bad, after all." He kissed me softly. "Be still." Standing, he disappeared into the shadows.

* * *

The medics appeared with a stretcher and various doohickeys for checking me out before I could contemplate getting my feet under me. They pronounced me in need of stitches and wheeled me through the foyer on a gurney. Elise waited just outside the doors.

"Are you okay?" she squealed. "I couldn't find you and then people were shooting at each other. Some guy in a bulletproof vest told me I had to stay out here."

"Mathers. It was Mathers."

Her face twisted into a mask of horror. "Why?" she choked out.

"Money. Sex. Power. They make people crazy."

"Jasmine loved Mr. Mathers." She bowed her head, sobs shaking her shoulders.

"Which is why she let him up in the loft with her." I nodded, the last pieces of my puzzle arranging themselves. "Elise, I need that box. Can you bring it to me?"

She ran for the dorm and I asked the medics to hold up. They grumbled but complied. Huffing, Elise settled the box next to me and brushed her fingers across my forearm. "Thank you."

"Thank you," I said. "I'm so sorry about your friend."

I turned my head on the way out the door and caught sight of Brady and a tiny blonde—Chloe. They huddled beneath the larger-than-life portrait of Golightly.

Whose vice was vanity.

32

Thunder rumbled through a slate sky, soft rain pattering the roof as I limped to the coffee maker Sunday morning.

"Splenda and milk?" I asked, turning to the table where Kyle had his leg propped on the extra chair.

"However you take it is fine." He smiled around a strip of bacon. Swallowing, he took the cup. "You didn't have to make me breakfast."

"You got shot trying to save my life."

"But I didn't. Save your life. And you still got hurt. I didn't even get you the story. You did that."

I rolled my eyes. "Stop it. I've got a triple-banana-split scoop on Charlie this morning, and it'll get another layer when y'all get the weapons thing processed."

"Way of Life canceled services this morning on account of the ATF crawling all over their property." He grinned.

"Did you tell them to check the feed shed?"

The grin gave way to a laugh. "Could we interest you in agent training? That's where the money was. In the bags. See, in an operation like that, they deposit the cash a little at a time with their regular banking, and then withdraw it in odd amounts and pay the mob. So the taller stacks were the cash they needed to clean, and the shorter ones were what they already had. Mario Caccione was there last night to pick up the money."

"I still can't believe it." I shook my head. "You're a hero. Again. But I like my job. And I dislike guns."

"Too bad, because I'm getting you one," he said.

I laughed.

"I'm serious," Kyle said. "This was the last near miss you get to have without a weapon."

I fluffed the pillow under his leg, which had a shredded knee and a newly-sewn-up popliteal artery thanks to Don Mario (who was deader than dead. Shooting an ATF agent with four others present, not the smartest move. Especially when they weren't shooting at you to begin with). "Landers sent me Mathers's background—turns out, it was a thirty-something white guy. He just wasn't hiding in Shockoe Bottom."

"You're a good detective, Nichelle." Kyle caught my hand and smiled when I straightened up. "You're a better cook. And a pretty good nurse. How's your shoulder?"

He had one arm in a sling and a cast from hip to thigh, and he was worried about me. "I'm fine." I extended my arm with some difficulty, thanks to various sutured layers of skin and muscle in my shoulder. "The stitches in my leg hurt more this morning. My real concern is what this is going to do to my wardrobe. They told me to keep the scars out of the sun for three months."

"Now, that's a shame."

I leaned on the edge of the table and picked up my coffee. "Overall, I'd say my weekend hasn't been half bad. Bob loved my story. Ordered me to take the rest of the weekend off. Girl Friday has been fired from the PD. Not that she's going to take her blog down, but at least she has to get her information like everyone else. Aaron said Mr. Galloway is coming for his daughter's body tomorrow—with her old boyfriend, who is paying for the funeral out of his 'shop of my own' savings. And Picasso—whose real name is Aidan Caruthers—is out of jail and in an empty dorm room at RAU. Jenna got him into the art department as a teaching assistant."

"Nice work, Lois." Kyle nodded.

"I have exclusives lined up for a week. Landers picked up Deputy Buck's cousin this morning for trying to kill us Thursday. Got his plate number from the gas station video. He has a pretty good lead on the other murder, too. Seems Cecilia had a brother who was killed by a weapon she'd traced to this Mafia family through files at her law firm. They help cover up the money laundering. She had scans and a journal on her laptop, all ready for the authorities. And there's a guy in Mario's command who had it out for the retired cop who found the body. Landers thinks he killed her. Hopefully I'll have that story this week."

"My team is dismantling the Caccione crime family. At least, we're trying to before someone steps up to take Mario's place." Kyle winked. "That'll make a hell of a headline. And I'd say you have the inside track."

"I'll take it." I turned to refill my coffee.

"I'm glad you're okay." Kyle's voice thickened and he cleared his throat. "You stepped outside yesterday and I was afraid I'd never see you again."

"Back at you, friend."

He shook his head. "I was scared when you left here the other night. And nothing scares me."

I dropped my eyes to the floor. "I'm sorry, Kyle." The words hung in the air, the double meaning not lost on him.

He sighed. "Who is that guy, Nichelle? No bullshit." He had his cop face on, and I knew it was only a matter of time before he put Joey together with my "Mafia source" after yesterday. Maybe he already had, but I couldn't tell.

Strictly speaking, Mathers's death wasn't an ATF case, and I doubted the Fauquier Sheriff would have the guts to ask me much of anything after Deputy Buck almost got me killed. So I played stupid.

"We're sort of seeing each other, I think. But it's a new thing. I know next to nothing about him." Every word true.

"I see." He smiled, his eyes sad. "I want you to be happy."

"And I want the same for you. Though Jenna's staff isn't exactly where I think you should shop for a girlfriend." I picked up his empty plate and dropped it in the dishwasher, the single violet rose in the vase on the windowsill sending a spark through me when I stood. Darcy and the rose had been in the house when Kyle and I got home in the middle of the night. No note. No text. No call.

I closed my eyes, the roar of the gunshot that killed Mathers echoing in my ears for the nine hundredth time. Joey had killed someone. Right in front of me.

Still, I missed him. And needed to skirt the questions I knew Kyle had about what happened in the sanctuary. I suspected he knew it was Joey. But had he seen him? Could he prove it? Joey is a master of being unobtrusive, and Kyle was busy bleeding.

If I wasn't already crazy, this could very possibly hurl me over the edge.

Emily's words rolling in my head, I pasted on a bright smile and turned. "Let's get you settled with ESPN."

Kyle hobbled to the living room, where I flipped on the TV and arranged sofa pillows under his bum leg.

"I'll check on you in a bit," I told Kyle as I patted Darcy and turned for the hallway.

Perching on the edge of my bed, I opened the dresser, digging under folded unmentionables for a faded, yellowed piece of stationery.

A thousand questions whirled through my head, starting with "Why?" and ending with "Was my father's last name Brady?"

I threw a glance at the clock. Ten-thirty. The sun was up in Malibu.

My fingers flew across the keypad, and I punched talk before I could chicken out.

"Hello?" The voice sounded so much like my mom it stopped my breath.

"Hello?" she asked again.

I cleared my throat. "Um. Mrs. Clarke?"

"Yes?"

Time to grow up. Or start, anyway.

"My name is Nichelle. I—I'm your granddaughter."

COVER SHOT: Nichelle Clarke #5

Cryptic online messages and a murder in a swanky condo complex don't strike crime reporter Nichelle Clarke as related-until a gunman sends a hospital into chaos.

"...if you're a fan of mystery, you simply must read this series..."

When a body is discovered in a high-rise in Richmond, Virginia, crime reporter Nichelle Clarke races to the scene. The victim is a brilliant doctor with an unusual past. But before Nichelle can decide what to make of the murder, the local police radio is filled with a dreaded distress call.

There is an active shooter at a nearby hospital.

The gunman has taken hostages on a patient floor, and gives the police a single demand.

He wants to speak with Nichelle.

In person.

Get your copy today at
severnriverbooks.com/series/nichelle-clarke-crime-thriller

ACKNOWLEDGMENTS

I had a blast writing this book. Loosely based on events I covered as a reporter many years ago (and later had the opportunity to learn more about through a welcome twist of fate), it was great fun to send Nichelle to do things I wish I could have.

First up, the details wouldn't have been possible without the help and honesty of the fabulous Jane Deer. Thank you for trusting me, and for sharing.

More thanks to my brilliant forensic biologist friend Jody Klann for her help (again) with the science behind a murder investigation.

My books wouldn't be the same without my eagle-eyed beta readers, who help me see the story so much more clearly: thank you hugs to Gretchen Smith, Larissa Reinhart, and Julie Hallberg.

Big thanks to Andrew Watts and the team at Severn River Publishing: Your creativity and ingenuity, and your devotion to Nichelle's stories, are nothing short of amazing.

The months when I created this book were not the easiest of my life, and you wouldn't be holding it if my girlfriends hadn't been there to prop me up and keep me sane. Julie Hallberg, Sarah Dabney-Reardon, and Nichole Dwire: I am thankful every minute to have such strong, amazing women to brighten my days. Love you girls.

Always first in my heart, my wonderful family: Thank you, littles, for understanding when mommy needs time to hang out with Nichelle. And to my best friend, my partner, and my biggest fan who doesn't actually like to read: thank you, Justin, for making it possible for me to chase this dream. I love our life together, and all my crazy adventures with you. Many more await—the best is yet to be.

As always, any mistakes are mine alone.

ABOUT THE AUTHOR

LynDee Walker is the national bestselling author of two crime fiction series featuring strong heroines and "twisty, absorbing" mysteries. Her first Nichelle Clarke crime thriller, FRONT PAGE FATALITY, was nominated for the Agatha Award for best first novel and is an Amazon Charts Bestseller. In 2018, she introduced readers to Texas Ranger Faith McClellan in FEAR NO TRUTH. Reviews have praised her work as "well-crafted, compelling, and fast-paced," and "an edge-of-your-seat ride" with "a spider web of twists and turns that will keep you reading until the end."

Before she started writing fiction, LynDee was an award-winning journalist who covered everything from ribbon cuttings to high level police corruption, and worked closely with the various law enforcement agencies that she reported on. Her work has appeared in newspapers and magazines across the U.S.

Aside from books, LynDee loves her family, her readers, travel, and coffee. She lives in Richmond, Virginia, where she is working on her next novel when she's not juggling laundry and children's sports schedules.

Sign up for LynDee Walker's reader list at
severnriverbooks.com/authors/lyndee-walker
lyndee@severnriverbooks.com

Printed in the United States
by Baker & Taylor Publisher Services